SHADOWS

Recent Titles by Kenneth Royce

BREAKOUT*
LIMBO
THE PROVING GROUND
REMOTE CONTROL
THE AMBASSADOR'S SON*

*available from Severn House

SHADOWS

Kenneth Royce

This first world edition published in Great Britain 1996 by
SEVERN HOUSE PUBLISHERS LTD of
9–15 High Street, Sutton, Surrey SM1 1DF.
First published in the USA 1996 by
SEVERN HOUSE PUBLISHERS INC of
595 Madison Avenue, New York, NY 10022.

British Library Cataloguing in Publication Data
Royce, Kenneth
  Shadows
  I. Title
  823.914 [F]

  ISBN 0-7278-4878-X

Typeset by Hewer Text Composition Services, Edinburgh.
Printed and bound in Great Britain by
Hartnolls Ltd, Bodmin, Cornwall.

With acknowledgements to

Dr Tim James

for his contribution

Chapter One

The pistol was a 7.65 mm calibre with an eight rounds magazine and an uncomfortable looking ribbed hand grip. It was far from new but had the appearance of being well cared for, and the soft fingered hands that roamed over it, did so with both familiarity and affection. The woman checked the pistol expertly before screwing on a specially made silencer and then placing it on the dressing table. Sitting in front of the mirrors and crossing her long legs, she began to examine herself; that was the order of things.

She knew she was attractive. There was something fascinating about her cool image as if there was more to find but was well concealed behind the shielded gaze. And some would find the slight mystique disturbing as if too much was hidden and they would wonder why. She was not vain about her looks but knew how to capitalize on them, and when the mood took her, could be a magnet to any man.

When she started to apply her make-up she deftly changed the contours of her lips so that her mouth changed shape. Her eyebrows too, were subtly changed, and by the time she had finished with her cosmetics, there was a difference about her that was difficult to pinpoint. She then inserted brown contact lenses to cover the natural colour of her eyes. These actions were done with cool appraisal and quite clearly, not for the first time. A wig completed the transformation making the final effect startling. She was stunning. Friends might recognize her, but even they might be fooled for a short while and certainly from a distance.

Once satisfied with her appearance she carefully removed the long, false, scarlet-coloured fingernails to reveal natural, polished short nails; too long a nail might foul the trigger guard or crack. She sat still for several seconds reflecting on what she must do, but showing no reaction to the deadliness of her thoughts. Her composed image stared back at her through the mirror, but there was no indication of whether or not it pleased her until she rose.

It was time to go. She gazed round the room, picked up the pistol, slipped it into a wide pocket of the jacket she wore over her expensive, low cut black dress, checked herself in a cheval mirror, and slowly crossed the room to let herself out. She locked the door behind her.

Ronald Walsh MP, unlocked the door and entered the hotel room. He stared round thinking it rather grotty, not up to his usual standard: three star rather than four or five. But he had long since recognized that he had to be ultra careful. It was not too long ago that the trash press had caught him out and it had almost cost him his parliamentary seat, lost him his family and wrecked his marriage. The marriage was dying on its feet anyway, but they had managed to keep up appearances for the sake of the children; others believed he had exploited the children to save his skin. Money was not his problem, he had plenty of that, it was women.

As he traversed the room he accepted once again that it was impossible for him to change. He could not help himself and really did not want to. He enjoyed his escapades but they were being forced further and further underground. His liaisons were dangerous but added to an excitement that stimulated and significantly increased his pleasure.

He was not a good-looking man. In his mid-forties he still had a good head of hair, but that was his redeeming feature. His male friends wondered how he had made so many conquests, although he was seemingly not always choosy. He sat on a bedside chair and glanced at his watch; he was a little early and he was an impatient man.

He hoped it would be worth the wait. He had to travel north later that night so this was a fit-in job to while away the time, rather than go to his home before the trip. He had used the agency before and they had always been reliable.

He rose, crossed to the window, and stared down at the street, then backed quickly away. There was an office building opposite and he had a well-founded fear of long distance lenses; there was no morality about the modern day press. The irony of the reflection did not touch him. The appointed time passed and he began to get edgy; his features showing something of a man used to getting his way. He fiddled with the radio and found some soft music.

He returned to the chair just as he heard someone at the door. There was a faint sound and as he moved towards the door he realized that a key was being turned. He backed away and waited. A brunette came in, but was turned away from him as she closed the door and relocked it. She turned to face him just as he was admiring her legs.

He saw the image of her, and was confused by the familiarity of her features but without instant recognition. His reaction was one of immediate pleasure followed by a slow, engulfing shock which brought with it fear. And then he realized but still could not comprehend why such changes had been made, especially to the eyes and hair. Something had gone terribly wrong, for he did not believe in so massive a coincidence. It was as though he was looking at her sister and then he saw the pistol in so steady a hand and a coldness about the expression. He felt the blood drain from his face.

He stepped forward, an awkward smile appearing. "What on earth . . .?" But that was as far as he got. He felt the pain in his chest as she fired twice and he knew he was slipping. He stared unbelievingly at her as he crumpled but was dead before he hit the floor. One leg was twisted under him but his head had caught the edge of the bed and remained propped so that he stared at her sightlessly; disbelief, surprise and fear all somehow retained in his gaze.

3

She stepped forward showing no distress or any form of reaction, and crouched before him to go through his pockets, using his own handkerchief with which to hold what she extracted. His wallet bulged with money but she left it there. She was searching for some kind of identification but found none. He had been careful. But not careful enough. She put everything back, stared down at him quite dispassionately for several seconds before saying, "You were stupid, Ronnie. Nobody will miss you."

She removed the silencer and returned it to her pocket with the pistol. She retained his handkerchief to open the door and to wipe the handle before leaving the room and locking the door behind her.

The body was not found until the next morning when the cleaners went in; the room had been booked for the night as a crude cover. Identification took some time. Ronald Walsh was not a well-known public figure, was far from being a household name, and had never held office in his years as a Member of Parliament.

The evening press started off with 'Man Found Shot Dead In Hotel Room'. It was not front page until identification was made later that day, and even then it was a suspicion rather than a certainty. Finally the police persuaded Walsh's reluctant wife to visit the morgue, after which the headlines changed dramatically in time for the following day's national press. Everyone guessed that Walsh had tried one woman too many, but would any of them consider him worth killing?

Politically, whilst severely shocked, most of his old acquaintances were not sorry to see him go; he had been an embarrassment to the government and even to his faithful constituency. He had not been deemed a 'character' like some philanderers, and as one unnamed MP put it, he was a "pain in the arse". But it was still fodder to the opposition, and over the last year or so, too many mistakes had been made by individuals who should know better, and each time the government ratings went down, as the party fell into disarray much to the satisfaction of the opposition. There had been too many upsets one way or the other and now there had been murder. The popular press would dig the dirt until the public lost interest, but this was a juicy one which could fill space for some time; there were too many possibilities for it to go away.

Scotland Yard were working on it of course. And they were quick to find the agency who had supplied the call girl. The hotel receptionist had filled in some details. He had assumed that the room was wanted for a liaison, although he had not actually seen anyone go to the room, for there had been a substantial tip and an arrangement about picking up the room keys, and a great deal of discretion had been used. But it was at the agency that enquiries floundered.

The girl who had been booked for the assignment had cried off sick and had telephoned in to the agency, who had found it too late to find a suitable replacement. The agency had tried to contact their client, failed, and had then telephoned the hotel. The receptionist had promised to advise Walsh, who was of course, using another name, but evidently had failed to do so. When questioned, the receptionist denied he had received any such call. Either the receptionist or the agency were lying, or at best, covering a genuine mistake.

Many, including some sections of the police, believed Walsh had got what he deserved; his family were now free of him without continuing a charade, but it was not going to be easy explaining it to the children. People like Walsh left a long legacy of suffering.

George Bulman, who had read about the murder with a mild interest, was enormously surprised when he was telephoned by the Home Secretary's PPS to arrange a meeting. He did not know the man, wanted a reason to persuade him to stir from an old clock he was working on, and all he got was a vague reference to a recent murder that he would like to discuss with Bulman.

5

It was early December but exceptionally mild, and Bulman wore only a lightweight raincoat over his sturdy frame when he called at the apartment off Northumberland Avenue. It was on the second floor, the location itself enough to make it very expensive. After ringing the bell, Edward Marshall opened the door to greet him.

Marshall looked his part, thick wavy grey hair, tall, city image, intelligent eyes and a firm handshake. "I believe your tipple is scotch," said Marshall as he waved Bulman to a club chair while he went to a Sheraton sideboard to pour the drinks. "Malt?"

"When I can get it. You've done your homework."

"Don't be so modest. You're well known. And for good reason. You're bigger than I imagined." Marshall returned with the drinks. "I've put nothing in it. Cheers." He sat opposite Bulman and raised his glass as he appraised the rugged, crusty face and the eyes in folds that smothered the questioning look.

"Now I recognize you," said Bulman. "You've been on telly."

"A few times. So have you. Are you still running that private agency of yours?"

Bulman was about to put down his glass but found the spirit so good he decided to hang on to it. "What agency? I dabble. At the moment I'm sorting out an antique clock for a friend. Don't make them like that any more." He gazed round the room, noted the bronze clock on a mock Adam mantelpiece and said, "If you have trouble with that silk suspension over there give me a buzz."

"With pleasure. The detective agency—"

"I've never had a detective agency. I was with the Yard for a good many years. Have done odd jobs for MI5 and even MI6 on occasion, but I don't like the way they work; helping them is to find yourself the victim. I haven't done anything for some time."

"Really? That's not what the Deputy Commissioner of

6

Police told me, nor the Home Secretary and the US Ambassador."

"Yes, but I got caught up in that to help an old mate of mine in the FBI."

"I thought he was CIA."

"He might have been. You know how they move around out there. It's a wonder they get anything done. Where is all this leading?"

"Nowhere, while you're being so evasive." Marshall smiled. "Maybe it's because your glass is empty. I'll get you another." Marshall rose and took Bulman's glass and over his shoulder said, "Are you looking for a job in your old line? You were once a detective superintendent in the Murder Squad, weren't you?"

"Done a bit of everything. You're Home Office for God's sake, has the Yard closed down? You have a complete police network at your fingertips. Or is there something you don't want them dirtying their fingers on?"

Marshall returned with the drink, and smiled as he said, "What a suspicious fellow you are." He sat down, crossed his legs and gazed up at the ceiling.

Here comes the bullshit, Bulman reflected, and waited to see if he was right.

"Ronald Walsh," Marshall pronounced. "A squalid ending for a squalid man. But his death carries problems we could do without."

"We? Government?"

"Indeed. I wondered if the case might interest you?"

"You mean the Yard boys are all away on refresher courses or on holiday? Manpower shortage?"

"I was told you were blunt. Are you interested? Generous expenses and well paid. Some of it up front."

"Well that's blunt for a politician. But not blunt enough. I can't possibly match the facilities of the Yard. Which could mean the detectives working on the case do not have the full story. Are you holding out on them?"

"They would soon find out if we were. Nobody has the

full story. I understand you have a network of old lags and informers second to none."

Bulman shook his head slowly, careful not to spill his drink. "Not any more. Not for a long time. Some are even dead. I really don't think I can help you. And, anyway, nobody appeared to like this guy. What's so special about him for you to go to this trouble? Why bother?"

Marshall mused for a few seconds, avoiding Bulman's questioning gaze. "We think there's a hidden agenda here. Shadows that don't match the contours of the apparent."

Bulman offered a crusty smile. "That's bloody poetic. I'm sorry, Mr Marshall, I don't know what your problem is and you have certainly not made it clear. I don't think I can help you, but I wouldn't mind another malt while I finally make up my mind."

Marshall crossed to the sideboard and brought back a decanter, placing it on a side table beside Bulman. "Help yourself, but don't let it fog your judgment."

"I can't remember if it ever did that. Spit it out so that I can see what's on offer."

Back in his own chair, Marshall picked his words slowly. "It is possible that Ronnie Walsh's murder is more complicated than it seems. We don't think it's a straightforward killing by a call girl, whatever her motive. And it certainly was not robbery; his wallet was still on him and crammed with notes. He had no identification, but in those circumstances he was hardly likely to carry any." Marshall paused, watched Bulman carefully before saying, "We think he was assassinated."

Bulman was at last fully attentive. "A contract job? For whatever reason? He wasn't important enough by all accounts. Was he?"

"No. Not politically."

"Are his businesses sound? I mean, wasn't the man filthy rich?"

"Very. And so far as we know, his businesses are thriving at a time when so many are struggling. It is difficult to see how business is connected with this. It must be something else."

"But you don't know." Bulman stirred in the chair. "I still cannot see why the whole issue should not be left with the police? This meeting is crazy. Is there an aspect that you suspect and don't want them to find out? If there is I would need to know it. Are you afraid that the police will find something they will have to reveal? Or that the press will winkle something out, and you would like me to find it first? Just what chance do I stand for God's sake?"

"What chance did you stand last time out? You were up against worst odds than this. It would seem that you have a knack of grasping the general form of a problem very quickly, and are able to look for answers to questions which nobody else has grasped."

"Oh, sure, I'm a right clever dick. You're laying it on a bit thick, you must be desperate."

"Just give it a try. You can always pack it in. Whatever you're paid will be nonreturnable."

"That was the shrewdest remark you've made so far; someone has told you I don't like packing it in. Do you know what type of gun was used?"

"No. But I can find out."

"And nobody saw anyone go into Walsh's room?"

"That's how I understand it from the police."

"How do we know it was a call girl? It might have been a man."

"Because of the call girl agency connection. It was a girl who went sick. We must assume that Ronnie Walsh was expecting a woman."

"I'll need to know the name of the agency and the name and address of the girl who went sick. And the name of the hotel receptionist who is involved. I'd also like his duty times."

"I can get those details for you. Does this mean you will do it?"

9

"I want no restrictions of access to anyone who I think might be able to help. Anyone."

"You're not thinking of contacting any of your old police friends?"

"Anyone. Anyone at all, and that includes politicians. If I feel I'm being blocked at any time, and that's happened before, I'm out. I want a totally free hand and the money in cash."

"That would have been done anyway. For obvious reasons we don't want an open liaison."

"Who would I report to?"

"Me. I can give you an ex-directory number. If I'm not there just say 'shadows' to the answering machine and I'll contact you as soon as possible. Are you on?"

"I've been on since I entered the room, so I'm already on back pay; I need the money." Bulman finished his drink, ensuring that the glass was empty, then he rose. "You're not holding anything back? Anything I need to know?"

"That would be rather counterproductive, would it not?"

Bulman shrugged. There was already a nasty feel about the affair. There always was. He was only asked when it was bloody hopeless, and almost always, extremely dangerous. But this one had more than a nasty little tang to it. He did not believe that Marshall was holding any actual evidence back, but he was sure that he had not heard the full story. Counterproductive or not, Marshall was holding *something* back.

Chapter Two

Bulman learned that the hotel receptionist's name was Bert Cooper, and that his car was parked in the small staff yard at the rear of the hotel where Bulman now waited. As Cooper was still on a late shift, it was midnight before he left the reception desk to go through the rear exit to the car-park. Bulman watched Cooper come into the yard and pick his way through the indistinct dark humps of the parked cars. Bulman moved swiftly and quietly for a big man. As Cooper was about to put the key in the lock Bulman closed up behind him and put a powerful arm round his neck.

"Don't shout, Bert, or I'll break your bloody neck. I just want a word, OK?" Bulman wrenched the keys away with little trouble, and whilst still gripping his man, turned the key and opened the door. He retained the keys, then told Cooper to lean across the seat and release the passenger door lock. He bundled Cooper into the driver's seat, locked the door and ran round the other side before Cooper could move. He sat beside him and said affably, "Now don't worry. I'm not going to hurt you unless you're difficult. A few words and I'll be off. Switch on the interior light."

Cooper fumbled, but the dull light came on and was sufficient for Bulman to get a better sight of Cooper. Bulman placed an arm along the back of Cooper's seat.

"Who the hell are you?" Cooper demanded, beginning to recover.

"Well, you know I'm not the police. They've already talked to you and you've given them the load of bullshit we told you to say. They probably did not believe you;

11

they'll be back and I have to make sure that you keep your nerve. I represent the people who paid you a small fortune to tell porkies, to make sure you told the right ones and that you keep your story straight for the police. An insider told me that you did a good job on the Bill. Just keep it up. OK?"

Cooper did not answer at once. In his mid-forties, he had led an uneventful life until now, and was not sure how to deal with it. He was also afraid and not at all sure about the big gruff man by his side. "I don't know what the hell you're talking about. Leave me alone." There was a tremor in his voice.

Bulman grinned. "Good man," he said. "Cautious under pressure. That's good. And that's all we are asking you to be. That's what I came for, to make sure you can handle it. Just keep your nerve and you won't regret it." He turned to face the front and put one hand on the door catch. "I'm sorry I was so heavy-handed, but we could hardly meet in the hotel, and I needed to put a little frightener on you just to see how you reacted. You did well, Bert. Just keep it up and don't worry about the coppers. You've nothing to fear from them." He opened the door, turned his head. "You OK?"

Cooper nodded, looking to his front.

"You're not worried?"

"I could have done without the aggro. There was no need for that."

"You're probably right. I guess it's just my way." Bulman slapped Cooper's shoulder. "Nice meeting you. You're doing a great job." The temptation was to push further, to try to get some idea of who had approached Cooper in the first place, but he would have given himself away and Cooper would have been warned. It would have to wait, but he had at least established, to his own satisfaction, that Cooper had been bought. He had not expected it to be so easy, but then, he was not confined to a set of rules and guidelines.

*   *   *

12

The following day he rang an old friend, Detective Chief Superintendent Walter Beatty at Scotland Yard. As Bulman was on unqualified expenses he took his friend for lunch at an expensive restaurant off Victoria Street, not too far from the Yard.

"Can you afford this place, George?" asked the big, balding detective as they shook hands.

"Well, I remembered you liked your grub, and didn't think you'd come unless I took you somewhere special. You've put on weight."

They sat down. Beatty said, "Well I'm virtually desk-bound these days." His round features creased into a grin. "I overheard one of my sergeants say that since I've been promoted, all I do is sit on my arse and growl. I thought he was talking about one of the police dogs, but it was me." They laughed; it was a shortened version of an old joke. "But grub or not, it's nice to see you, George. I miss the old days."

"So do I at times. We were good together."

From behind the huge menu Beatty said, "As your style is usually the nearest pub, someone else must be paying for this. So George, what do you hope to get from me?"

"I wondered if you knew anything about the Walsh killing?"

"The MP who couldn't keep his trousers on? His extra-marital activities have interested the Security Service for years. He'd have been considered high risk but he remained on the back-benches and few people trusted him anyway. There's not much to know. But why should you be interested?"

"One of his relatives asked me to snoop around. It seems that she's worried about his past. I thought it was a bit late for that, but maybe she jumped in bed with him sometime; everybody else seems to have done. It's probably some family aspect she wouldn't want to get out."

Having decided what he wanted to eat, Beatty put

the menu down. "You're just as big a liar as you always were."

Bulman beckoned the waiter. "Well, it's more interesting than giving you a line about a client's confidentiality. What do you know, Wally?"

"It seems to be pretty open and shut. In some way or other, he upset a call girl sufficiently for her to top him."

"What sort of gun was it?"

"Ballistics say it was a 7.65 calibre. Possibly a CZ vz 70."

"Chuck that at me again."

"It's difficult to be precise about the actual make. The weight of opinion is that it's Czechoslovakian. In looks very like the Walther PP. They can't be sure, though." Beatty stared hard at Bulman. "This is for old times sake, not for publication, George."

"When have I ever let you down? Were the shots wild?"

Beatty looked surprised. "Have you heard something?"

"No. Have I touched a sore point?"

"A strange point. Two shots were fired. They both hit the heart and were so close together they almost touched. The entry wounds were almost as one. It's possible, of course; two shots fired very quickly, but unusual."

"That's a bit of classy shooting for a call girl, isn't it? You don't think she was a pro?" Bulman ventured almost casually.

"Oh, she was a pro all right, she must have been on the game or he wouldn't have let her in. There had been no struggle. We're trying to draw up a list of his bed mates to see if any of them is an expert shot. But it's a formidable task. The public only get to know of the well-known women, but by all accounts he was not always that fussy. It's an almost impossible job digging out his mistresses, and will take a long time." Beatty smiled. "If we ever complete the list it would win an entry in the Guinness Book of Records. It was a wonder he hadn't been done ages ago by a revengeful husband."

"Maybe he was."

"You could be right. Nobody is too excited about it. And there are a lot of people who would prefer for the murderer not to be found."

"Anything else?"

Beatty held his body back as the starters arrived. When the waiter had gone he said, "One small curious thing; he had no handkerchief on him. Apparently, to him, that was tantamount to going out in the noddy. He was a bit of a fop. There were no prints on the door, even his, other than those the hotel staff put there when he was found. So they must have been wiped clean."

"So that's what the handkerchief was used for? Not very professional if it was a contract killing."

"I never mentioned a contract killing. On the contrary, it indicates the opposite, someone killed him but had not prepared too well, or it had been done on the spur of the moment. I think the call girl agency has told the truth. But whether or not the girl who was originally booked has done, is another matter. She certainly did go sick and stayed home that day. I think the hotel receptionist on duty at the time was paid to close his eyes to the assignation. That's not unique and does not make him an accomplice to murder. I think Walsh didn't want to be recognized and probably fixed it through a friend. I don't think the receptionist did see him or anyone else go to that room that day; he made sure that he didn't. We'll be having another go at him."

"And that's all? No imminent arrest?"

"This is going to be a long one, George. The man's life was too complicated and littered with straddling women. But we'll get there."

They ate for a while, and then Bulman said, "You know, Wally, you're pretty casual about the standard of the shooting. Call girls don't go around toting guns, nor are they known to be so uncannily accurate with them."

"We don't know to what degree he upset her. I'm sure he upset a lot of woman, and, as you say, husbands and

15

boyfriends. Whoever it was went there for the express purpose of killing him; it did not arise out of something that happened at the time; she'd hardly be armed by coincidence. As for the accuracy, it was extremely close range and maybe she is just a bloody good shot."

Bulman chewed slowly, studying his friend who was concentrating on his food. "Why do I get the impression that you're talking a load of bull? Or has sitting behind a desk blunted your copper's perception?"

Beatty smiled and continued eating. "This is the nicest fillet I've had in years."

"You'd enjoy it even more if I told you who is paying for it." And then Bulman asked, "Is there something iffy about this case? I wouldn't expect you to tell me what, but is there an element of unusual secrecy about it, because that's the feeling I'm getting?"

Beatty ignored the question, thereby confirming Bulman's suspicion. The two men knew each other extremely well and had once been a formidable team. When Beatty had finished eating, he wiped his lips and said, "You must accept, George, that you are no longer in the force and that I still am. I have no reason for telling you anything except as an old friend and the expectancy that any pointers you may pick up will be passed on to me."

"That goes without saying."

"No it does not; it will depend on who is employing you and I don't go for a relative of the deceased bit." Beatty leaned back and eyed Bulman bleakly. "I'll throw you a crumb. So far as we know Walsh's present mistress is a cracker called Anna Brenning. She comes from East Germany but already spoke excellent English before she came. He set her up in a place on the fringe of Kensington and Earl's Court. An interesting woman."

"You've spoken to her?"

"Not personally. Two of my team went. She was a possible suspect but wasn't in the country at the time he was killed. She had gone to see friends in Germany."

"Verified?"

"Oh, yes. There are one or two more checks to make, but there is already sufficient evidence to confirm her story. You can try her if you like."

"Why would I do that if she has established an alibi?"

"Somewhere for you to start." Beatty shrugged. "She may not have done it, but she might have some ideas she might tell you rather than us. When she was living in Germany I think she had a nasty brush with the Stasi, when they were in control, so policemen are not her flavour of the month. I think you should think up a better story than acting for a relative, though. By all accounts she's highly intelligent; must have been after his money."

"Is she in the directory?"

"Yes, under her name. Walsh wouldn't want his to be used. The apartment was probably owned by Walsh, but done through a dummy company, so it's difficult to prove, but we're still working on it. I'll leave the address on your answering machine."

Bulman was not sure whether his old friend was trying to help or deliberately mislead him; Beatty would not throw him an important witness. But it was all he had managed to get and it would have to do.

Bulman returned to his flat in North Kensington. It was on the first floor of one of those Edwardian terraced houses, in one of the old squares close to the Portobello Road with its antique markets. He had eaten and drank too much and felt drowsy, but noticed his answering machine blinking and checked the messages. Anna Brenning's address had already been recorded, which meant that Beatty had phoned it through as soon as he had returned to Scotland Yard. But it was not Beatty's voice.

Bulman sat down and dozed and it was quite dark when he awoke. He sat thinking that he would not get too far with Walsh's murder, but he needed the money and would

17

keep going until such time as Edward Marshall decided he was wasting government funds.

The following morning, crisp and bright with a heavy frost, he took the underground to Kensington and walked from there. The apartment was not far from Olympia and tucked away behind the main road. It was in a short terrace with railings above the basement and steps leading up to the heavy front door. There were only two names against the entry box and a third with a blank card. He rang the blank and knew at once by the trace of accent that he had chosen correctly. "Anna Brenning?"

"Yes." Absolutely no hesitation. "Who is that?"

"My name is George Bulman. Could I have a word with you, please?"

"What about? I don't think I know you."

"You're right. I don't believe we have met. About Ronald Walsh." He expected her to hang up.

"Are you a reporter?"

It was a reasonable question. Why wasn't there a long queue of reporters blocking the entrance? Her association with Walsh had been well concealed by both Walsh and the police. That was strange in itself. "No. And I'm not the police either. Just a few words. I'm middle-aged, overweight and harmless. You will be perfectly safe."

"Oh, I know what you look like, Mr Bulman; but you may not be as harmless as you say."

Bulman felt caught out. He was getting slack. When he hastily examined the porch he could now see the television scanner high up in the corner and aimed straight at him. He thought quickly and gave a grin and a wave.

"Come on up, Mr Bulman. Top floor."

He heard the buzz of the lock release and pushed the door. Bulman went up to the top floor, and found an unmarked door along to his right with a spyhole centrally placed. There was no other door he could see so he rang the bell.

"Come in." It was as though she had been waiting behind

18

the door for him. He stepped past her into a small hall. "Go through," she said, closing the front door.

His first glance had been enough to see that she was a striking woman most men would turn their heads to see. And yet she wore old jeans and a sleeveless cardigan over a patterned silk blouse displaying no sign of glamour. Her copper-coloured hair was short with a fringe, her eyes a striking pale blue, her lips, smiling quietly, soft and well shaped.

"Now that you have had a good look, what is your impression?"

A younger man might have floundered but Bulman offered one of his crusty smiles and said easily, "You're by far the best thing I've seen this frosty morning. May I sit down?"

She stood by the doorway, hands clasped in front of her, the smile freezing a little as she said, "Not until I'm satisfied about you. How did you hear of me? Great pains have been taken to keep my presence here a secret, which is why there are no reporters camped out in the street. So who told you about me?"

"It is not as secret as you think. I can't tell you who told me and I don't think it matters. It is not something I intend to tell anyone else. Ronald Walsh may have left pointers to you."

"He was too careful a man."

"Not careful enough, evidently. He was obviously not prepared for what happened to him. You don't seem too upset by his death."

"You are very blunt. I was his mistress not his wife. I am an East German, I needed some sort of security here and he was able to give it to me. But it is none of your business." Anna Brenning walked up and down, hands still clasped in front of her, and she remained close to the door. "Perhaps you had better sit down." She unclasped her hands and sat on the arm of a chair as Bulman chose a comfortable seat.

For a while she studied the space between them, while Bulman studied her. She spread her arms in a gesture of resignation and said, "You must be wondering why I let you in. I want to know how you found out about me and this address. Even his friends did not know."

"I'm sorry but I can't tell you that. You have my name, from that you can make enquiries to check my credentials."

"You said you are not the police, is that true?"

"Absolutely. I was once but that was some time ago."

"Perhaps you still have friends in the police. That might be my answer. If it is, then there has been a betrayal of confidentiality. I shall formally complain."

"Friends or not, the police would not give me such information. Does it matter? I'm here to see if you can offer any leads as to who might have destroyed your meal ticket."

"I'd hardly do it myself; I relied on his financial support and now it's gone. Have you a business card?"

Bulman was taken by surprise. "I don't use them; never seen the need."

"But you are a private detective? You must have an office somewhere."

"I don't run a business; just odd jobs for friends. You must have known something about Walsh. He had a reputation for philandering; did you know about it or any of the other women?"

"I see no need to answer any of these questions. Just who are you working for?

"OK. I'm working for his wife." There was little chance that Anna Brenning would ever contact Ronald Walsh's widow. "She thinks the police might sit on a few things because he was an MP, and the Government can do without any more embarrassments. She could be right. Finding a murderer is one thing, revealing more of his shenanigans quite another. Not unnaturally she wants to know what he was up to and with whom. Does she know about you?"

"Not so far as I know. But she will now, won't she, because you will tell her."

Bulman was impressed by her composure. "You are naturally worried about your position. I might eventually have to tell her, but I'll only do that if I'm convinced it will help her to know. If you are able to provide some rough pointer to who might have killed him it could help me make up my mind."

"That's emotional blackmail, Mr Bulman. It's true I am worried about my position, someone has killed the goose who laid my golden egg, but it could take time to trace the ownership of this apartment, and until that is established and I am given an eviction order, I will stay here. That could be for some time. So your threat is hollow. Anyway, I simply don't know." She shrugged expressively. "Of course he had other women. I knew that before I moved in. It did not worry me, provided he was careful. And knowing gave me a little power over him, added security that might one day be useful."

Anna rose and from his sitting position, Bulman thought she was quite tall. She stood in front of him. "I suppose you think I am disgraceful."

"It's none of my business. I can understand why you did it. So you can't help me?" He felt a little sorry for her.

"I too, would like to find his killer. Whoever it was has complicated my life at a time when it was at least stabilized. Now it is not. I have told you more about myself than I told the police. I am quite lonely now; I needed to talk to someone."

"Are you here illegally?"

"If I was, the police would have acted on it."

"OK. Do you intend to return to Germany?"

"Not while I can live here. Why are you asking questions that have nothing to do with Ronald's murder?"

"I wondered if you ever go back for a visit; whether your friends are still there."

"I was in Germany when poor Ronnie was killed. I was

21

over for a few days." Anna gave an icy stare. "The police have checked so that will save you the trouble."

"To see your mother?"

"My mother is dead. Look, I would like to help you. I want to know the answers too, you know. How can I contact you if I think of something?"

Bulman scribbled his telephone number on to a page of a note pad and passed it over. "I'm not too far from here. One thing puzzles me, though. You were obviously something special to him, but you know he had other women. Was he in the habit of using call girls?"

"I never questioned him about his women. I simply accepted them to keep the peace and this apartment. We both knew what we were doing."

"You might have known; he got himself topped."

"Topped? Killed?"

Bulman nodded. "It is the motive that worries me. He had enough money to keep everybody happy, so what upset someone so much that they kill him? Perhaps there was a side to him that few knew about."

"There were many sides to him. It was not my function to find out how many; I simply satisfied a need. Me and others."

Bulman rose. "Did the police tell you that the call girl he booked cried off sick? Whoever took her place did the job."

"They did not go into detail. They were more interested in where I was at the time."

Bulman nodded. He made a more apparent inspection of the room and said, "Well, he certainly set you up well. How will you cope for money?"

"I shall be all right for a while. He was never mean."

Bulman thought she was well in control of herself. No false tears, no expression of rage, she was coping very well. She was obviously intelligent, spoke English as if the language was her own; what had reduced her to living with a creep like Walsh? Surely she could have done much better.

"It was the best offer going at the time," she said, as if reading his thoughts. "There was nothing for me in Germany, and it takes time to get established here. I had to fill the gap and it was the only way I knew." She smiled more fully and it was captivating. "At least you showed more interest in me as a person than any of the police or even Ronnie. Thank you. Perhaps we will meet again."

"Good luck." He shook her hand and left taking the stairs when the lift did not respond. When he reached the street he reflected that she had left an impression. He wondered how Walsh had found her and realized he should have asked. As he walked to the nearest underground station he considered that she had shown no fear; her future, one way or the other, did not seem to worry her. And that to him, left a question mark. Most mistresses would have shown some form of remorse, if only a false show. But, really, he had got nowhere except to have met her, when perhaps he could not have expected to have done. And that in itself raised another query.

Bulman decided to see the call girl who had cried off from seeing Walsh. By the time he reached his flat, he discovered he was left with more questions than answers. As he pushed open the street door, a man stepped from a porch across the street, made sure Bulman did not reappear, then walked back to a car parked awkwardly in too small a slot. He climbed into the passenger seat and the driver pulled out.

Chapter Three

The next morning Bulman rang Edward Marshall on the
special number, the answering machine clicked in and he
simply said "shadows". The return call came surprisingly
quickly. Bulman asked Marshall for the name of the agency
and the name and address of the girl who had cried off the
day Walsh was murdered. He was given them straight away.
He was so impressed that he said, "Have you anything else
there that you can give me to save me ringing?"

"Now, now. I knew you would want them, so made a
point of having them ready. Have you got anywhere?"

"Oh, sure, it's all wrapped up. Just tying the ends."

"No need to be sarky. Just keep me in touch."

Bulman called in on the agency that morning and got
nowhere. The police had already been twice and the once
good-looking, hard-faced ex-prostitute who ran the place,
saw no reason to give someone like Bulman, who had no
real authority, the time of day. And she was direct about
it. Once he had spun his stories and failed to impress her,
she simply told him to "Piss off". She had enough problems
with the recalcitrant girl and the police, without strangers
like Bulman poking his nose in.

Bulman accepted defeat gracefully, even laughed at being
beaten, and made his way to the girl's address. Connie
Smith, if that was her real name, lived in Islington in
one of those houses that had been upgraded when fashion
reversed itself in an area that had spent years in the social
wilderness. Now it was smart, and expensive cars parked
along the street proved the point.

24

Again there was an absence of press, when one might have expected a crowd outside the house. Someone was keeping the lid on very tightly indeed, and in an age where large sections of intrusive press printed fiction as fact rather than miss out, that could not have been at all easy. Walsh was getting infinitely more protection in death than he ever had in life. Why was he worth it? He had been one of those men so disaster prone when relating to keeping his assignations private, that it had become a public joke, even from his own colleagues. So how had he been so successful in keeping Connie Smith under wraps and why was it so important now?

The police had already called here, and neighbours would have noticed even if the cars were unmarked and the officers in plain clothes. It was a quiet street, few people visible, but Bulman did not feel alone as he rang the bell. When there was no answer he stepped back to view the windows. There was no curtain twitching. He rang again, a prolonged burst which must have been heard through the house.

He stepped back again. There was no back way that he could see. There was probably a small back garden which backed on to another back garden in the next street. A woman's voice close by asked, "Are you the police?"

Bulman had not noticed the adjacent front door open. A well-dressed woman in her mid-forties stood there. "Yes. This is Connie Smith's place, isn't it?"

"Yes. She's gone away."

"Oh, dear. Do you know where, or for how long?"

"No. Is it important that you get in? I mean is it her or the house you want to see?"

That was a strange question. "Why do you ask?"

"She left me the keys. She always does when she goes away. I can let you in, but I would have to come with you to make sure everything was all right."

At first Bulman thought she saw him as an excuse, as an opportunity to nose round, but as she already had the keys there was nothing to stop her doing that anyway. It was

25

curious. "Well, it would be to her benefit if I could contact her. She might have left a forwarding address inside." He thought that if she had, the neighbour would already have found it. "Let's have a look," he said cheerfully.

The neighbour introduced herself as Lorna Russell. She was quite well spoken, smart and not unattractive. She opened the door for him and he preceded her into quite a large hall with doors on one side and a wide staircase on the other. It was expensively carpeted.

"If she left an address it's likely to be in the music room," said Lorna, who clearly knew the layout and led the way to an end room. "The police have already seen her, but you must know that." She opened a door and stood aside, suddenly realizing that she was alone with a stranger. "I should have asked to see your identity card," she said belatedly.

"Yes you should have," replied Bulman stepping past her. "Don't worry. I'm Detective Chief Inspector Allen. There has been a development she should know about, which is why I want to contact her." He gazed round the room. There was a stacked hi-fi system at one end with mini speakers, but nearer to him was a desk covered in newspaper adverts.

"She was always answering ads," said Lorna. "She was always getting catalogues for this and that. Not short of money." And then the question she had been dying to ask: "Is Connie in trouble?"

Bulman smiled to himself. Lorna had let him in, not to view the place which she knew only too well, but to get him alone to find out what she could. He moved over to the desk and sat down before it. At the back, almost hidden by newspaper clippings, was a framed photograph which had been knocked over. He stood it up where he thought it should be. A pretty brunette stared wistfully into space. He thought a soft lens might have been used to ease the lines. This must be a photograph of Connie Smith, but he hesitated to ask, for as a policeman he would have her description. "Pretty woman," he said.

"Yes," agreed Lorna. "Of course she is photogenic. That's a bit flattering and probably taken some time ago. You did not answer my question; is she in trouble?"

Bulman started to sift through some of the clippings. "That would depend on what you call trouble."

"Well, there are some around here who think she is on the game. She does go out at strange times, mainly at night. And she's very quiet about what she does."

Bulman tried the desk drawers; they were locked. "Have you seen men come here?"

"Oh no, she doesn't bring her work home. They say she's a call girl. But I think she's very nice. Always been pleasant to me. What has she done to bring the police round?"

Bulman continued to rummage through the papers on top of the desk. "I'm not sure that I should tell you. Are you sure you have no inkling of where she might have gone?"

"I'm not sure that I should tell you," mimicked Lorna. "I wouldn't want to get her into trouble."

"If you're withholding information you are already in trouble." Bulman pushed the chair back. "I tell you what, I'll do a deal with you. Providing you promise not to tell anyone else, I'll tell you as much as I dare without getting myself into trouble, if you can point me towards her. She won't get into trouble from me, I promise you. And you can also give me the keys to this desk."

Lorna considered the proposition for about five seconds and said, "All right. You first."

Bulman clasped his hands. "Connie is a very fine lady. She runs an animal sanctuary down in Berkshire. For some crazy reason, animal activists think there are experiments being performed on some of the animals and have set most of them free. Many of the smaller animals will perish, they can't cope on their own. Some have already been found dead. Her house there has been vandalized, and a barn set fire to and destroyed. That's what my colleagues called about earlier.

"Since then," Bulman continued, "we have arrested two men and a woman, and we need Connie to see if she can identify any of them. One of them seems to know her personally. There is a fourth person involved, the ringleader, who has sent a message to the local police that he'll kill Connie unless the others are released. It's probably an empty threat but he is known to us and is the type of maniac who might just do it. Now you understand why we must find her."

"Oh my God, I had no idea. Poor, Connie. You can be so wrong about people. Have they recovered any of the animals?"

"Some. They are still searching. We've called in a zoologist to help, for some are rare specimens. Come on, Lorna, she hasn't returned to the sanctuary, so where is she?"

"She sometimes went to a little cottage her sister owns in Hampshire. I don't know the exact address. I think it's in the Wallops or somewhere."

"I'll have to go through the desk. She must have it written down somewhere. I suppose the poor girl is so distressed she couldn't cope and just ran off. The keys, Lorna. Please."

"I haven't got any desk keys."

"You've deceived me. I gave you information nobody but a police officer should have."

Lorna, believing she had been smart enough to get what she wanted, was now clearly worried.

"Look," said Bulman sternly, "everybody has suitcase keys; go and dig some out. As many as you can. We can but try. Go and have a look, Lorna, we're running out of time."

"I'll see what I can do."

When Lorna had bustled off, Bulman quickly located the kitchen, found an ice pick and a steak hammer, and returned to the desk to break the locks open. He found the Hampshire address quite quickly, but he also found a bank statement and some old chequebook stubs. He was immersed in them when Lorna returned.

At first he did not hear her, for she moved very quietly and he was concentrating. When she spoke he started, feeling caught out.

"You've opened them," she accused.

He looked up, irritated now by her presence. "I found some of my own keys fitted. So I got on with it. I've found the address, but thought I might find some evidence that might link her to the man still on the loose." He hoped that his body bulk hid the ruptured locks. He put his hand over the one nearest to her.

She stood beside him with a bunch of small keys on a ring. "I'm sorry, Lorna, but time is vital. But you have been most helpful. I'll just make a few notes and I'll be off."

He was forced to do it from memory as Lorna was in no hurry to move again. But if he started copying from the bank statement she would at once become suspicious, and he wasn't at all sure if she was already at that stage. He scribbled down what he could remember, closed the drawers, stood up, and said, "There's no point in locking them again, they contain nothing of material value. I'll explain the situation when I catch up with her. Anyhow thanks, Lorna. Do you want me to tell her how you helped or would you rather be left out of it?" He was virtually herding her towards the door.

"You'd better leave me out of it. If things turn out right I'll let her know myself."

Just before they left the house Bulman jotted down his home number and passed it to Lorna. "If she does contact you, could you let me know personally? She might not want to contact the police as such. I happen to admire what she is doing and I think I can help her without a load of officialdom. Just give me a bell."

He returned back home, went to the nearby lock-up and reversed out his ancient, but well-cared-for Daimler Sovereign, the same car Spider Scott had wanted him to

29

burn to destroy evidence not many months ago. He drove down to Andover on the M3 and from there picked up the signs to the Wallops.

He found the Salisbury Road, motored a few miles until he reached the Army Air Force Museum at the approach to the Wallops, took the mini roundabout and turned right past a village church and then right again. The mainly thatched cottages were often badly marked or numbered but he did not want to draw attention to himself by asking someone, although there were very few people about.

He eventually found the cottage. It was well isolated from the rest, on the edge of farmland. The name board hung sideways as if vandals had tried to tear it off the wooden gate which needed painting. There was no garage that he could see, but there was a red Ford parked round the side of the cottage suggesting someone was in. He turned the Daimler round awkwardly in the narrow lane and managed to tuck it behind a tall privet hedge on the far side of the cottage and actually in part of the field.

It was impossible to walk quietly on the gravel from the gate to the low cottage door. He had to duck under the overhang of thatch forming the porch. There was no bell on the low oak door so he raised the horseshoe knocker and gave it a slam.

Nobody answered so he slammed harder. The thud must have been heard right through the house. Nobody came. He waited a while before deciding to explore.

The garden was badly neglected and rose bushes struggled through shrubs, withered heads still hanging on. The paved path which ran round the cottage was largely overgrown. He followed it round, peering into windows as he went. The interior appeared to be cosy enough, though lacklustre, and, like so many cottages with low ceilings, it was dark inside.

He continued round, looking for an open window or an unlocked door. The rear garden was not large, but was screened by a tall beech hedge which gave maximum privacy. A window was ajar at the back and when he

30

looked through saw that it was the kitchen. The door was closed, but when he tried it it opened. He went in and repeatedly called out.

On the kitchen counter the kettle was still plugged in and when he touched it it was still warm. A mug lay on its side with the coffee spilled out. He passed into a lounge, quite a large room which had probably been converted from two. A newspaper lay opened on the floor as if someone had put it down to do something, perhaps answer a knock on the door. He stood in the hall and called out again.

He stood there waiting; there was a bad feel about the place, as though the cottage and its inhabitants had suddenly died of age. It was easy to imagine, as he surveyed walls that needed cleaning and the drabness of the furniture; it needed sprucing up. There was a heavy smell of smoke and the wood fire in the huge open grate was still sparking and spitting.

He ducked under a beam and climbed the stairs. He found the main bedroom quite easily and it was the brightest room in the place. A modern shower cubicle had been erected. He pulled the screen back but it was quite empty. There was another bedroom and a box room. He went downstairs again, and wondered what to do. He gazed through the windows; the cottage was not overlooked; it was well screened and secluded. An ideal retreat. If Connie Smith had come here, perhaps she had gone shopping, in which case she should know better than to leave the kitchen door unlocked and a window open.

Having come so far Bulman was reluctant to let go so soon. He went outside again. There was a deafening roar as seven helicopters flew overhead in formation, having come from the nearby military airfield. Once they had gone the silence was complete again and he started to poke around the garden. The weather had been so mild for winter that the ground was soft underneath, and sometimes slippery. He saw what appeared to be skid marks in the grass and he headed towards the rear of the garden where the ground rose into a neglected rockery.

He found the body of a woman apparently tucked behind the rockery, but closer examination suggested this was where she had finally fallen and had died. Her terrible condition could suggest no other cause but murder. It would have been impossible for anyone to self-inflict such ghastly wounds. Her clothes were torn, presumably as a result of a frantic struggle, and her face was deeply lacerated, rivulets of congealed blood down her face and neck. Her fingernails were broken and bloodied where she must have raked her attacker. Blood was spattered on the rockery suggesting she had fought desperately for her life and had dragged her murderer all over the place. Her plucky effort had not been enough to save her.

Bulman touched her only to satisfy himself that there was no pulse and to get some idea of body temperature. There was stark fear in her staring eyes; she had been terrified before dying. He did not close the eyes, it was an expression the police would need to see. She had not died easily, had clearly fought for her life and her murderer must bear the marks of such a fight. Even with her face so badly scarred and with blood clotted hair stranded across her features, he was sure of one thing; this girl was not Connie Smith.

Bulman sat back on his heels staring at the corpse. So where was Connie Smith, and who was the dead girl? What worried him most was the certainty that the murder had not been done long before his arrival. The body was not yet cold and the kettle had been warm. He had seen no car come from this direction on his final approach to the cottage. Once on the Salisbury Road no car would stand out anyway, but it must have been a near thing.

He could see no obvious sign of how she had died, only of the struggle. He resisted the temptation to move her, so went round her once more. He could not be sure, but by the way she was huddled with one arm across her stomach she might have been knifed. There was no indication that she had been sexually assaulted.

Bulman straightened. The policeman in him demanded that he should immediately ring the police. The independent loner demanded that he should find out what he could while he was here. There was nothing he could do for the girl. He stared down at her, horrified and puzzled. Years on murder cases made no difference; mutilated bodies still made him feel sick. He pulled on his woollen gloves and walked slowly back to the cottage to begin a careful search.

He could find no photograph of the murdered girl, but he did find an unframed one of Connie Smith tucked away in a drawer. So at least he had come to the right place. He searched diligently, room by room, drawer by drawer, putting everything back as he found it knowing that the police would also search. Apart from women's clothing the cottage was fairly basic and, as a retreat, perhaps that was the idea.

He found a black wig in one of the drawers. There was no wig stand that he could see. And in a dressing table drawer among the make-up in the main bedroom he found a set of contact lenses in their little box. They might have interested him had anyone actually seen who killed Ronald Walsh MP, but there was no connection. And then he found the pistol tucked into some rolled up stockings. He was no great authority on pistols but he had good eyesight and was able to read the make. It was a Presne Strojirentsvi; a CZ vz.70. Now that was one hell of a long coincidence and he did not accept those odds.

He carefully wrapped the pistol up in its stockinged cocoon. He hoped nobody missed it during the police search. He went back to the girl and took a long look. Was he looking at Walsh's assassin?

Chapter Four

The discovery had taken him no further forward and, as yet, there was no positive indication that the two murders were connected. Yet he was sure that they were; the question was in what way? Had they both been killed for the same reason? He began to think that there must be a witness to Walsh's murder as yet unknown, a more positive witness than a hotel receptionist who had turned a blind eye to make sure he saw nobody enter Walsh's room, and a more positive witness than a girl who had agreed to pass up a 'trick' for someone else to perform. They must both have been paid considerable sums of money.

There were no apparent pockets in the clothes of the dead girl, nothing clutched in her hands. Forensic would surely find skin tissue under her nails, but would not inform him. He took one last look to try to record her features under the ghastly wounds and then walked back to the cottage. There was no point in going round it again, so he left by the kitchen door and went round the side to the red Ford.

All the doors were unlocked. He climbed in, rummaged through the shelves; a packet of chewing gum, paper tissues, torn road maps; there was nothing unusual. The driver's seat was very tight for him, too far forward, suggesting the car belonged to the dead girl, which was no great discovery. He climbed out, made a note of the registration number, and wandered back to the cottage. He already knew the telephone was in the cramped hall, and he dialled 999 and briefly reported the murder. He returned to his car and drove off.

He had come down to find Connie Smith. He was satisfied that she was nowhere in the cottage or gardens, so where was she? And was she dead or alive? By the time Bulman reached London he was disgruntled and worried. The killings were coming too easily and nastily. He had the strong sensation that someone was closing the doors as he reached them, which meant they knew about him, in which case he might try one door too many.

He decided to go out for a meal and went to a Chinese restaurant not too far from his apartment. When he got back there was a message from Detective Chief Superintendent Walter Beatty asking him to ring him back. When Bulman did Beatty was off duty and it would have to wait until morning.

After a restless night he cooked a full breakfast and took pot luck in ringing Beatty again. Beatty was quite amiable. "A witness has come forward, a girl. Reckons she saw someone enter the hotel at a time Cooper, who was on duty that night, maintains he saw nobody."

"A witness has come forward? How? Did you advertise for one?"

"Don't be funny, George. Our boys have been chasing the local brasses in the area. This one says she saw a brunette enter the hotel about six the evening Walsh was murdered."

"That it?"

"Well sod you, George. I'm doing this for old times sake, show a bit of gratitude."

"I don't suppose she noticed the colour of the girl's eyes?" Bulman had meant it to be half flippant believing that Beatty was throwing a crumb in the hope of getting something back.

"Yes. Brown. She had a good look, for all the brasses are known to each other, and this was one she did not know."

"What made her think the brunette was a brass, for God's sake?"

35

"It's sad when a man like you loses touch. It takes one to know one. Have you got anything for me?"

Bulman ignored the question. "Is there any chance of my seeing this witness?"

"Now you're pushing your luck. I've stepped right out of line to tell you about her in the first place. With my rank I should know better."

Bulman had already thought that; Beatty was far from being a fool, and Bulman began to wonder if he had been prompted to tell him about the brass by a higher authority. Someone like Edward Marshall MP for instance, with the backing of the Home Secretary. "And that's supposed to be helpful is it?"

"Well it points to a woman doing the job."

"You already accepted that."

"So now we know it was a brunette. Or at least see the distinct possibility."

"She might have been wearing a wig."

There was a long pause and Bulman could hear Beatty's laboured breathing. "Do you know something?" Beatty asked at last.

Bulman weighed it up. "I'll answer that for the name and address of the witness."

"You know I can't do that. I can have you for withholding information. Come on, George. Cough."

"What information? The offer stands. And don't piss about, Wally, this call is costing me a bomb and we're getting nowhere."

"I'll give you her street name and her beat. That's the best I can do. And I'll give you the colour of her hair. Now what do you know?"

Big deal, reflected Bulman, jotting the details down. He thought carefully before saying, "Contact the Hampshire Police, Andover area. They will probably contact the Yard in due course once they've made a connection, but that might take time and I'm saving you that time. My information is that a woman has been murdered, and

36

that she possessed a black wig and brown contact lenses. She might also have a gun that will interest you."

"*George, what the hell have you been playing at?*"

The roar forced Bulman to hold the receiver away from his ear. Bulman said sweetly, "Come off it. You know bloody well that Connie Smith did a runner. But it ain't her." He hung up before matters became more complicated. He considered that he had saved Beatty time and had given more than he had received, but it was the best he could expect. At least he had a tap-in to some of the Yard's information.

There was nothing Bulman could do until evening, when a red-headed prostitute called Sheila might possibly be operating on her beat, which included the hotel in which Walsh was killed. He could not really see what he could get out of her that Beatty and his men had not already obtained.

It was drizzling when he went out that evening to search for the volunteer witness. With only a name and hair colour which might change nightly, he was not hopeful. He used the hotel as a starting point.

The trouble with brasses, he thought, was that they knew how to make use of the shadows as well as any villain. Now you see them, now you don't. And he had the tremendous disadvantage of looking like a policeman, which he had been for so long. The girls could pick the Bill out in the dark. This was a time when he needed his old beat skills and that was going back a long time.

He roamed around, gradually getting wetter and more miserable. He spotted the odd pair of legs in doorways but none of the girls became actually visible. They clearly did not see him as a potential client and almost certainly as a copper, so there were no beginners on the early beat that night.

He stood hopefully in the hotel entrance for a time, but nobody came or went, and suddenly life had ceased in what would otherwise be a fairly busy area at this time. Finally a young girl did sidle up to him, and flashed him a smile under a coloured umbrella. Before she could start her routine he said, "I'm looking for Sheila. Where can I find her?"

"By looking, granddad. I was about to do you a favour."

She flounced off before Bulman could say anything more. Granddad. That hurt. But it seemed that Sheila was around somewhere. He went walking again, during which he received from the shadows a hissed, "copper", and worse, "filth". It never used to be like that.

Finally he saw a pair of legs, almost fluorescent in the dark, at the top of some steps under a porch. He climbed the steps and said to the girl standing there, "I am not a copper even if I look like one. I'm looking for Sheila and will pay for the right direction. I mean her no harm."

"How much?"

"A fiver?"

"Mean bastard. Twenty."

"That means I don't eat for a couple of days." Bulman pulled out his wallet. "This is extortion," he added as he peeled off a couple of tens.

"I'm doing you a favour, pop. You need to diet."

That dismissed a generation at least. "So where can I find her?"

She held out her hand for the money and it disappeared into the darkness. "What do you want with her?"

Even close to, it was difficult to see clearly under the porch. He could just make out the pale shape of her face, and what little light there was, gave her eyes an attractive luminosity. "That was not part of the bargain. I just want to know where she is."

"It's just that she's a friend of mine. I'm trying to protect her."

"Tell me where she is or give me back my money, and don't think I'd have qualms in taking it back, anyway you like. Look I just want to ask her something. No sweat."

"I'm Sheila. Who are you?"

At first Bulman was furious, then he laughed. "You crafty cat. A nice one, Sheila, but it wasn't worth more than a fiver. You volunteered as witness to a girl going into the hotel up the road about six on the evening that MP bloke was murdered. Was that on the up?"

In the poor light he could not see her stiffen, but he did sense a change of atmosphere. She stepped away from him, and for a moment he thought she was going to run. He said quickly, "If you do a runner you'll never work this patch again."

With a slight quiver in her voice she said, "You said you weren't the Bill."

"I'm not. I just sound like them. I'm making enquiries for another party. There's no need to get het up. Did someone approach you to spill that yarn about the brunette going into the hotel? Or did you actually see her? I mean, with your business acumen you would have struck a hard bargain."

"Only the police have that information. You must be one of them." Sheila's attitude had changed completely. She now sounded scared and perhaps that supplied the answer.

"If someone nobbled you that means two sources have that information. I just want a straight answer, Sheila. The police will already have considered the possibility and will probably come back to you. I might be able to head them off; I have contacts in high places."

"What does it matter what I told the Bill if you're not one of them?"

"I don't care what you told them; all I need to know is if someone used you to give them a bum steer."

"You've asked your question and I've given you an answer."

Bulman said, "I'm not passing judgement. You would not be the only person recently who has misinformed the police. There was one not a million miles from here. Come on, Sheila, just nod if you don't want to say anything."

"Do you mean Bert, at the hotel? He's tired of answering questions; he's done a runner."

"When?" Bulman was alarmed.

"He didn't turn up for duty last night. We had quite a good contact with him. We are all tired of answering questions. A randy MP gets topped, what's the big deal? Someone did his wife a favour. Maybe it was her."

"Sheila, if Bert's done a runner then maybe so should you. If you were paid to lie to the police it might backfire. Whoever paid you might find life easier if you weren't around any more."

"They'd have done it by now. Stop trying to scare me."

But it was her fear that gave her away. She had been nobbled, thought Bulman. "They would not use you as a witness and then kill you directly after; it would be counterproductive. Push off for a while, Sheila. They'll have you marked down for later. You carry your equipment on you, ply your trade somewhere else." He gave her a nod in the dark and went down the steps.

He went to the hotel to make sure Bert Cooper had left, and found that Sheila had told the truth on that count. As Marshall was picking up the bills, he went into the dining room and had dinner there. Three people, he reflected, one cancelling an appointment, one suddenly losing his sight and seeing nothing, and one bearing false witness. Two of the three had disappeared. The hotel management had tried to contact Bert Cooper by phone, and had even sent one of the staff round to his flat to make sure he was not ill; he apparently lived alone. Bert had taken all his stuff and had cleared off. Had the money he had received been worth it? When intimidation started from practised people, no money was worth it.

When he got back to his own apartment Bulman left a telephone message for Edward Marshall without using the code, and insisted that they meet as soon as possible. They met the next day at midday in a small apartment off St James's. Marshall was annoyed from the start. As Bulman removed his topcoat and threw it over a chair prior to sitting down, Marshall said, "I'm not at all happy about this. I was hoping there would be no need to meet."

The place was cramped, nothing special, apart from location. Bulman was not impressed by the furnishings or Marshall's attitude. "Why not? What's so special about meeting? Why is all this so bloody secret? And do the police know it's secret?" Bulman was annoyed too; as yet he had not been offered a drink.

"I'm sorry. I'm having a bad day. Now what problem is so urgent that we have to meet?"

"I've done what I can and have come to a dead end. Two witnesses have disappeared, a woman has been murdered, and a brass called Sheila has been paid to give false evidence. Someone wants us to believe that a brown-eyed brunette did the job. There is a lot of manipulation behind Walsh's murder, and I would say a good deal of money. The only thing I'm satisfied about is that it is far from being a *crime passionnel*. I can't get anywhere. That murder has far deeper roots than a woman taking her revenge."

"Do you know who the murdered woman is?"

"You mean the police haven't told you? I find that strange. I don't know who she was, but would guess it to be Connie Smith's sister. I reckon they got the wrong woman, unless she was also involved. The other thing I find very strange is that the Detective Chief Superintendent on the case happens to be an old friend of mine. Now there's a coincidence."

"Come now," Marshall was more relaxed. "You must still have many friends in the police after all the years you put in. Had it not been Beatty it might have been someone else you know. Just a piece of luck he was one of your best friends." Marshall glanced towards a small table which had some bottles on it but made no move towards it. He could see that Bulman was far from convinced. "It seems to me that you've done remarkably well," he said at last. "In a very short space of time."

"Possibly. But I can get no further. I simply don't

41

understand why, with the massive weight of the Met behind you, you should use me as well. It's bloody stupid. I'm relying on them for scraps of information. I can't carry on like that."

"The Yard are looking for a murderer and if they find one their job is done. They want a conviction. What I want is to know what Ronnie Walsh was up to besides bedding a variety of women. That might mean finding the murderer, but it is my belief that motive will not be easy to establish, and that there may be far more than one. The police will be happy with any motive, but I won't be. I've asked Beatty to help as far as he can. I know your record, George. I know what you've done already. Knowing who did it has never been good enough for you, which is one of the reasons you left the police. You could have been a psychologist had you so wanted. I'm fully aware of your success at Open University. Bear with me, George."

Bulman was surprised at Marshall's insistence and it confirmed to him that he was still not being given the full picture. "Let's get this straight. You really want me to find out what Walsh was up to apart from women? From me you want his hidden background not his murderer? Have I got it right?"

"To a degree. Digging out his background and finding his murderer might well be compatible. The lines must cross somewhere."

Bulman shook his head. "It still doesn't make sense. If the police are interested only in a conviction without having to rake up too much of his background, why worry? What the police don't know nobody else will worry about. Let it stay buried. You're obviously afraid of something coming out about our Ronnie that could be political dynamite otherwise you wouldn't care." He was watching Marshall closely as he spoke and added pointedly, "You're afraid of it brushing against other involved parties. MPs? Ministers? So why don't you use the Security Service? Shit, you're using me for a cover-up."

"Don't be ridiculous. If I was sure of that I wouldn't need you at all. Just keep digging away. You've worked on gut feelings; that's exactly what I'm doing. Don't give up, George."

Bulman shook his head. "You don't seem to understand that I have no more leads to follow. I haven't got teams of officers I can put on surveillance to keep an eye on the witnesses. It's a disgrace that they have been allowed to run."

"You won't even sleep on it?"

"I have been sleeping on it. Right at the beginning, I think it was you who said that we are dealing with shadows. Take it from me that these shadows know how to create confusion and to close the door tightly behind them. I'm stumped."

"You are not afraid that something might happen to you?"

"In what way?"

"After the experience that put you in hospital when you were protecting the US Ambassador, I thought you might be worried that something similar could happen. I would understand if that were the case. You do appear a little concerned."

Bulman rose angrily. "I'm concerned because you haven't offered me a bloody drink. Let's just forget the whole thing. I'll send you a bill." He strode towards the door.

That might have been the end of it, except that Bulman was annoyed with himself for allowing his distaste of officialdom in general to get the better of him. His feelings were mixed when Marshall called on him that same evening. It was so unexpected a step that it made him at once suspicious and thereby interested. A PPS calling at his apartment was a first, and he considered, a careless if not a desperate move.

In spite of his mood, he offered Marshall a drink as the politician lowered himself on to a Queen Anne chair, and decided to include the liquor on the bill. He intended to

43

make it as uncomfortable as possible for Marshall and did not even ask him why he had called.

They sat drinking quietly and were almost at peace with each other when Marshall eventually said, "I've had an idea. You have a friend, a retired burglar, called William Scott — "

"Spider Scott," Bulman cut in. "Forget him, he's on holiday in the Bahamas with his wife, Maggie."

"Yes, I know that. I checked before coming. But there is another man; Jackson. I believe he is called Jacko. If he's available, he could do your leg work for you. And he could watch your back, too."

"Watch my back? What the bloody hell for?"

"That was badly phrased; help you then. Run around for you."

"I haven't complained about the leg work. As I understand it, Jacko is a bit of a nutter, ex-SAS."

"You've heard of him then?"

"Oh, yes. He's another one the Security Service have used almost to extinction. We operate in entirely different ways. I have no use for such a man." And then with some surprise Bulman said, "Was it that notion that brought you slumming over here? That wouldn't persuade me to change my mind."

"I think you should at least speak to him and not prejudge." Marshall added, "Nice whisky. Extraordinary fellow, our Jacko. Incredible shot." Before Bulman could cut in, Marshall hurried on, "I went to Hereford once with the Home Secretary. The SAS put on demonstrations for visiting VIPs. A little showpiece. One of them is to seat a soldier in a chair with a blank board behind him. Another picks up a submachine gun and shoots his colleague's outline on the board while the fellow doesn't blink an eyelid. "Marvellous shooting." Marshall was trying to see if Bulman was impressed. "But the general idea is to show the tremendous confidence and reliability they place in one another; the absolute trust."

44

"Bully for them," said Bulman dryly. "I wouldn't know one end of a gun from another. I'd probably shoot myself, I'm so useless with guns."

"I just thought that support like that might give you a sense of security."

"You're beginning to frighten the hell out of me. Why would I want security? Just what are you not telling me? Have you really come out of your way just to tell me that? Are you so desolate?"

Marshall was uneasy. "I haven't handled this at all well. My object was to reassure you not to dismay. To offer you someone else to work with who would earn his keep. Someone you could rely on."

"Maybe I just have that effect on you." Bulman smiled. "You've done the opposite. I can't work with other people, or at least not unless they are my own choice. I really don't understand why you called. Can't you find another sucker?"

"I'm disappointed in you. I was led to believe that you had staying power. I'm sorry I've wasted your time. But I'll leave you Jackson's address just in case you change your mind."

Marshall closed the street door behind him, and stood for a moment on top of the shallow steps while he pulled on his gloves.

A man in a doorway diagonally across the street watched Marshall slowly descend the steps and walk a few yards to where he had parked his car. When the car moved off with a puff of exhaust smoke obscuring the rear lights, the man did not move for a while and then his gaze shifted to the first floor window he knew to be part of Bulman's apartment. When Bulman's silhouette showed against the drawn curtains he made sure nobody could see him, then pulled out a gun with a laser sight and raised it until the red light shone on the window pane just in front of the shadow.

45

Chapter Five

After Marshall had gone, Bulman wondered at the politician's persistence; he would not have called on a whim. He walked the room, unaware that a laser sight was aimed at his shadow as he passed the front window. He was far from being a coward, in fact, although he would have scoffed at the idea, he was a brave man. His bravery sprang from the fact that he did not like being beaten by a problem, even if physical violence stood in the way. But he never looked for trouble and saw himself as useless when violence erupted; too often he had been on the losing end of it.

He could not stop his mind from working, and that was one of the problems. Anyone who really knew him, also knew that they had only to arouse his curiosity to make an otherwise indolent tendency to function. And there was no doubt that Marshall had done that. Marshall had not accepted Bulman's resignation from the job without actually voicing it; he had merely rekindled Bulman's interest. And the hint at danger intrigued Bulman enough not to run away from it.

He poured himself another drink and cursed Marshall for calling. He sat down and unknown to him, the man across the road put his gun back in his pocket, but remained where he was until he was relieved by another man.

Bulman agonized for some time, wondering if it was actually feasible to continue. Eventually he picked up the phone, the answering machine cut in and he announced himself as "shadows" before saying, "I'll want time and a half, no arguments about expenses, and I want a complete

46

dossier on Walsh covering the last year. Where he's been and particularly who with, if it's known. But his travels should be recorded. I'd also like details of his business interests, and I'd like to know whether you think he has interests which are not recorded. I also want a complete run-down on Anna Brenning. I might contact Jacko; I'll think about it. If I do, I want freedom to negotiate what he is paid, if he agrees to help, which is probably bloody unlikely."

So Marshall had won. Bulman laughed aloud; maybe it was fifty-fifty, he had after all upped the ante for he had no doubt now that Marshall would pay. His attitude had changed and he knew that whatever happened now he would not change his mind again. He was in for keeps in spite of a deep foreboding.

The information he wanted arrived by hand at ten, next morning. It was quite a bulky envelope and the contents must already have been prepared. There was a handwritten slip clipped to the dossier of Anna Brenning which read: 'This information was not available when we first met or I would have handed it over then. It does show that I have not been idle.'

Bulman started on the bigger file first. Walsh was involved in all sorts of companies and in many held controlling interest. He could not expect balance sheets of the various companies, and probably would not have understood them had they been supplied. But Marshall had supplied a rough index of the companies' success or failure rate. It seemed that everything he touched turned to gold. There was no doubt that he had possessed a remarkable business acumen. There were failures, if Marshall's notes were accurate, but small companies probably used for tax advantages, were the only ones to indicate no obvious success.

Bulman went through everything Marshall had supplied and could only come away with the impression that Walsh would not have wanted for anything ever again; he'd simply had a gift for making money, and his companies would

47

seem to be reputable traders; there was nothing 'iffy' in their products. Walsh had been an upright business man running upright businesses of some magnitude. Why then, had he not been more successful as an MP, as many a man of far less achievement had been knighted or more? In recognition terms Walsh had been bottom of the league. And yet the dossier showed him to be active, and often patron in several worthwhile charities.

Bulman was certain that the list of female conquests was incomplete, and each name was accompanied by a scribbled note that there was no actual proof of any of these affairs and the women involved had laid no complaint; it did not add whether possible husbands or boyfriends had complained. Some of the names Bulman recognized and surprised him; Walsh must have possessed far more than business acumen. There were no men involved, at least none were mentioned, so he had not been gay which cut off one line of enquiry. The list must have been compiled by MI5 rather than the police, who would not care how many women Walsh had slept with. Until now. If the police were to enquire about each woman, then they had a job on and Bulman was sure that most would deny any such connection.

If MI5 had made the list for security reasons then they would have chapter and verse of meetings. This information had not been supplied and Bulman was not at all certain that he needed it. All he required was an indication of a relationship and this he now had. As he studied the list he realized that he had a small army of would-be assassins, and some, he was sure, were capable of it. But he did not think the truth lay with them. One notable omission was Anna Brenning, but Bulman took the charitable view that she was not on the list because of her separate dossier.

Had it been Walsh's notorious womanizing that had precluded him from honours? Why should he be singled out? There was a whole history of womanizing politicians, long lists extending either side of Lloyd George, who had received honours. Bulman pondered this before turning to Anna Brenning's sheets, without really getting anywhere yet he felt it was important to know, and he would have to tackle Marshall about it; maybe he had slept with one wife too many. Later he would go over Walsh's papers again but meanwhile he concentrated on the German.

She had been a young radical, not quite of the gun and bomb toting variety, but had expressed her views under a harsh and brutal Communist regime and had been sentenced to one year's imprisonment for speaking out of turn too publicly. But, inexplicably, she served only two months. When the wall came tumbling down and the Stasi, the hated East German Police, went running in all directions, she was able to 'finger' some of them, much to her delight. What changed her life completely was when the Stasi records were eventually released, and she discovered that both her mother and her brother had been reporting her to the Stasi for years.

Bulman lowered the report. Finding that her own family had been betraying her all along must have had a devastating effect – even if she had not been close to her mother and brother. He read on. It was soon after this discovery that Anna came to Britain to try to start a new life, and she had achieved that by high class whoring. Bulman began to have a certain sympathy for her. Betrayed by those closest to her was bad enough, but it inevitably meant that she had lost her family at the same time. There could never be any form of trust again.

The Home Office had obviously taken a lenient view of her reasons for wanting to stay in Britain, for she was clearly far from being an illegal immigrant. There was no mention of when she had been allowed in or whose decision it had been in the Home Office. Nor was there any mention of her running affair with Walsh. Bulman knew of it, Marshall knew of it, but both only after the death of Walsh. It suggested that this was one affair MI5 had not discovered. And yet Walsh had been seemingly cavalier about his other affairs or Bulman would not have the list he was now holding.

He reached for the phone and rang Anna Brenning. The answering machine clicked in and after the bleep he said, "Anna, if I may, this is George Bulman. Would it be possible to see you again?"

Anna's voice cut in and said, "Hello, Mr Bulman. Of course you can. I leave the machine on to filter calls. Why don't you come round for coffee tomorrow about ten?"

He thought quickly. "Could you make that afternoon tea? Or would that be inconvenient?"

"That'll be fine. See you about three, then."

He rang Marshall and left a message asking for particulars of who exactly in the Home Office had given Anna Brenning permission to stay in Britain, and were there any conditions attached. He hung up. Of course it could have been a civil servant, but it still needed answering; unless she had been working for the SIS while in Germany, which would raise a whole lot of questions.

He then rang 'Glasshouse' Willie Jackson. He knew more about him than he had let on to Marshall. Some called him Glasshouse, because he had finished up in a military prison, but most called him Jacko. Bulman was aware that Jacko owned an agency which hired out clothes to theatrical and film companies. He seemed to exist quite well by it, unless he had other activities, but anyway the business had been going for some time and operated out of an old warehouse near the docks in London's East End.

A girl answered the phone and he asked if he might speak to Mr Jackson and told her that his name was Bulman. She asked him to hold on and then came back to ask, "Are you Mr George Bulman?"

"Yes. Don't tell me he's heard of me."

She asked him to hold on again and then came back saying, "He said he doesn't talk to coppers."

Bulman had heard the click of a second receiver being lifted and could hear the faint breathing of another person.

"Bullshit," he said. "He's spent half his life talking to coppers. Anyway, I'm retired."

"You knew I was listening," Jacko cut in.

"Your breathing can't be as even as it used to be. Can I come and see you?"

"What about?"

"I'll tell you when I see you. You have been recommended to me."

"That narrows it down. What about lunch tomorrow?"

"It would have to be early, I've an appointment at three."

"Busy little Bulman. Do you know the Hot Pot in Soho?"

"Most of the villains and coppers in London know it."

"Twelve o'clock, OK?"

Unknowingly, Bulman was seeing Jacko at his best as the two men shook hands. The excess weight Jacko had acquired after leaving the services had been trimmed down, the hair was now cut short again, and his granite features had the patina of good health. Jacko looked what he was, tough without being belligerent.

Jacko led the way to his favourite corner table, and it was clear from the nods and smiles on the way that he was well known there. They sat down and a waiter appeared almost immediately. Two large scotches quickly appeared as if they had been waiting for them. Jacko lifted his whisky and said, "Cheers, at least we have something in common." He noticed Bulman's gaze drift to his hand holding the glass. "It was broken in training," he said, waggling his little finger. "Still gives gip sometimes." And then he added, "The grub's not bad here, what will you have?"

Bulman had taken a liking to Jacko almost on sight. He looked round. "In the old days you had to cut your way through the fog to get inside the place; reaching a table needed bushcraft."

Jacko laughed. "They installed air-conditioning. Made

51

all the difference. The place is almost respectable now."
He did not pick up the menu as if he knew it by heart,
and he was still waiting for Bulman to make up his mind.

"Fillet steak, petite pois and saute. The meal is on me."

Jacko gave Bulman a shrewd glance. "Who's your client?"
He smiled and the toughness vanished at once, eyes full of
mirth. "I wonder what we know about each other? I'm
bloody sure we must have worked for the same people on
occasion."

"I'm bloody sure you're right. And survived to tell
the tale."

Jacko nodded sombrely. "Just about. What is it you
want?"

"I want to hire your services."

"What services? I'm in the theatrical clothes hire
business."

"I know, but you've done the odd caper to stave off
boredom. I thought you might keep an eye on me. I'm
old and crotchety, slow of movement and thought, and
generally an easy target for anyone who feels inclined."

"You are also a crafty bugger. From what I hear
you are none of those things. I don't do minder work.
Never have."

"It's not exactly bodyguard work, there's much more to
it than that. I need help. And I want someone to go to
Germany with me."

The meal arrived, and they ate in silence for a while.
Neither man wanted wine, both content with another
whisky. "I don't need the money," said Jacko suddenly.
"It's not what motivates me."

"Then what does?"

Jacko finished chewing, leaned back in his chair and
eyed Bulman thoughtfully. "Very little these days. I have
a girlfriend, a cracker, far too good for me and I don't want
to lose her through some bloody pointless caper."

"Is she the solicitor? Should be modelling but prefers the
law? You're a lucky man," said Bulman, "and I certainly

52

wouldn't want to break up your love life. So there's no way I can interest you?"

"No." Jacko shook his head.

"Then why the hell did you agree to meet me?"

"I'd heard a bit about you and I thought it would be interesting to meet you. I was right. But I'm not for sale."

Bulman made no further comment until they were on coffee. "Your brother died in an air crash, didn't he?"

Jacko immediately stiffened, eyes hard and at once formidable. "My brother has nothing to do with you."

"In fact he has," corrected Bulman benignly, watching Jacko closely and very aware that if he was not careful he could drive him to explode. "It was following his death that you went berserk, was drummed out of the SAS, and finished up in the glasshouse. Nobody in the SAS understood it at the time. He must have meant a great deal to you for your career to have been ruined by the disaster that struck him."

Jacko was quietly fuming. It was as well they were in a public place, for just then he wanted to throttle Bulman for raising something he had been trying to get out of his system. "You'd better change the subject or better still piss off."

"I knew about your brother. And I managed to keep his name off the form sheet. It wasn't his death that drove you mad but what led up to it, the futility of it. Calm down, Jacko. I know what your brother meant to you."

"If you did you wouldn't have brought him up."

"Maybe it's time you faced up to it."

"Faced up to it?" Jacko's voice was rising. "What do you think drove me over the edge, but the fact that I faced up to it? He was twenty-two, for chrissake. What a waste."

"You must have blamed yourself at the time, or you wouldn't have gone bananas. How could you possibly have been responsible for him mixing with the wrong crowd? You were a serving soldier, not his keeper. Didn't he fail

53

his medical when he tried to follow your footsteps and join the forces?"

It was clear that the whole memory of the circumstances of his brother's death was still a forbidden issue, even after so long. But at least Jacko seemed to get a grip on himself as the tension left him all too slowly, much to Bulman's relief. "He wanted to join the RAF but his sight was defective," Jacko said.

"He could have gone into the ground forces couldn't he?"

"He wanted to do better than me, to become a pilot. He had it in him, education, ability, desire. But lousy bloody eyesight. So he took private flying lessons which needed money. I guessed what he was up to, but there was nothing I could do, I hardly ever saw him. He was into ferrying drugs wasn't he?"

Bulman nodded. "What the hell did you think you could do? You wouldn't have talked him out of it. He wanted to fly and this was a way he could do it. He hadn't obtained his licence at the time he crashed into the sea. The cargo went down with the plane. We let it go at that. I just wanted you to know that we knew and that we sometimes have a heart. I was still in the force when this happened."

Jacko was silent for some time, while Bulman hoped he had laid a ghost. Eventually Jacko said, "Thanks for keeping him off the records." He grimaced. "The boys at Hereford couldn't understand why it affected me so much, but they didn't know what he'd been up to. Maybe the truth should have come out."

"It wouldn't have helped anyone. There was no point. The plane was monitored from the time it left Holland. We were waiting for him to land but he never made shore. A drug haul had finished in the drink, and the drug squad were satisfied because they knew who, in Holland, had sent it out. Later they got the gang. And it saved a good deal of paper work. You'd be surprised the lengths to which we'll go to save some of that."

54

"Is that how you found out about me?" Jacko asked quietly.

"Partly. But I knew an oppo of yours, Sam Towler."

"Sam?" Jacko brightened. "A bloody good mate. I suppose he told you all that crap about me outlining my mates with bullet holes."

"Oh, sure. He also told me you sat in the chair while others had a go."

Jacko was smiling at the memory of Sam Towler and then said, "He's another one the Security Service tried to screw up, the bastards, they almost got him." He gazed at Bulman suspiciously. "This isn't a caper for Five, is it?"

"They're not my contact but to be honest, how the hell can I know?"

"So nothing's changed," Jacko said dryly. "Even if I was prepared to help, how can I protect you? You wouldn't expect me to carry an unlicensed gun and they are the only kind around."

Bulman was startled; he had not been thinking in terms of guns. "No, of course not. You just being around should be enough." Bulman scribbled his address on a paper napkin and pushed it across to Jacko.

Jacko pushed it back. "I haven't said I will help. And, anyway, I know your address; I checked after we made the date."

Bulman looked disappointed, and stuffed the napkin in a pocket. He finished his coffee.

Jacko said, "You were hoping I would change my mind because you helped my brother?"

Bulman managed to look guilty. "To be honest, yes. Well, I was hoping. A bit of a low trick, I'm sorry."

Jacko was still smiling. "Yeah. Bloody low. But it worked. I'll give you a hand if I can."

Bulman brightened. "Terrific." He did not add that his trick was lower than Jacko realized. It was not Bulman who had kept Jacko's younger brother off the crime sheet but Beatty. Bulman had not been in the drug squad at the time, but he well remembered Beatty talking about the affair because it had finally turned out to be a success story, and the reason Jacko's brother had escaped mention was that it could never have been fully proved that he was flying the plane. Neither the plane, nor its cargo was ever recovered.

"Do I get to know what it's about?" asked Jacko. "I need to know what I'm in for."

"It's about the murder of Ronald Walsh. The Yard are taking care of the murder and I've been asked to find out something of his background, the bits nobody knows about."

"The dirt?"

"The obvious dirt has been around some time; it's the well hidden we're after."

Jacko was puzzled. "And they don't think the Bill can find that out?"

"I don't think they want the Bill to find that out."

"Who's your contact?"

"Home Office is as far as I'll go."

"Well, we all know what that means, Bulman."

"I don't think so. Five are well capable of conducting their own enquiry. Although with the guy dead they might have lost interest. By the way, you can call me George."

"I've never called a copper by his first name in my life, and I'm not starting now." Jacko smiled. "Thanks for the lunch."

They went out into the street and a weak sun was struggling through the clouds. They shook hands and Bulman walked down Dean Street towards Shaftesbury Avenue, while Jacko stood outside the Hot Pot watching Bulman's big figure until he was out of sight before turning thoughtfully away.

Bulman was running late and had difficulty in getting a cab in Shaftesbury Avenue. It was almost half past three before he rang the bell of Anna Brenning's apartment. He

56

apologized profusely as she let him in, but she appeared to be unperturbed.

"Got held up," he said. "I'm so sorry." As he sat down he could see that Anna had taken pains over the tea; there was a silver tray and teapot, biscuits and cake. He was still full of lunch but forced himself to eat cake.

Anna was dressed in tailored slacks and a jumper, and could have made the front cover of most quality magazines. Bulman was again impressed with the selectiveness of the late Ronnie Walsh, but perhaps money really could buy anything.

"Have you found out anything more about this apartment?"

"No. As long as the rates are paid I don't think there is a problem." The slight German accent was just a little more pronounced than he recalled.

Bulman put his cup down. "As you know, when you first got permission to stay in the UK, you had to provide your background. You obviously did this to the satisfaction of immigration and I have read the report. You had a hard time over there."

"You've been investigating me? Again?" Anna appeared to be more surprised than upset.

"I'm sure you expected it. It's inevitable. I think the police are chasing their tails and you were Walsh's main passion, that is obvious. It must have been a terrible shock to you when you read the Stasi reports about your mother and brother."

"Spying on me, you mean?" Anna's features had tightened and in a strange way this made her more attractive, as the bone structure became more pronounced. She held on to her feelings very well but had paled a little. "I'd rather not talk about it. It's been over for some time and I don't want it resurrected. It's too painful."

"I'm sure that it is. But it still formed part of your application for entry, so you must have talked about it in some detail when you applied to come here. You must have run into a quite compassionate official; they hear so many stories that they are usually as hard as nails."

"They were very understanding, yes. Do we need to go on with this?"

"Did Walsh help in any way? I mean he was a member of Parliament. Did he try to influence the Home Office?"

"I did not know him then. This really is old ground, Mr Bulman. Had I known that this is what you wanted to talk about I would not have invited you here."

Bulman threw up his arms in surrender. "I'm sorry. I know you're having a very trying time. Is your mother and brother still alive?"

For the first time Anna lost her composure. She was uncomfortable and did not want to answer. She stood up and offered him another cup of tea which he declined. "The answer is," she said at last, "I really don't know. I severed contact with them as quickly as I could." She folded her arms around her and shuddered. "I don't want to see them again. They don't exist to me."

"I understand."

"Nobody can understand." It was the first time she had been sharp and Bulman glimpsed the underlying toughness. "Unless it has happened to them." She turned to stare at him blankly. "Has it happened to you?"

He shrugged. "No, but we've all had our problems."

"Not like this one. We are talking of a mother's betrayal of her own daughter. It is impossible for anyone to imagine. *Anyone.*" The last word was uttered with venom.

"I really didn't mean to raise bitter memories. I should have been more considerate. I am sorry, Anna." He felt like moving towards her, to put his arm around her. Just then, she appeared to be so vulnerable and needed someone. So he did just that and put his arm round her shoulder and she buried her head into his chest and quietly wept.

She eventually eased herself away from him, wiped her eyes and sat on the arm of what appeared to be her favourite chair. "I shouldn't have broken down like that; it was disgraceful. I'm so sorry."

Bulman smiled. "Maybe you needed to cry. You're quite right, it's impossible for someone else to imagine such a betrayal, particularly if you were ostensibly close."

"We were all close, I thought." Anna shrugged. "Oh, I know I was a bit of a rebel, but it was nothing really serious and I was not in a position to do the regime any harm. It was all young student talk. I would like not to talk of it any more."

"Of course. I think I will have another cup of tea." And while Anna poured it he asked, "Have you had any more thoughts on who might have killed Ronnie Walsh?"

She passed him the cup. "Yes, I've had many thoughts, but none of them fruitful. I think he was killed by someone from a side of his life about which I know absolutely nothing. He kept me in this expensive cocoon, and I knew nothing about him or his friends and enemies outside these walls. Inside them he had no enemies." She picked up her cup and gazed steadily at Bulman as she added, "To be honest I don't want to know about them. Life is already complicated for me."

He nodded in understanding and was therefore surprised when she asked, "And how are your enquiries going? Are you making progress?"

It had been dark for some time when Bulman returned to his apartment. He went in, switching on the lights as he went and turned up the heating before taking off his topcoat. He went into the lounge to switch on the television and nearly jumped out of his skin when he realized someone was already there.

Jacko was sprawled in one of his chairs waiting for him.

"God, you almost gave me a heart attack. How the hell did you get in?"

"Your locks need changing. Anyone could get in. You

haven't even got an alarm. Did you know you're being followed?"

"Followed? Who would want to follow me?"

"That's why I came," said Jacko helpfully. "I was going to phone, but then I thought that as you have a tail, you might also have a bug on your phone. As it turned out you haven't, nor in your flat; I've checked." He sat up. "I could murder a drink. Haven't had one since lunch time. I noticed them as you went down Dean Street. They are probably outside now. Didn't they teach you anything in the Bill?"

"Oh, yes. Surveillance. But not being on the wrong end of it." He moved towards the array of bottles on the small sideboard. "Who are they?"

"Well, the two I saw look like Slav hit men."

Bulman froze in mid-stride.

Chapter Six

Bulman turned. "*Slav*? How do you know they are Slav?"

"Because they look bloody Slav. High cheekbones and death masks. Not a smile between them. These aren't your average Slav, these are hard cases." Jacko stared at Bulman in exasperation. "Slavonic," he added. "They could be from almost anywhere in Eastern and Central Europe; Poles, Czechs, Bulgarians, Serbo-Croates, even Russians."

"I know what a Slav looks like," snapped Bulman. Instead of continuing to the sideboard he veered towards the windows.

"Don't be daft," snapped Jacko. "Don't twitch those curtains. In any case you won't see anything down there in the dark."

Bulman nodded briefly and stepped towards the drinks. He brought two large whiskies across, handed one to Jacko and sat down to face him. "Slavs?" he said again. "Why bloody Slavs? And why bloody me?"

"They can't follow a complete murder squad; you're probably all they've got. Why are you so surprised? You're trying to dig up dirt and that means Walsh was involved with dirt and that means other people."

Bulman felt disgruntled. "I haven't dug up any yet. I'm no threat to anyone."

"What about the German girl? That's dirt?"

"Yes, but everyone knows about his women. There may be others well hidden. I don't think we're looking for that kind of dirt. But Slavs?" And then he added, "Well they must know their way round London. There are still a large number of unemployed Eastern Bloc secret police and the like." He recalled the last time he had come across one. "And hit men, but most of them are being used in mainland Europe and even in the States. My information is that we are now clear of them here."

"I wouldn't bank on it."

"Did they follow you?"

"No. I kept a look out but took evasive action anyway. I brought nobody here."

"What should we do?"

Jacko flung a leg over the arm of his chair. "Well, that depends on whether you want them to know that you know or not."

"If they are hit men they might try to knock me off any moment. I want rid of them."

"I don't know how long you've had them, but my guess is that if they wanted to top you they would have done it by now. Perhaps they don't see you as a threat – yet. Your problem is to accurately gauge when you do become a threat. Meanwhile don't let them know that you know."

"Slavs!" Bulman was trying to establish some kind of connection. "That's thrown me a bit."

"You can always get your friends in the Bill to pull them in or make life difficult for them."

Bulman said, "I must have taken them to Hampshire with me, to Anna Brenning, the hotel, to you, everywhere. I've left a trail anyone could follow."

Jacko was grinning. "Well, you were a copper. It's not your fault that you're thick. All coppers are thick. It's just one of life's disadvantages."

"It's not funny, Jacko. I don't want my head bashed in again."

Jacko became serious. "Do you want me to stay a couple of nights? My girlfriend is busy on a difficult brief at the moment, so I could square it with her. At least you now know they are there."

Bulman shook his head. He rose slowly and walked over

to the windows without going too close. "It's kind of you, but it would not be fair."

"I thought that's what you hired me for? To keep an eye on you?"

Bulman gestured. "It's shaken me, that's all. I wasn't looking towards Central Europe but nearer to home. It's come up from behind."

"Some of these Eastern European boys were well taught. They could be red hot at the art of shadowing. They were amongst the best, whatever anyone else says."

"Some of them," Bulman said bluntly. "I didn't spot them because I didn't expect anyone. But you spotted them first time." And then at a complete tangent he asked, "How many call girl agencies do you think there are in London?"

Jacko finished his drink. "How long is a piece of string?"

"I'm serious."

"Well, I don't suppose we'll find any in the Yellow Pages. You're thinking that this girl Connie Smith has to work to live, and might try another agency?"

"At last you're talking sense."

"She could go to any big city."

"Maybe. But she's a Londoner. She'll be at home here. She could change her appearance; wig, that sort of thing." He offered Jacko a twisted grin. "Female disguises seems to be the 'in' thing. Connie had to go somewhere and she has to live."

Even in prison uniform Veida Ash was a striking woman, belying her forty years. She had naturally fair hair and a complexion to match, good legs in spite of the low heels she was forced to wear, and sky-blue eyes which could harden icily. She was escorted to a room used for special visits, and sat at a plain wooden table waiting for the visitor to occupy the opposite chair. A wardress stood behind her.

It was a few minutes before the door opened, and a tall, middle-aged, dark-haired man entered. He had the

63

appearance of a civil servant and in a way he was. Veida had not seen this man before, and she immediately wondered if he tinted his hair as there was no sign of grey.

Without looking at Veida he placed a briefcase on the table, undid the clasp but took nothing out. He then looked up, his gaze above Veida's head to the wardress, who then left the room, locking it behind her.

"An evening call. That's unusual. Now we can have sex in private," said Veida. "I hate an audience, don't you?"

The man looked her straight in the eye, his gaze as disconcertingly unblinking as her own. He smiled and it reached his eyes, crinkling them round the edges. "That would be interesting, if not enjoyable. But it wouldn't reduce your sentence." And then he added impishly, "And you'd be left screaming for more. So I'll spare you the agony and refrain."

"With difficulty, I hope," replied Veida.

"Of course with difficulty. You are an attractive, intelligent woman. But, sadly, I am not here to discuss sex, yours or mine. My name is Derek North. You can call me what you like."

"Have you just joined the Security Service, Derek?"

"Do I look as though I have, Veida?" He was quite agreeable to the foreplay, he wanted her co-operation, and she did not get to see too many people these days; it seemed that few wanted to be associated with her, in case they were sucked in with her.

"It's just that I haven't seen you before, and you're not like the others. I find you attractive and I'd like you to stay. I should be able to arrange a double cell."

He remained smiling. "Having to serve twenty-five years in a women's prison would make any man appear attractive to you. But thank you just the same. And I would love to stay. But duty calls I'm afraid."

"Good old duty. What a bind."

"Had you stuck to yours, you wouldn't be in here. What a waste of talent." North gazed across the table with a degree of admiration. "You ran the biggest crime syndicate in Europe, Germany, Poland, even Russia, and all through the contacts you made through the section you controlled in the SIS. That took vision, considerable ability, the power of persuasion, and an enviable toughness and dedication. Unfortunately, it also required immense greed. How sad. You must miss your comforts, Veida?"

"Not really. I have half the staff on my payroll. I admit I miss the actual freedom of movement, but I can send out for food, have my own radio and television, and all the comforts a cell can hold. I have medical care when I need it, so I make up in other ways. Besides, Derek," Veida gave him a brilliant smile, "I don't intend to stay here for anything like twenty-five years. I'm just feeling my way."

"And still controlling the empire of villainy you had before being imprisoned."

"Some of it," Veida conceded. "A very large chunk was decimated and I'm having to rebuild. It keeps me busy, though, and I shall never, ever, be short of money. What was it you wanted, Derek?"

"The same the others wanted, I suppose." He sighed. "You were not too co-operative with them. I hope I might do better. It is in your own interests, after all."

"You want me to give you names of my operatives, organizations, offshore banks, money hidden under the bed, and generally betray everyone I ever worked with. How can that be in my own interests, Derek?"

"You might get your sentence reduced, for starters."

"I'm not interested in my sentence being reduced. Apart from the fact that I intend to reduce it anyway, I would want it in writing and the precise number of years to be deducted stated, and we both know that can never be done. So I'd be left with promises. Well you can stuff those, Derek, I know too much about promises. There is nothing you can offer that would ever make me change my mind."

"Not even the welfare of your bastard daughter?"

Veida sat quite still but was clearly shaken. "That was

a very low blow, Derek. My daughter has nothing to do with what I do. How did you dig that up?"

"You've been delivering low blows for years, and still are. You can have no complaint. As for your daughter having nothing to do with what you do, does she pay her own considerable school fees? Provide her own finance, home? It's all paid for with dirty money, although I'm sure she doesn't know it. She doesn't know who her mother is either, does she?"

"Don't you dare tell her." Veida had paled considerably, but years of dealing with crisis enabled her to keep her nerve. "You wouldn't sink that low."

North was watching her very closely; shaking her was one thing, breaking her quite another. "I can promise you that we'll sink no lower than yourself. That's fair isn't it?"

She could have sworn at him, used expletives which would have told him he had scored. When in the SIS, she'd had a reputation for ice coolness and she was not going to lose that now. After the first shock she was already planning. "What is it you want of me?"

"Come, Veida, you know very well. We, and that includes most European police and intelligence forces, want to destroy what is left of your still considerable empire, which is a peculiar mixture of villainy and corrupt politics."

"You could never be sure of what I told you. I am saying that to save you the trouble."

"We're perfectly capable of judging by results. We'd expect you to keep a little back for yourself, and I've said that because you are already thinking it."

"So you'd be prepared to kill off a young, innocent girl's life just to screw me?"

"That depends on what you call innocent, but basically, yes, we are prepared to do so."

"I need time to think this out."

"Of course. We can give you until this time tomorrow."

"That's nowhere near enough."

"That's more than enough. You've probably already

decided on who you can spare to send to the wall."
North was very relaxed. "We're serious, Veida. It took
time and a few trips to Germany to dig out your daughter,
but we have the doctor and the clinic. And the father. Don't
underestimate us, it's too big an issue for us to pussyfoot
around. Nobody knows that better than you."

Veida tried to smile but found it too difficult. "So
they sent in the Godfather," she said bitterly. "You're
good at it."

"And so are you. I'm waiting for an answer."

"I'll see what I can dig out by tomorrow."

"Don't be too selective; we don't want minions."

"You realize that they will try to kill me in here once the
word is out?"

"You mean like you had Terry Shaw and Katz killed
while they were inside? Don't expect sympathy. I'm sure
your money will buy you all the time you need. There's
just one more thing." North waited for a reaction, as if she
might expect a catch to what he said. When she continued to
sit stonily he went on, "You'll have heard about the death of
Ronald Walsh MP; have you heard anything from inside as
to who might have done it?"

"I knew about him long before he was killed; all that's
surprising is that he lived for so long." Veida gave him a
cool stare. "Why on earth would I know anything about
that? How can I know from in here? My visitors are
restricted to a trickle, because they think they will be
followed home and persecuted by you lot just for seeing me."

"Maybe we can come to an arrangement about your
visitors. I just thought you might have picked something
up; there are plenty of brasses in here; we could reimburse
you if you had to pay out for information. We would
consider it helpful, and listen to ways to ease your
burden here."

"If I hear of anything I'll let you know. I will want it down
on record if I do help. But it was time that philandering
bastard was put down by a woman."

North fastened his briefcase and slowly rose. "I didn't say it was a woman. Nobody knows for certain."

Veida smiled again. "Give me credit, Derek. We do listen to, and read, the news. And everyone in here is sure it was a woman, you should come more often." And then as a departing dig she added, "Did they tell you I'm having a fax put in here?"

He moved to the door, but before tapping it smiled and said, "They didn't need to. I suppose I've burned my bridges for the sex? I'm so sorry. Until tomorrow."

When Jacko left Bulman's apartment he stood under the canopy of the porch at the top of the steps, much the same as Marshall had done the previous evening. Even though he was in the darkest part of the porch, unseen from street level, Jacko well knew that he had been seen coming through the street door when the light would have been behind him. That someone was across the street he was certain, even though he could see nobody except those who passed by.

Jacko's life had been on the line too often for him not to obey his instincts. At first he wanted to deal with it, then he recalled what he had told Bulman, and decided ostensibly to ignore it. Let them think he did not know. He went down the steps slowly, stood at the bottom, glanced up and down the street without looking across it, and then turned and walked away, head down, hands in pockets.

There were a few people about. The rush hour was long over and things had quietened down. He knew before he turned the corner that someone had detached themselves to follow him, which meant that there must have been at least two men watching Bulman's place and one would have remained. He kept his pace even, listening, trying to exclude casual footsteps from the evenly paced, almost imperceptible, footfalls behind him.

Jacko had been making for the main road where there was plenty of movement and traffic, and where it would be much easier to lose someone who might be following. But because it was Jacko's nature to confront rather than cut off his tail, he decided without making a conscious decision, to ignore the advice he had forced on Bulman. So he stuck to the backstreets, realizing he would have to indicate a direction or be rumbled.

He headed further from the main streets into the more deserted roads and squares. With far fewer people it was easier now to be certain that there was someone following and that he was now across the street. Jacko had to make a move and it had to be the right one. He made a show of checking his watch under a street lamp and quickened his pace from then on as if he was late. He reached a corner and sprinted behind the row of parked cars and crouched behind one of them on the street side.

He heard, rather than saw, his man come into view, then the panic increase in pace and finally a run. Through the windows of the car he saw the figure dash past and he followed along the car line. His timing had been right for there was nobody else about, but that was a situation that would not last. He quickened his pace, certain that the man would return once he recovered from his sudden panic. And that was what happened.

The man, realizing that Jacko was unlikely to have got so far, returned slowly but had now produced a flashlight which he shone into doorways and along the car line. Jacko crouched, waited, then eased himself between two cars, and waited again. It was easy to follow the advance of the torch. He timed his jump to perfection and struck a wicked rabbit punch at the base of the man's neck. The torch went spiralling into a pattern of flashing loops before hitting the street and snuffing out with a crash.

Anyone else would have gone down at once from the blow, but the man was big, protected by a topcoat. He fell to his knees and swung round to catch Jacko's legs in one movement. The fight that followed was ugly, mostly silent, and intense.

69

As soon as Jacko realized that he had failed to flatten the man he knew he was up against someone trained in the same way as himself, and his opponent had the weight. But Jacko had forgotten little and had kept himself fit. It was savage.

A young couple coming upon them decided to turn back and run away. The two men struggled on, neither willing to give in until Jacko saw an opportunity to crash the other's head against some basement railings, and even then it took several attempts before the body went limp and started to twitch.

Jacko looked around breathlessly. There was no time for rest, he had to get the fellow off the street fast. With a great deal of effort he dragged the body up the steps of the nearest house praying that nobody would come out.

It was hard work and he had to rest half-way up. Footsteps came towards him, and he hastily sat on the steps beside the unconscious body. He managed to lift the trunk of the body until the head lolled against his shoulder. Somehow he held it there as two men passed at the foot of the steps, one of them seeing the shadowed tableau half-way up the steps.

"You all right, mate? Your friend looks dodgy. Do you want a hand?"

"It's OK. He never could hold his drink. I'm just resting before I get him in."

"We'll give you a hand," said the second man, not wanting to be left out.

"No. Thanks just the same. Let him get the fresh air for a while. Once the warmth hits him he'll probably be as sick as a dog."

They moved off and Jacko now took his hand away from the man's back where he had been holding him up. He could feel the blood trickling over it and realized it must be from the fellow's head and that worried him. He rose and grabbed under the armpits to try to lift the body to the top and then under the porch.

He finally pulled the body into the far corner of the porch. Now safe from view from anyone at street level he hoped that nobody would come out of the house. He had to carry out a search of the man's pockets purely by touch for he had no torch and the other one had smashed. The best he could do was to remove anything he could find and stuff it in his own pockets to examine later. He found the pistol almost at once as it was the bulkiest item. It was unusually heavy and as he groped he guessed it had some kind of night sight, or perhaps a laser mounted on it so that it felt almost top heavy. And he found a silencer attachment soon after. When he was satisfied that he had emptied the pockets he rose shakily and steadied himself against one of the supporting pillars.

He was still feeling the effects of the fight. He gazed down at the dark lump. Although the breathing was shallow and the pulse feeble, Jacko believed that the man would come to with not much more than a gigantic headache and some loss of blood. Anyway, there was nothing he could do without getting himself into trouble.

He half stumbled down the steps. He could feel the blood on his hands, but he probably had it spattered all over him, so he would have to avoid taxis and public transport. At the foot of the steps he straightened up and considered the best way to walk back to his own house in north London without touching the main streets. It was some distance. He was so depleted that he briefly considered stealing a car. The thought was driven out when he suddenly heard a police siren approaching and he saw the distant reflection of a blue flasher. Had the young couple who had ran past them telephoned the police?

Jacko tried to break into a run away from the approach of the police car which was suddenly much nearer than he realized, the beams bouncing on the corner building behind him. He was spattered in blood, a good deal of it not his own, and he carried a pistol and a silencer and stolen items. He cursed Bulman then. His

71

life had stood on its head in less than a day, and if the police caught him he was in deep trouble.

As the car skidded round the corner with siren wailing, it produced more people at windows than a summer's day, and Jacko knew it was far too late to run.

Chapter Seven

Jacko was used to physical crisis and survived them by
expertise, a great deal of courage, following his impulses,
and some luck. If he kept moving away he would be the only
person in the street who was not focused on the police car.
The car slowed down and pulled in. A policeman climbed
out while the driver doused the lights and switched off the
siren which died in a decreasing wail, before joining his
colleague. Some of the people leaning out of windows
shouted down at them. Most had heard nothing but the
police car, roused by the siren just under them.

A few people were now in the street, and Jacko was
relieved about that as he stood near the other end gazing
towards the activity further up. Overzealous, and downright
inquisitive neighbours, also helped him by occupying police
time. The police were trying to find out about the fight.
There would never be a better time, and he slowly backed
away until he could slip round the corner. And then he ran,
as far away from the scene as he could, cutting through side
streets, alleys, anything that offered a confusing route of
escape. It would not take someone long to find the body
in the porch.

It was after midnight by the time he reached his home
in North London. Getting away from the scene had been
only part of the problem. As he dare not use transport
his walking had taken him a very long way round, and
increased the possibility of bumping into a beat policeman
or patrol car. He unlocked the front door and stood with
his back to it once inside the hall.

He did not want to put the light on. Georgie would be asleep upstairs and he did not want to disturb her. He had left a message on the machine to let her know he would be late, but she would not be satisfied with that if she saw him now. He felt his way along to the downstairs cloakroom, closed the door behind him and switched on the light.

Jacko was shaken by what he saw. There was blood spattered over his face and clothes, and his knuckles were raw and still bleeding. He began to wonder whether his opponent was in a worse condition than he had thought. Murder crossed his mind. Oh, Christ.

In the small confines of the cloakroom he stripped and scrubbed down as best he could. He bundled up his clothes, switched off the light and crept out into the hall to fumble for a topcoat off the stand. He groped his way down to his small study at the back of the house. He closed the door, switched on the lights and put the topcoat on against the cold, dropped his clothes in the knee hole, after removing the various items he had taken.

By this time Jacko was near exhausted but that was another condition he had learned to cope with. He sat at his desk with the coat wrapped round him and examined what he had. The pistol was a .357 Colt Trooper revolver model 7. What was more interesting, was that it was mounted with a laser product target designator. It was mounted above the barrel, covering the area of the normal foresight and ran back to an extension that held the batteries. He balanced it in his hand and guessed it to be about four pounds in weight. To him it was top heavy and cumbersome and would need specialist training to handle effectively. He reckoned that the sight would be set at about twenty-five yards which would be usual for this type of weapon. These pistols could not take a silencer, so he was left wondering what the silencer was for. He could hardly have missed another gun in the pockets even in the dark. But somewhere there had to be another weapon.

For the rest, there was a wallet with forty-five pounds in

it; the address of the call girl agency scribbled on a piece of newspaper; and a receipt for eight hundred pounds which was not made out to anyone and the signature was totally indecipherable. There were also two packets of extra strong mints; some chewing gum; a bunch of keys, two were Chubb, one a deadlock, and what must be car keys all on the same ring. Nowhere was there any sign of identification and this did not really surprise him.

He was studying the items on his desk when Georgette Roberts walked in. She stood in the doorway in a dressing gown looking down at him, frightened at what she saw. "I thought you had given all this up." Her voice had a tremor.

He stared up at her, thinking she still looked terrific even in the middle of the night without make-up. But it was a safety reaction to the real fears he had on realizing what he had on view. "I have. Are you going to let me explain?"

Georgie was leaning against the door jamb, arms folded. "Are you going to explain now or do you want the time it takes me to make some coffee?"

"I can explain now —"

"Before you do I don't want any lies, darling. I'm a lawyer; I dare not get compromised as I did before. I helped you then but I can't keep pushing my luck. I don't want to be struck off." Before he could answer she added, "Just look at the state of your hands; they need attention. And the bruises on your face. Just what the hell have you been up to?" She was awakening as she took more in and there was nothing to ease her feelings; what she saw was all bad news. She sank into the nearest chair while he told her what happened.

Georgie listened with an expression that suggested she had heard it all before. Trouble followed him around; no, that was not true, he looked for trouble without really knowing it. As he tried to explain, stumbling here and there when something did not sound right and he tried to justify himself, she knew she would always love him and that it was very unlikely that he would change. But could she risk losing everything she had worked so hard for, by continuing to live with him? She was already fighting a rearguard action against colleagues who were blatantly sexist and resented a woman, especially a very bright one, continuing to be one of their number. "And that's it?" she said at last. "Just out to see a friend and you finish up beaten and bruised and with somebody else's gun. It could happen to anyone."

Jacko was tired, in pain and miserable. "I know it sounds daft. But Bulman was one of the Yard's best coppers. He's absolutely on the up and up. I have to help him; I'm committed."

"Because he helped your brother?"

"My brother was very important to me. You know that, Georgie. He could have died with form hanging over his memory."

"Can you believe Bulman?"

Jacko considered it. "Yes. He's cagey but I think he's basically honest."

"Just as you are cagey and basically honest. But you can still spin a story when it suits you. Do you think that was what he did?"

"I haven't spun you a story, Georgie. OK, I could have evaded the guy but it would have happened again."

"So what happens next?"

"I'll bring Bulman up to date and then I think he wants us to go to Germany. I'm not sure when. Let me see this through, Georgie. The guy's in trouble. I didn't realize how much when I agreed to help but I can't ditch him now. He's a bloody good detective, but he doesn't even know how to turn the other cheek. I won't involve you in any way. Really."

"I'm involved by just being your lover. I don't want to be a widow before we're married. Oh, Jacko, for one so tough you really are an idiot."

"That's why you love me," said Jacko, risking a grin.

Georgie rose and came over to him. "Just remember that

76

you haven't got the strength or back-up of your colleagues any more." She looked at the gun on his desk and shuddered. "People who carry that sort of sophisticated weapon around with them usually intend to use them and know how to. You should sit in at the courts some day."

He did not reply to that; she might even have been quoting something he had told her earlier.

Georgie added, "You are Bulman's back-up but who is yours?"

About the same time as Jacko reached home, Veida Ash made a telephone call on her mobile phone. She was well aware, as were all the prisoners, of the huge controversy on the leniency of treatment in some of the men's prisons. Privileges, such as phones for those who could swing it, weekend visits home, shopping expeditions, food brought in, home brewing and other aids to prisoner comforts had outraged most of the nation, but continued while the Home Office tried to grapple with the problem and to blame anyone they could outside their own walls.

No one yet had mentioned anything about women prisoners and for that the female inmates were grateful to the men for the distraction away from their own benefits. Women of Veida's education and position did not always fare well at the hands of the tougher breeds of female inmates, and some could be very tough and violent, but they soon discovered the aura Veida carried that made her different. And some were afraid of her. Her toughness and skills were quickly recognized, and in no time she had acolytes running round for her for which services she paid in a variety of ways. Her immense wealth held sway and formed a barrier even against those who would have liked to throttle her.

Nevertheless, she took nothing for granted and was careful not to offend the establishment in the prison. She heaped the blankets over her head as she dialled, leaving clear space for the aerial. She punched out a number. It was some time before a woman answered having been roused from bed. "Veida," she announced. "Can you hear? I'm having to keep my voice down."

"I can hear. Just. This must be urgent."

"It is. I've got to sacrifice a few people and I need you to move very fast on it. I've had to work out who can go and who can't. Difficult. I must show that some of the main contacts are on offer but I want them warned so that they can disappear for a while. I'll give the signal when they can return to business. But a couple of the bigger fish will have to go or it will become too obvious. Have you heard all that?"

"I've heard."

"Nothing in this country. Certain sections in Germany, Poland, Czechoslovakia, Romania and Bulgaria will have to wind up for a while. And maybe a small one in Russia. All main sections must be advised if it takes all night. Now jot these down; sections three, eight, ten, seventeen and eighteen to go to the wall. Maybe they can be resurrected later, but there is nothing I can do about it. If they don't go I might be restricted and that could affect far more. Just don't tell them anything. Contact Eric; he'll know exactly what to do."

"Are you sure?"

"I wouldn't be on the phone if I wasn't sure. It's a pity, but there's a lot of pressure on. These things happen and we have to be realistic."

"It will be done. I'll contact Eric at once."

"Destroy that note when you've finished. To make it easier to accept, I've worked it out that financially those sections are the best to go. They are not big spinners."

"Some of them might have potential."

"That's for me to decide. Just do it."

"Of course."

Veida was quick to notice the coldness of the reply and was reminded of just who she was dealing with. "Any problems I should know about?"

78

"The police are still looking for Walsh's killer. But you will have read about that and seen it on TV." There was a low laugh. "I wonder who did it? And there is a man called Bulman who is poking around."

"Bulman? George Bulman? I met him a couple of times when he helped Five and the SB. He was a sort of liaison at one time. What sort of poking around?"

"Walsh's murder."

"Why would he be doing that with the Yard on the job?"

"I don't know. He seems to be doing a separate line of enquiry. I can't see him getting anywhere."

"Don't underestimate Bulman. Do you know who is using him?"

"He told me he represents Walsh's relatives."

"You mean you've seen him?"

"He's been to see me twice."

"And you believe him?"

"I don't know. It makes no difference."

"Unless Bulman's lost his marbles it could make quite a bit of difference. Have the police stopped coming?"

"It's too early to say."

"You should have told me about Bulman."

"You know I have to wait on you. You asked and I told you. It's the best I can do. Anyway he's being monitored and we can always deal with him if it comes to it." Again the matter-of-fact coldness, almost as a warning.

"Try to keep in touch with him, and if you sense real danger you'll have to risk calling me. Good-night." She more than matched the other's coldness and her implied warning was deeper.

After the call, Veida lay on her bed feeling the frustration of being confined. At times of crisis like this she had to rely on delegation at which she was good, but right now she needed the freedom of direct control. That she could still command from a prison cell what was still a considerable criminal force in Europe, spoke highly of the respect she

79

attracted but also her considerable expertise and the myriad contacts she had made abroad while with the SIS. She did not want to organize a hurried escape; it must be well planned and at the right time; it was too soon now. But just then she needed it as never before.

Jacko rang Bulman early next morning. He'd had little sleep and had risen early. Jacko said, "Do you think you can get over to my warehouse by the docks without bringing anyone with you?"

"Can't we meet someone nearer?"

"By nine. I've something to show you."

Bulman got his car out. He hated driving in the London traffic but accepted that Jacko would have his reasons for the venue. He watched his mirrors but could pick out no particular car following; the traffic was forever changing and he would be the first to admit that he would never have made a patrol car driver when in the force.

He did his best, and some time later eased his way along the row of seemingly derelict warehouses which for several years had been due for demolition and rebuilding, and were just a street away from the docks. He drove over uneven cobbles past a series of huge blank doors until he saw the sign, 'Costume Hire'. He pulled in alongside the opposite wall.

There was a bell at the side of the double doors and he rang and waited until a young, cheerful girl opened an inlet in the main door and asked him his name. He was expected and went in, past rows of historic and modern costumes and dresses, until he reached glass-fronted partitioned offices, one each side of the walkway, and was shown into the largest, to be told that Mr Jackson would not be long, which irritated Bulman having been told the urgency.

It was another ten minutes before Jacko arrived. Bulman was about to complain, took one look at the facial contusions and the bandaged hands and asked, "What the bloody hell happened to you?"

"Had a run in with one of your watchers. Coffee?"

Bulman nodded and Jacko went to the glass-panelled partition and made drinking signs to the two girls in the other office.

"They went for you?" asked Bulman, sitting down opposite Jacko's surprisingly clear desk.

"Not quite." Jacko told him what happened.

"So much for not letting them know we know," observed Bulman in disgust. He glanced at the hands. "And you didn't get it all your own way?"

"No. He was a tough sod. I've been waiting for news on the radio or TV for some mention, but haven't heard a thing. They must have found him."

"Unless he walked away from it. You obviously did."

While Jacko considered that, he produced from a drawer the items he had taken.

Bulman almost recoiled at the sight of the gun. "Jesus! And he was opposite my pad?"

"With another bloke. By the way, you didn't shake off your tail. I was tucked away in a side street at the entrance to this one. I saw you arrive and I saw the guy behind you. He stayed parked round the corner so I had to take a longer way back here to avoid him. That was why I was late."

Bulman sighed. "I've never been good at shaking people off, mainly because I don't see them in the first place. It does show that there's something to find out, but what does it really mean?"

"It means," said Jacko, "that you've put the fear of God into them if they've put armed men on to you."

"And now they know you are helping me which puts you in the front line."

"Oh, sure. But they'll have learned lesson one; we're no pushover and they've lost a weapon and maybe a man out of action for a bit." He indicated the items on the desk. "There's no identification among that lot. But they obviously knew where to contact Connie Smith."

"Was the guy foreign?"

81

"He didn't introduce himself. It was dark, his back was to me when I clobbered him and from then on I was too busy to take notice. Anyway his looks would have given nothing away; there are plenty who were born here who look foreign. The point is he didn't speak. Neither of us did and that suggests he was well trained; well I know he was. We're up against pros, mate. You have only to look at the gun." Jacko suddenly flat handed the desk. "I wonder if the other gun dropped out of his pocket while we were at it?"

Jacko placed a newspaper over the gun as the coffee arrived, and they sat in silence across the desk from each other for some time. Eventually Jacko said, "I'm in deep trouble with my girlfriend, Georgie, over this. But I said I'd help and I won't go back on my word. And I'm still chuffed for what you did for my brother."

"I'm grateful to you." Bulman did not want to talk about Jacko's brother.

"So what happens next?" asked Jacko. "I can't take them out one by one, and it's clear they intend to keep you in sight. It's worse than having a restraining order."

"I have a list of Walsh's trips abroad, but what happened during them is scanty on detail. And the less obvious people he met. I must find out more on that score."

"You mentioned Germany. Is that still on?"

"Maybe. But I want a little more information about Walsh himself first."

"So the German trip is not about him. Anna Brenning?"

"I'll fill you in when I'm more sure of it myself."

"You don't seem certain about any of this," Jacko observed, putting down his mug.

"I'm not. Walsh headed a huge conglomerate. A good deal of detail will only be known by his business colleagues, and I'm damned sure that they won't give me the time of day if I try asking them. I have no authority." Bulman was brooding, then suddenly looked up. "Do you know any decent forgers?"

"I'm not a bloody villain."

"I know you're not. Do you know any?"

"A couple. Haven't seen either for a bit."

"Do you think one of them could make a Board of Trade identity card? It would have to be convincing. And it would have to be a rush job." Bulman took out his wallet and extracted a credit card case from which he took a small photograph. "Passport mug shot. That should do."

Jacko grinned as he took the photograph. "You're asking me to break the law? And you an ex-copper. That's dishonest."

"I know. Can you fix it?"

"Sure. What about the goons who are on our tail? If they've detached one or two on to me, do I lose them or take them with me?"

"Lose them. It's going to be difficult operating in a strait-jacket and we'll be showing our hand to them. We should go to ground."

"That can be done, but we'll have to be bloody certain that we really lose them or we'll be taking them to the other pad.

"OK. Whatever is necessary."

"Give me a few moments to sort things out with the girls, as it looks as if I'll be away for a bit." He pushed his chair back on its castors. "I've got some film people coming in this afternoon but the girls can take care of them." He stood up. "I'll show you where you can put your car for a while."

"But I shall need that," Bulman protested.

"Not if you want to lose them. Follow me."

Behind the warehouse was a long strip of concrete where a small extension had been built. The door was on the far side, so it could not be seen from the corner of the main building. The place was mainly full of empty cartons and clothes racks, but holding central position, clear of any protrusions, was a red Ferrari. Jacko had only to set eyes on it for him to produce a smile.

"A beauty isn't she? I was doing a favour for someone,

just like you are now, and the guy I was watching took umbrage and blew my old Ferrari up. There are still blast marks out the front. As we got to know each other better he acknowledged his mistake and bought me a new one. Nice eh!" Jacko climbed in and switched on. Thunder filled the building, then it ticked over like a cheetah purring. He reversed out.

The two men went round the front and immediately someone at the far end of the block slipped out of sight. "They're getting careless," said Jacko. "Get the Daimler out of sight round the back. I'll stay here to keep an eye on matey."

Bulman did not like leaving his car where he had no direct control, but drove it round and parked it where the Ferrari had been. Jacko came round a little later and locked the door. They returned to the main building by the back route, and Jacko made his arrangements with the girls. "Right," he said, turning to Bulman. "Let's get out of here."

Bulman climbed into the Ferrari, finding it difficult for his large frame. As he strapped up he said, "I must go back to my place for some things."

Jacko swore softly. "I can't believe you. Do you want to lose these guys or not? That's the last time you see that place until the job is done." He switched on and the smile came back. "Let's go. Let's tie the bastards in knots."

There was no way they could avoid driving round to the front and Jacko did so with relish. He could afford new tyres any time he needed them and he took the corner in a controlled skid. Bulman held on to the door as Jacko accelerated towards the corner around which was the follower's car.

Bulman quickly acknowledged Jacko's driving skills and reflected that his new friend provided what he lacked. He hoped it would work.

As they flashed past the corner the other car pulled out behind them, and both Bulman and Jacko noticed that there were two men in it and that the driver knew his job. He would also know that once on the main streets, Jacko would have to obey the speed limit, and the speed capability of the Ferrari would be of less importance.

Bulman looked back over his shoulder. Suddenly he yelled. "They're coming at a hell of a lick! For chrissake, the mad bastard is going to ram us. And the other one has his gun out. Bloody hell!"

Chapter Eight

Jacko had a fixed grin on his face, his eyes darting from the road to the central mirror. "That's not a standard engine they've got under that bonnet," he said coolly. "The cheeky monkeys."

Bulman was still gazing back at the advancing car, now almost on their tail but not quite making it, and he realized that Jacko was just easing away. "It's no time to play games," he yelled. "They've only got to make a yard and they'll hit us."

"That's right," said Jacko, just keeping ahead. "I want to get a good look at the guys in the car so that I'll know them again."

Bulman looked back with more purpose. He knew neither of the men, although it was difficult as they both wore caps pulled down. "Don't mess around, Jacko. You've only to miscalculate a bit and they'll have us piled into the wall."

"What wall?" Jacko gave a sudden burst of the accelerator and the following car dropped back just as the wall petered out and they were heading towards the docks. Before then, Jacko did a right turn at speed, burned up his tyres and took off towards the City.

"This car's the wrong colour," Bulman bawled, slightly relieved. "They'll see us a mile off."

"And that's as near as they'll get in a few minutes. I don't know who the passenger is but I recognized the driver. An ex-E Type racer called Lofty Peel. Used to race at Thruxton amongst other places. Everyone wondered how he got his bloody long legs in the car. He was good but not good enough to make Formula One and I think that was his ambition. He'd be right up our tail if he was in a car like this."

"He almost was," said Bulman sharply. "Strange. I've grown to the idea that we are dealing with foreigners."

"You have to have local drivers otherwise they'd all be on the wrong side of the road. I knew he'd operated getaway cars for some of the boys, but this seems to be a new departure."

"How would they get on to him? There seems to be a lot of knowledge of our underworld in this, yet I don't think it's a villain's territory. The hit maybe, but someone is pulling an awful lot of strings somewhere." Bulman looked over his shoulder again. They were now deep in traffic and Jacko was happy behind the wheel of a car he cherished, relaxed and able. For once Bulman felt comfortable; Jacko was handing it well and clearly knew his way around London. They left the traffic turmoil of the City and headed for the West End taking whatever detour Jacko felt necessary.

Jacko said, "Lofty tried to ram us because he knew he could never keep up once I got going." But in spite of his easy attitude Jacko was totally alert to what was going on around him. He continued, "Good racing drivers are not necessarily good road drivers and they can go bananas in heavy traffic. In a getaway the routes are carefully planned as if you didn't know. But he's still there. A good way back but sticking to it."

Bulman had never really got used to the reversed position of being chased rather than chasing, even as a passenger in both cases. But he felt confident with Jacko at the wheel and at last sat back and let him get on with the driving.

They finished up in one of the better parts of Lambeth. It was an end of terrace house with the luxury of a recessed garage which had a high wall hiding it from the side street. Jacko opened the garage by remote control and the car was tucked away and the door dropped behind it. They went into the house by a side door from the garage.

"You seem to know your way around," said Bulman.

"I own it. I usually rent it out but it's between tenants at the moment; it won't be occupied for another two months."

The house was tall and narrow and comprised three floors of small rooms most of which, it seemed to Bulman, had been decorated by someone flying a kite on crack. Garish was a word that came to his mind.

After Jacko had showed Bulman round, nominated his bedroom *en suite*, they returned to the lounge. As Bulman sat down Jacko said, "Just make yourself at home. There are plenty of ready meals if you get hungry. I'll be as quick as I can."

"Where are you going without me?" Bulman was taken by surprise.

"I've got to trace a forger called 'Balls Up' Balfour. Marvellous forger but always cocked up the distribution. The last I heard, was that he is getting on and is arthritic, so I don't know if he's still operating. I believe your pal Scott knows him, which means you probably do too. If he's no good I only know one other. And I want to pay Lofty Peel a visit when he returns home. There's nothing you can do, Bulman, until I've done those things; I don't want anyone with me who looks like a copper. Just make yourself comfortable."

"Are you sure you shook off that car?"

"Oh, yes. Be good."

When Jacko had gone Bulman was left with the strange feeling that he had been set up away from his own familiar ground. It was a passing thought, but made him realize how little he really knew about Jacko. In some ways Jacko reminded him of his ex-burglar friend Spider Scott, but Scott was basically a gentle person and had never used violence on any of his jobs. Jacko was far from gentle and had taken no time at all to prove it. They were both superb drivers for possibly similar reasons. Bulman began to doze and accepted he would simply have to let Jacko unfold as they went along.

Jacko had a beige-coloured Ford in a lockup just a block from the terraced house. He drove to Soho and after a settled negotiation, parked the car at the rear of a garage in Brewer Street. He walked the short distance to Frith Street and trundled up some stairs between a video shop and strip club, where he had last known Balfour to live. He knocked on the door of the second landing; the paint had peeled off years ago so nothing had changed. The door was opened by a young untidy man with a straggling beard who certainly was not Balfour.

"I'm looking for Balls Up," said Jacko.

"How well did you know him?" The voice, through weak lips which were almost hidden by wisps of the beard, was educated.

"Did? Does that mean what I think it means?"

"Ah, the man actually understands the language. He died eight months ago. You couldn't have been a friend or you would have known."

"I'm sorry to hear he's dead. He was a fine artist." Jacko stood there wondering where to go next.

"In every sense. I've still got some of his copy paintings. Are you interested?"

"Not in his paintings." Jacko took a chance. "It was his other work that interested me."

The gaze from the pale eyes darted over Jacko's shoulder. "You'd better come in. I'm his nephew, Sonny. He left me what he had."

Jacko had not set foot in the place for years, but little seemed to have changed from what he remembered. At first sight the place was a tip, paints and paintings and oily rags everywhere. He had to pick his way carefully into the room. At a glance he could see just how fine an artist Balls Up had been. Nobody had ever found out why he turned to forgery; it was rumoured that he simply liked the challenge.

Jacko took another chance as the young man was about to speak. "Are you as good as your uncle was?" He could see nowhere to sit down.

"At least as good. He taught me over the years but I have a natural aptitude for it."

"Reproducing masters, or more mundane forgeries?" Another chance.

"Both. It runs in the family." The weak eyes had suddenly strengthened. "You didn't come here to chat. What is it you want done?"

"He used to keep dummies of various identity cards, coppers, that sort of thing. I wondered if you had any examples of the Board of Trade. Cash is no problem."

"Nor is the job if you have a passport snap. When?"

"Today."

"There's not much of the day left. I can't do it."

"Tomorrow then, here is the snap."

"This face rings a bell," said Sonny, studying Bulman's snapshot closely.

"He's got one of those mugs everybody thinks they've seen before. What time tomorrow?"

"Ten, if I work late tonight and get up early tomorrow. They can't be rushed. This will cost you."

"Of course. C.O.D. By the way, you don't happen to know an ex-racing driver called Lofty Peel? Used to be getaway for a few blag jobs."

"I've heard of him. Vaguely. Why?" Sonny was still studying the photograph.

"I want to make contact. I've got some work for him."

"It's time I knew who you are. You have the advantage."

"That's because I knew your uncle. I'm Jacko. Ask over at the Hot Pot, they'll know me. What about my locating Lofty?"

"I don't know where he hangs out but I know a man who might."

*　　*　　*

90

It was quite a smart hotel. The subdued ribbon lighting was tastefully scripted into the words Sands Hotel, not to be confused with, nor related to, the hotel of the same name in Las Vegas, although to the gullible the suggestion was there with the potted palms in the vestibule visible through the heavy glass doors. The location was tucked into a no man's land between North and South Kensington in one of those long discreet streets of mixed properties.

Jacko had found it very difficult to park and had gone round in big circles before finding a spot reasonably close to the hotel. He had checked with the hotel reception that Mr Peel was staying there but was not in his room; he had forgotten Lofty's first name if ever he had known it. As he was not dressed for waiting in hotel foyers he went back to the car. It was half-past eight, there was no moon and no rain and it was cold, the recent mildness suddenly vanishing. All he could do was to wait and hope that Lofty appeared.

It was quite a busy street trafficwise and seemed to be a regular route for taxis which made surveillance that much more difficult. He considered raising Bulman on the car phone but really had nothing to report. From time to time he started the engine up to get some heat into the car. And he was hungry.

He was used to waiting, had done it in Northern Ireland, virtually buried in a field close to a farmhouse for days on end without relief, but this was a different kind of waiting and he grew restless at times. He mused while he waited, his gaze on the entrance of the hotel all the time. Lofty must be doing fairly well to live in a nice hotel like this. There was no sign of the car that had followed them, Jacko had checked on foot up and down.

He would have waited all night if he thought that during that time Lofty would have appeared, and as he did not believe that, he put a time limit on it. Midnight. That seemed reasonable enough. With the passing of time, concentration became more difficult and he had to fight off drifting.

A taxi pulled in about thirty yards past the hotel and someone got out and paid the driver. It wasn't until the cab moved off and the man started to walk towards the hotel that Jacko recognized Lofty as he passed under a street light. Jacko scrambled out of the car not bothering to lock it as he raced across the road, dodging traffic; he must reach Lofty before Lofty reached the hotel.

Jacko kept his head down and aimed for a spot the other side of the hotel entrance so as to block Lofty off. He reached the pavement and kept running, aware that Lofty was drawing closer and as yet not suspicious as far as he could see. He pushed a hand inside his jacket and took a grip on the Colt which he had thrust inside his waistband.

Lofty stepped aside to let Jacko go past, calling to him to look where he was going, and the next moment he felt a gun barrel boring into his ear as he was pushed back against some railings.

"Don't struggle or I'll blow your head off." Jacko could be menacing without really trying, and most of the time meant what he said. "Now put your hands in your pockets and keep them there." By this time Jacko had put his free arm round Lofty's shoulders to satisfy passers-by. He lowered the gun to the rib cage where it was less evident. "You nearly scratched my Ferrari," snarled Jacko feeling an instant stiffening of Lofty's frame.

"No, I held right back. I wouldn't have touched you."

"You lying bastard. I managed to just keep ahead of you. Now cross the road with me, we're going to have a talk."

By this time Lofty was showing more fear than when he had first felt the gun. "Someone's waiting for me in the hotel. They'll come looking."

"Bullshit. Move."

They reached Jacko's car, a friend helping a drunk, and Jacko said, "Climb into the passenger seat."

Lofty climbed in, looking for the half chance.

"Now move across to the driver's seat."

"I can't. It's too difficult with my legs."

Jacko leant down and put the gun on full view just in front of Lofty's face. "Do you know where I got this gun from? One of those pudding faces who was with you in the car. Would you like the same thing to happen to you? No. Well bloody well move across."

Jacko slid into the vacated seat before Lofty had a chance to slip out the other side; it was a crucial moment. "Strap up."

"Where are we going?" Lofty was really anxious now.

"What does it matter? Somewhere nice and quite. Head south out of London. There's plenty of juice."

"Can't we talk here?"

"One of your mates might pitch up." Jacko handed over the keys. "Just drive off while I think."

Lofty pulled out and the jerk on starting told it's own story; as the minutes ticked by Lofty was more concerned. His ability to drive took control once they were moving and he made good headway south.

Jacko had positioned himself at an angle so that he never removed his gaze from Lofty who did not like the attention. Jacko well knew the longer he drove the more nervous Lofty would get and would wonder what would happen when he stopped. From this point Jacko said nothing, ignoring the anxious glances, the odd questions, but making sure he had full view of Lofty and that the gun was also on view.

They headed south towards the coast, with Jacko leaving the route entirely to Lofty who eventually burst out, "Look, I must have some bloody idea of where I'm going. We've been on the road for well over an hour and you haven't said a bloody word. Where am I supposed to go, for God's sake?"

"Once you're the other side of Croydon head for the country. Find a nice quite lane where we can chat,"

Lofty did not like the sound of that and he nervously licked his lips. "This is crazy," he said, "coming all this way. There was no need. We could chat anywhere."

93

"Yes, but the gun might be heard. I don't want that."

In the pale glow from the instrument panel the sweat beads could just be seen on Lofty's forehead. A trickle ran down his cheek. His gaze darted between the gun and the road. They were south of Croydon by now, but not quite out of the built up area. Lofty pulled in sharply and sat back, gaze forward. They were in a short, tree-lined residential road and it was quiet here, the houses well spaced and only the odd car on the street.

"That's as far as I go," said Lofty in a shaking voice. "If you're going to shoot me you can do it here."

"Who said anything about shooting you?"

"You want to be somewhere where the gun won't be heard. Well, I won't oblige."

"That's only if you don't help me. Get on with it, just a few miles more."

"No. I might just as well top myself."

Jacko was trying to keep it light but could not remove the menace of the gun nor wanted to. "I don't understand you. You used to hare round a race track risking your life every time and thinking nothing of it. Now look at you. Drive on."

"I had my life in my own hands then."

"You still have. You have only to co-operate and I want you to do that where we won't be interrupted. For both our sakes. Just a few miles more." When Lofty hesitated Jacko added, "I don't want to shoot you, Lofty, that just complicates things. So don't make me." There was a sharp bite to his last words.

Lofty mulled it over and drove off slowly. They eventually found a lane with a side track off it which Jacko told Lofty to take. They entered some woods and suddenly it was very quiet, and very, very dark away from the headlight beams.

Jacko switched on the interior light and told Lofty to douse the others. Now they were sitting in an illuminated bowl with the dimmed shape of trees rising beyond the windows. The cold started to creep in as soon as the engine was cut.

"Let's keep it short," said Jacko. "You know what I want to know so let's get on with it. Who's paying you?"

"I don't know. I really don't. I'm contacted by someone who is virtually an agent, who tells me where to go and to do what they want. The terms are the best I've ever had." He half turned to Jacko. "It's mainly driving, a job I enjoy."

"So you have no names. You are operating blind which everyone knows is suicidal. Were you that broke? I heard you'd given up the horses."

"I've cut them down. Look, the money's very good and they pay on the nail."

"Who's your agent?"

Lofty hesitated then said, "Benny Walker."

Jacko had vaguely heard of the man. Everyone had agents these days; footballers, villains, there was no end to the middle man. "Are they paying for the hotel?"

"No. I'm between moves. I'll be there for another week, that's all. I'm sorry I can't help."

"No, you're not. And I haven't finished with you. If these guys give no names what do they do for accents? What nationality are they?"

The length Lofty took to answer was at least indicative that they weren't British. "It's difficult," he said. "I'm not good on accents. I can tell an engine by it's sound but voices aren't my thing."

"Have a shot and don't try to mislead me."

"I've met two of them so far; I reckon they're Russian."

"Russian? You sure?"

"Of course I'm not bloody sure. It never occurred to me to ask." There was now a resignation about Lofty that surprised Jacko, who believed that Lofty was at last trying to be helpful.

"Tell me what you can about them."

"There's nothing to tell. I'm told where to be and at what time, a guy is there to see me and to tell me what to do. My

95

job was to tail you, and when he realized you might get away he told me to ram you. The gun he produced stopped all arguments; this guy intended to use it."

"It's a long way for such little info."

"That's what I've been telling you. I could have told you this outside the hotel."

"You could have but you wouldn't have. You'd have felt safer there and you would have been. Why are you suddenly letting up?"

Lofty shrugged, much more relaxed now. "I'm supposed to stay in the hotel waiting for a call. If they find me missing I'll be in trouble. These aren't people you mess with. I've decided the best thing I can do is to bugger off up north. I don't like the feel of this, and I didn't like being told to ram you. The guy is a nutter and is comfortable with a gun in his hand. Like you."

They sat in silence for a few moments while Jacko tried to decide what to do. He was still thinking when Lofty said, "I could have got you, y'know. I was holding a fraction back while telling matey I was flat out. I don't know where he got the car but it could go."

"What do you know of a scrubber called Connie Smith?"

"Never heard of her." Lofty considered again. "No. Rings no bell."

"And Bert Cooper? A hotel receptionist. Well a concierge, I suppose."

"No. Is there any reason why I should?"

It was the old cell system, but Jacko did not think that this was political; it somehow hadn't that feel to it. "It all depends on what you're wrapped up in, Lofty. But I believe you for what it's worth. I think you're right to go to earth. As soon as you get back."

"I'll collect my stuff from the hotel and then push off."

It was like listening to Bulman talking. "For a villain you're pretty naïve. Cut your losses and just do a runner."

96

"Sod you. You've put me up against the wall."

"If you're right about Russians I might have. I didn't know Russians are involved, but they do tend to tidy up." Jacko tucked the gun away. "Look, Lofty. I was going to beat it out of you if I had to and I'm glad that didn't happen. And then I was going to ditch you here and let you find your own way back which would have been better than having a hole in your head. But I'll take you back to town or drop you off on the way."

"So what's changed your mind? I haven't really told you anything because I don't know anything."

"You've told me more than you realize." Jacko leaned over and took the keys from the ignition. "Let's change seats." When he was behind the wheel he said, "Where does Benny Walker hang out?"

"He'll kill me if he finds out I told you."

"He won't know. In for a penny . . ."

Lofty still hesitated. "If Benny doesn't get me the Russians will."

"If you don't tell me, I'll go back to plan A and dump you here then ring the hotel to tell them where you were last seen, and that you won't be back and would they pass the message on to all callers."

"You bastard. I've tried to help you. You're making sure they get me."

"It saves me doing the job myself and gives you a reasonable chance. Now, where does Benny hang out?"

"He has a first floor office in Newman Street, the other side of New Oxford Street. Fronts as a male model agency." He sat listlessly in his seat, as if he had just passed a death sentence on himself.

Chapter Nine

During Jacko's absence Bulman found it impossible to relax. He ran up a huge phone bill in an effort to trace someone who might know more about Ronald Walsh than he had hitherto met. Co-directors of Walsh were obvious, but Bulman had the gut feeling that he would get nowhere with any of them unless he had much more authority than he possessed. The police would have seen those who mattered, and he doubted that they would discover much from the closed commercial circuit with the risk of the good name of the business empire being besmirched. But he did come up with a name: Freda Curtis, Walsh's Personal Assistant, who worked in the HQ of the holding company off Ludgate Circus in the City of London.

It was late by the time he obtained this information, and when he rang Freda Curtis she had already left for the day. There was nothing he could do but wait. He used the microwave to heat a ready meal, and sat down in Jacko's gaudy dining room at an expensive but highly polished table, and felt the loneliness creep back. Being alone was different in a strange house which somehow deepened the feeling.

Jacko returned at three-thirty in the morning. Bulman was still up but asleep in one of the chairs. He was not aware that Jacko had returned until the lounge lights came on.

"Sorry," said Jacko. "You should have gone to bed."

"I was concerned about you." Bulman was still half asleep but his priorities were clear. "What about the ID?"

Jacko, looking tired himself, said, "It should be ready by ten; now ask me what sort of a night I've had."

They drank coffee while Jacko brought Bulman up to date, and it was clear that both had clear-cut tasks for the day. They sat in opposite chairs and dozed off until dawn, and then stirred with difficulty.

Once shaved, Bulman looked at himself in a cheval mirror; his suit was crumpled and he realized he could not meet Freda Curtis looking like that, so he set about ironing. "You'll have to lend me some money. I must have a change of clothing once I've seen this woman."

"How do you know she'll see you?" They were having breakfast by now and feeling more human.

"I must see her. Personal Assistants know a lot about their bosses. I think his colleagues would show me the door, if ever I got anywhere near them; we're talking of some high powered people here. I suppose you'll be seeing Benny Walker?" He glanced over the rim of his cup. "Be careful, Jacko. You are not dealing with terrorists now. I know about Walker. He has a large following and forces some good deals for the boys who operate for the major fences. His Christmas card list would scare the hell out of the Commissioner of Police. His contacts aren't fanatics but hard boiled professionals who know their job, and there are some very dangerous ones amongst them. Touch him and you touch the rest. Don't underestimate him or his powers; you can't take on the whole underworld."

"Are you trying to scare me?"

"Yes. Use your brain and less of the gung ho!"

"Has he a rival? He can't be the only link man around."

"So far as I know, there's nobody anywhere near as good. There used to be a young pretender called Mickey Dunn. I seem to remember that Benny tried to put him out of business but I can't recall the outcome. I haven't heard of him recently. Maybe he's no longer in business."

Jacko left at half-past eight and returned at half eleven with the ID. He gave Bulman a slip of paper with the cost on. Bulman whistled and then shrugged. "I must admit it's very good."

"You pay for the best," said Jacko.

"I've been trying to raise Freda Curtis but can't get hold of her. I left the name on the ID."

They had a snack in the kitchen, after which Jacko went out and Bulman rang Freda Curtis again, and was almost taken off guard when he was put through.

"Yes, Mr Russell, I believe you have been trying to contact me. May I know what it's about?"

"It's a Board of Trade matter, Miss Curtis. There was no point in you ringing me back there as I'm constantly on the move. I'm sorry to trouble you and I know it's a bad time, but can we meet?"

"Shouldn't you be dealing with one of the directors?"

"I think that this is a matter where you might be of greater help."

"How urgent is it, Mr Russell? And what is this matter?"

He had to take a chance. "Your ex-boss, Ronald Walsh."

"Can you be more specific?" Her voice had changed slightly, as if mention of his name had an adverse effect on her, and she sounded guarded.

"That's difficult to do over a telephone. Clearly it relates to business or we would not be involved. If you can spare me the time it should not take long."

There was a noticeable silence and at one time he thought she might have hung up or was cut off at the switchboard. And then she spoke again, her voice more subdued, "I'm sorry for the delay but I've been checking my engagements. I'm tied up for the next few days except for three this afternoon. Can you get round here by then?"

"I'll make a point of being there. It is most kind of you."

"Fifteenth floor. I'll see you then."

Bulman put the phone down, both pleased and puzzled.

100

He was sure she had checked no engagements, and for some reason she wanted him there as soon as possible but wanted to give an opposite impression. He glanced at his watch. There was not much time left, so he tidied himself up as best he could then went searching for a cab.

The building was a modern high-rise office block all concrete and glass and, like so many in the City, on an old bomb site. He had only to approach it to feel he did not belong to this atmosphere of wealth and wheeler dealing. As he walked through the huge double glass doors he felt like a man who had just ironed his suit to look for a job; he was thankful then that he had ironed out the creases.

There was nothing so simple as just going up in one of the many lifts; his identity card was checked at reception and he was asked if he had an appointment. A girl phoned through while he waited, he was given a lapel docket with his name on it, and told to take lift number five to the fifteenth floor where he would be met. He was in another world, one that he had come near to whilst at Scotland Yard but which he had too easily forgotten. This had been Walsh's world and he hoped he could handle it.

It seemed to him that the lift doors were opening almost as soon as they had closed behind him, when he had stepped in with a small army of well-behaved executives passing small talk and being funny but polite. Bulman kept quiet, aware of the glances cast at his unemployable image. They all disembarked before reaching the fifteenth floor, and he was glad to be alone and left with a feeling that he'd had his hand in the till.

The doors pulled back with hardly a sound, and a well-groomed, good-looking lady stood before him with a questioning smile. "Mr Russell? I'm Freda Curtis. I thought I'd better meet you myself." She held out a hand and he took it thinking how firm but soft it was. He liked her on sight, judging her to be in her early forties, and, to hold her position, highly efficient. She led him to an office

101

which would not have disgraced a managing director of most businesses.

There were two desks, the smaller with a computer and printer. There was a television set in one corner, the latest share prices flickering out. On the larger desk were two telephones, an intercom with a bank of switches, and a fax machine. Behind the desk was a huge sheet glass window which appeared fragile but which was probably toughened to a very high degree for safety reasons.

"Do sit down, Mr Russell. Coffee?"

He had not noticed the small table in the corner with the peculator and cup and saucers. "That would be nice. Black, please."

Freda Curtis moved nicely, she radiated a quiet efficiency but there was much more to her than that. He realized he would have to be very careful indeed with her if he hoped to avoid being slung out.

She returned with the coffee, placing one cup on the desk in front of him. She sat down in a director's chair and gave him a warm but tired and sad little smile, and he could see that recent events had probably left their mark on her. He suddenly wanted to reassure her and reflected on how ridiculous that reaction was.

"Now what can I do for you? You mentioned that it was connected with Mr Walsh, God rest his soul."

"Indeed. I'm sure the police have called about the unfortunate murder." He noticed her wince. "I'm more concerned about the commercial angle, how it might affect business, particularly abroad. And I wondered about his more recent projects abroad and whether we can help at all, if anything needs putting right in any way."

"Can you be more precise?" Freda Curtis was puzzled.

Bulman reached for his cup and gave an apologetic smile. "I have to feel my way round this," he said with perfect truth. "It is not easy." He sipped his drink then put down the cup. He sat back and focused on a point between them. "As you know, part of our function is to give advice to businessmen going abroad, including the occasional dangers of doing so. Some countries are very difficult over paperwork, and suspicious, often quite unreasonably, making it difficult for our businessmen. We try to straighten out these problems, and where we can, pass on commercial tips we've received from the various embassies and consulates. In spite of what some people think of us, we do try to provide a service to the British industry." He reached for his coffee again to secure a little time.

"And?" Freda Curtis now seemed both slightly amused and confused.

"We wondered if Mr Walsh had experienced difficulties during some of his recent visits?"

"Is that a Board of Trade question or a police question?"

"I would expect the police to ask something similar. But my purpose is to find out any problems encountered by Mr Walsh, if any, and to be in a position to warn others. That sort of advice can be invaluable."

"I am not aware of any particular problems he had, except the usual delays at airports and red tape over visas and things like that. But you would expect those sort of problems anyway, wouldn't you, Mr Russell? Or have you not yet reached the point?"

"Mine was a fair question. It's amazing some of the real difficulties businessmen come up against abroad; some even life threatening. In fact there was a recent case where a company director was shot dead in Moscow. Nobody has found out why and no arrests have been made, except the usual round-up of known criminals as a token gesture and they were later released. There are incidents too, of intimidation."

"Mr Walsh told me of no such incidents. And I am sure he would have done, had they happened. So far as I know his life has never been threatened abroad, nor has he been intimidated. Is that what you wanted to know?"

"That would be more reassuring if someone had not

103

shot him dead." Bulman still sat there feeling that he had achieved nothing and wondering which line to take next.

She stiffened at that; his death clearly still affected her. "He was not killed abroad but here, Mr Russell."

"His death might have been instigated from abroad. If it was, it is something we would wish to know. Others need to be warned." Bulman could see that he was losing her goodwill, if ever he'd had it in the first place. She did not want to talk about Walsh's death, and she was disturbed. She must have known about his women, probably taken messages from them from time to time. It briefly crossed his mind whether she had been one of them but he dismissed the idea for reasons he could not immediately explain. She was clearly loyal to him and he supposed that was part of the function of a PA.

Freda Curtis composed herself, sat quietly drinking her coffee and gazed at Bulman reflectively. Suddenly she said, "Have we met before?"

"Possibly. Although you are not someone I would forget."

She smiled and the image of professional efficiency was replaced by spontaneous charm. "Are you a middle-aged smoothie, Mr Russell, or was that meant to be a compliment?"

"I'm no good at being a smoothie. I meant what I said."

"Well, thank you. But I'm not sure that we've got anywhere. The concern you have shown, ostensibly for the protection of future businessmen abroad, would be covered by a routine report after each trip. Are you sure you are not a policeman trying to find a connection with Ronnie's murder and his trips abroad?"

Bulman smiled back and his crusted features could be very disarming. "What a wicked mind you have, Miss Curtis. No, I am not a policeman."

"You are not Board of Trade either. They would not go to this extreme and if they did it would be with Mr Walsh's colleagues. Are you with the Security Service?"

Bulman remained poker-faced and could not believe his luck. He held on to his senses wondering how best to play the card she had just dealt him. He took out his Board of Trade ID and placed it on the desk before her.

She picked it up. "I see the photograph is very recent. You are still wearing the same tie."

He grinned and nodded approval. "Nice try. I'm faithful to my old suits and ties; tend to wear them until they drop off."

He returned the card to his pocket as she said, 'You still haven't answered me. Don't fool around with me because I am not impressed and your time is running out."

"You wouldn't expect me to admit to being with the Security Service even if I was. I'll come clean about one thing though, which I hope will make you understand. I do know that he was helping the SIS from time to time while he was abroad. That could have courted certain dangers."

"MI6? But the cold war is long over. You are a little outdated, Mr Bulman."

"There are many types of intelligence gathering; they are not all political or military."

"Well I suppose I should not really be surprised; he was a very intelligent man."

"Except in one respect." Bulman let it hang and again saw a cloud pass over her features as if she was holding herself in.

"You mean his women? Everybody knew of that weakness. But they did not affect his commercial judgement. Is there anything else?"

"It's fairly common knowledge that businessmen are sometimes recruited by the SIS to bring back useful information. They've even been known to act as couriers. Mr Walsh had the advantage of also being a Member of Parliament, so was perceptive to political values. I've come as clean as I dare. Was there any trip he made fairly recently from which he came back showing unfamiliar signs? Of all the people in the business you were surely the closest to him and would have noticed anything unusual in his attitude."

She sat back thoughtfully eying her cup, and the weariness and pain showed itself more than hitherto. He thought it might be the angle of the desk light casting shadows under her chin and eyes, but he felt for her then and cursed what he was doing to her.

She stared wearily across the desk, as if the interview had suddenly drained her. "Have you any idea of the legacy he has left me? And when I've sorted it out I don't know whether or not I still have a job."

"Surely you are too valuable to the company for them to let you go?"

"I carry detail of his private life that some of his co-directors would prefer not to be within these walls. They have been embarrassed enough, and the yellow press have really put the boot in. There is a whole war for ascendency going on in this monolith of business ethics. The knives are out, Mr Russell, and some of them are out for me."

She was too in command of herself to shed a tear, but Bulman had the impression that she would like to do nothing else.

"You didn't answer my question," he said gently.

She sat upright as if shaking off unwanted memories. "Yes, there was a time when he returned in a rather morose mood." She moved the cup away and clasped her long fingered hands on the desk. "He was moody for some days after coming back from Russia. As he wouldn't talk about it I assumed he had been given the shoulder by a woman and he was not used to that. In the end the mood lasted too long for that to have been the cause. I became the butt for his bad temper for a while until I threatened to walk out, and then he became contrite and apologized profusely and told me he was in a mid-life crisis. But it wasn't that."

106

"Did you ever discover what caused it?"

Freda Curtis had either made up her mind to talk freely and wanted to unburden to a stranger, or had decided that the loyalty she had enjoyed was dead and she could not rely on those who were left. Bulman reflected that he might just possibly have unplugged her.

"No, I never found out, although I did try because I was worried for him. He was usually so buoyant."

"Did he pull out of it?"

"I suppose he did. I think something had gone from him though, but that could have been my imagination."

"How long ago was this?"

"Eight months. Nine, maybe."

"Is it possible for you to give me the details of the trip? Who he went to see and for how long he was there and so on?"

"You are asking for company secrets. I can't do that. And isn't that a strange request from the Board of Trade?"

He was pleased to see her smile back, even a small one. "I would say it was very much an interest for the BOT. They may even have the details themselves. But as I'm here I thought it might save time if you gave them to me. Anyway, if they upset him over there I want to know. Really, can there be any harm in telling me about a trip he did so long ago?"

"You are very persuasive, Mr Russell. But my loyalties are very well defined."

"You were just complaining that you might lose your job. Are the loyalties all one way? Come on, what possible harm could it do? It's a question the police might ask."

She did not reply to that and he thought she appeared a little uncertain, and began to think the police had probably already asked. She pressed a switch on the intercom and said, "Sandra, please bring in the file on the Zotov Corporation." The switch was flicked back up and Bulman noticed again just how careful Freda Curtis was.

A young blonde in a miniskirt knocked on the door and

107

handed over a thick file to her boss, giving Bulman a quick smile in passing.

Bulman said, "I thought that would all be on computer these days."

"It is. It's a double record; computers can get fouled up. There is a lot here, I don't know what you can possibly expect to get from it."

"I'm mainly interested in the name of the company, presumably just the one as you mentioned only one, and the names of the people he met whilst out there."

"I can't let you take the file away. The best I can do is to let you use the corner of the desk over there and supply you with pen and paper to make some notes."

Bulman had just settled when a smartly-dressed, middle-aged man opened the door and put his head round to say to Freda Curtis, "Still busy, Freda? What can you be up to?" His tone was far from friendly, and he had obviously had a good deal of wine with his lunch.

"There's a lot to clear up, John, as you know."

"Really? Can Ronnie's affairs have been so far behind, or do you just like sitting there wishfully thinking?"

Bulman looked up at that. He was not in direct line with the door and had time to assess the caller; he was thinning on top, had an angular, supercilious face and a superior air about him. His tone had been cruel and his lips close to a sneer. Bulman had the file open, some sheets raised, and he must have rustled them for suddenly the caller's stony gaze was on him. At first John clearly could not believe what he saw. He stood leaning at an angle whilst holding on to the door and glaring at Bulman in disbelief – his gaze vacillating between Bulman and the file he held.

"Just who the hell are you? And what are you doing with a confidential file? I'm going to call security." He turned to Freda Curtis in fury. "Just what the blazes do you think you are doing?" And then to Bulman again, "Give me that file at once, and stay there until the police arrive." He crossed the room and picked up one of the phones.

Chapter Ten

Jacko found the entrance to the male model agency where Lofty had told him it would be. A few photographs of well-groomed men were pinned in a glass case beside the door. The entrance was totally unprepossessing, shabby, and the narrow stairs were not carpeted. Jacko stood back so that he could again read the faded and chipped sign above the door. Some agencies did appear as if they were on their last legs, possibly to convince their clients that they needed a higher commission rate, but this was worst than most. If this agency was a dummy for the hire of villains then no effort had been made to make it convincing.

Jacko mounted the stairs and they creaked all the way up. The agency was on the top floor with two doors leading off the narrow landing. It smelled musty up there. One door was marked 'Private' and the other, 'Reception. Please Knock and Enter'. Jacko made a deliberate mistake and tapped on the grubby 'Private' door and went in.

A man Jacko vaguely recognized sat behind a large desk which was covered in papers and studio mug-shots of men. The man was overweight with a slicked back head of hair, sallow features and rock hard eyes. The desk was backed by an outer wall with a small window and faced the inner door, presumably leading to the other office. The man was on the telephone when Jacko entered, but glanced up in surprise and made sweeping movements with his arm to indicate that Jacko should get out quick and go to the other office.

Jacko saw the key in the other door, eased his way round,

turned the key and slipped it in his pocket. The fat man's expression changed from one of impatient fury to that of deep concern; he quickly wound up the phone call with a promise to ring back and snarled at Jacko.

"What the bloody hell do you think you're doing?"

"Are you Benny Walker?"

"Who wants to know?"

"I do, you stupid bugger. Well are you?"

"Of course I am. Put that key back in the lock before you land in deeper trouble. Who are you?"

"I'm the bloke who's going to blow your ears off if I don't get some answers. Now tell your girl you're not taking any more calls until you advise her otherwise, and that you don't want to be disturbed."

Piggy eyes flickered with anger and podgy hands began to open a desk drawer.

Jacko pulled out the Colt and laid it on the edge of the desk as he sat in one of two chairs facing Walker. He knew that the gun itself was intimidating enough, but the bulky laser sight along the barrel was additionally scary because so many people had no idea what it was, except that it appeared to be deadly.

"Close the drawer," said Jacko. "Now tell your girl."

Walker flicked down a switch. "Lottie, I'll be tied up for a bit. No more calls and don't come in." He sat back eying Jacko, noticed the damaged hands, and was not sure what to make of him except to acknowledge he was dangerous. He was about to speak again when Jacko picked up the Colt and signalled him to silence as he leaned across the desk and flicked up the intercom switch with the barrel of the gun.

"Don't try pulling that sort of stunt again or you'll frighten Lottie to death. Now put your hands on the desk where I can see them." When the podgy hands were resting on the desk Jacko added, "I want the names of the Russians who use you to hire out villains."

The piggy eyes roamed in their layers of fat; there was

110

no fear in them, for Walker was still assessing the situation, still not sure of the man opposite him. Something of a smile touched the folds around his lips. "You're off your rocker. I don't deal with Russians. This is strictly local. I couldn't cope with foreigners."

"Well at least you didn't try the male model agency crap on me. Good lad." Jacko gazed over Walker's shoulder to a wall at the side of the window where more posed shots hung up. "There's a bloke there with too much shadow over his right eye. I'm going to lighten it for him. Take a look."

Walker turned in his chair with difficulty and said, "Just what are you talking about?"

"The guy just to the right of your head, the one with the smirk. His right eye is too shadowed, wouldn't you say?"

"Maybe the photographer wanted it like that. Just what are you playing at?" Walker's hand crept towards the intercom as he gazed awkwardly at the studio shot. And then he saw a red dot on the offending eye. There was a sudden roar and he felt a rush of air past his face and before he could turn his head he saw the offending eye taken out to be buried in the woodwork behind.

For a moment Walker was paralysed then he started to quiver, his jowls flopping as his jaw fell open. He could neither speak nor move as, presumably Lottie, started to rattle the door while crying out to ask if he was all right.

"Tell her you're OK. Tell her you dropped a light bulb." Jacko was now standing with his back to the door he had used to enter. "*Tell her.*"

Walker managed to stop his jaw moving and called out, "It's OK, Lottie. I dropped a light bulb I was trying to change. Carry on, love. No problem."

"You weren't very convincing, Benny. She won't believe you but at least she knows you're alive and is hardly likely to call the police, is she?" Jacko remained at the outer door because there was no key in the lock and he did not want Lottie coming round the other way.

Walker was slowly recovering. The explosion could have

been worse, but the small, overcrowded office and its fittings seemed to have muffled the sound. As a warning, though, it had been very effective and Walker seemed to be fascinated by the blank hole where the eye had been in the photograph.

"Impressive eh?" said Jacko. "I've a few more party pieces but I don't want to give you a heart attack or scare Lottie again." His tone hardened. "If you make me fire again I'll put a hole straight through your flab and give it some ventilation. Now, the names of these Russian guys."

Walker was recovering from the shock, his mind working faster. "You were crazy to pull a stunt like that. Do you realize the kind of contacts I have? Just who are you?"

"You'll probably find out in due course but it won't reassure you when you do. I've got contacts, too, Benny. And they all shoot like that; that is when they're not blowing up things. Look, all I want is a little information. One of your Russians put Lofty Peel on to tailing me and I don't take kindly to that. I won't to know who and why."

"So Lofty told you about me. I'll have him done."

"No you won't. The nearest I've been to Lofty is his image in a rear view mirror. I recognized him just before I took off. The guy with him had Russian written all over him. But we're wasting time, Benny. Cough up or I'm going to beat your head in and then go through this office until I find what I want. And if that means Lottie's office too then that's what I'll do."

There was a shifty look about Benny that prompted Jacko to add, "Don't wrong foot me; I want the names you have and the telephone numbers and addresses."

"I have none of those things." Benny held up his arms in protest as Jacko half rose from his chair. "Listen to me." When Jacko was reseated Benny continued. "Two guys came in about three weeks ago. I'd go along with the description of Russians, although I'd prefer just to call them foreign, I mean they could have been anything. One could hardly speak English and it was murder trying to understand him. The other one spoke much better English but with a very heavy accent. They had been introduced by an old contact of mine who made an appointment on their behalf."

Benny shrugged heavily. "The only thing I knew for certain was that they were not cops of any kind. There was something about them I understood and something else that worried me. I can't explain. They wanted a couple of drivers, like Lofty, and some heavies from time to time. That's all there is to it."

"No names? Just like that? Immediate trust? Who are you kidding, Benny? You only survive on caution."

"They had bundles of money, cash. That speaks a lot and promotes trust. They paid up front and never queried a fee, which puzzled me a bit for such hard cases. They just peeled off whatever I asked."

"Your greed blotted out the fact that you were compromising yourself to total strangers. You must have had means of communication?"

"They would phone me. Sometimes one of them would come in, but always after phoning. I haven't dealt with them that often. That's it. They're not the only clients I have who don't give names. I've a couple in the aristocracy I do jobs for; one of them a topping. I know who they are but they don't know that. It's usual business."

"So you take a lot on trust?"

"I have to."

"Does Mickey Dunn operate like that? I mean is he as careless?"

Benny's whole attitude changed at the mention of the name. "Mickey Dunn, what's he got to do with it? I thought he had died or something."

"You mean your boys didn't finish the job properly? He's very much in business. He knows these two Russian guys, too. But he has names for them."

Benny tried to control his fury. "That scumbag. Where's he hanging out now?"

Jacko laughed. "So now you want information from me. Why should I tell you? I got far more from Mickey than I've got from you."

"So he gave you names. What do you think that means? They could be names off a toilet wall. They don't mean anything."

"They're something to call somebody by. So what names did they give you that aren't worth a light?"

"Will you leave the room while I get the details?"

"No. You might ring up the cavalry. I'm not interested in your general business, just these guys. And I'm doing you a favour by keeping the Bill off your back."

Benny mulled it over, glanced at the Colt which was now back on the corner of the desk, chewed his lip for a few seconds more, and then pushed his chair right back and rolled back the end of the shabby carpet to reveal a floor safe, which had been positioned under his chair.

Jacko was amused; Benny was not only sitting on his money but his secrets too. While Benny's large back was turned towards him, Jacko grasped the Colt; Benny might have an armoury in the safe as well.

Benny reached back and grabbed a pen and a piece of paper, and turned his back on Jacko again. The safe was closed, the carpet was flicked back and then the chair was wheeled into place. At last Benny sat down, out of breath. He passed the piece of paper across the desk and Jacko saw the two printed names on it. "Penkov and Zotin," he read aloud.

Benny winced as if the whole world could hear the betrayal. "Keep your voice down. Are they the names Mickey gave you?"

"Yes, they are. These two are obviously spreading the load." Jacko was trying to see how Benny was taking it. "Well that makes good business sense, but I would say you get far more from them than Mickey does. Maybe they just use Mickey for insurance, you know, you might

114

be sick one day at a crucial time. Well, that's all I wanted unless you have the addresses."

"Don't push your luck. I've already committed suicide. And I'll find out who you are and I'll do something about you. You won't get away with this."

"If you've committed suicide that's the risk of the game you play, Benny." Jacko rose. "You cream off as an agent, but if a job goes badly wrong one day, the boys you recruited might come back for you when they get parole." Jacko moved towards the door. "If you find me and try taking a crack at me, well you might just lose a client; if ever I need a creeper can you fix me up?"

Benny's expression changed; he did not know what to make of that. "I know one or two. Contact me and don't bring that bloody cannon with you. We could have done business without that."

Jacko grinned and left by the way he had entered, leaving the gun in sight until the last moment.

As John raised the phone, Bulman, who had remained calm, called out, "Perhaps you had better see this first." He pulled out his forged identity card and held it up knowing it was too far away to be read.

John wavered, shooting a questioning glance at Freda, and getting no help from her, he crossed towards Bulman who remained seated but kept the card held high. John took the card, studied it suspiciously but was not quite sure what to do about it. "Board of Trade. What on earth would they want with us?"

"If you don't know that, then perhaps you are out of touch with the functions of your own company."

John handed the card back. Where before he had been furious he was now dangerously cool, his gaze icy as it met Bulman's. "I think you had better explain that."

"I've already explained that to Miss Curtis. I don't feel obligated to go through it again. I'd have suggested that you ask her, but as you have shown publicly your lack of

confidence in her then I really don't know what to suggest."
He rose slowly, tidied up the papers in the file, retaining
the sheet with the few notes he had made, picked up the
file and handed it to John. "As this seems to have affected
your manners you had better have it back. I'm not used to
being treated in this way, Mr . . .?"

"John Parre," Freda called out. "He's on the main
board."

John was back to glaring again. His initial onslaught had
been on Freda, someone he knew he outranked, but Bulman
had come as a Joker in the pack and he was still floundering,
not quite sure which way to jump but not willing to lose
authority. "You have absolutely no right to that file without
the authority of a director, Mr Russell. I suggest you get
your people to make a formal request, giving reasons."

Bulman inclined his head. "I'll make my report. Perhaps
I can leave now without fear of assault or the threat of
police." He moved round John who seemed to be rooted,
profusely thanked Freda for her help and told her he would
be in touch. She gave him a secretive little smile and he
found himself sorry to leave.

Once in the street, he leaned against the wall and broke
into a mild sweat, but was satisfied that he had at least
made a note of some names from the file.

In Freda Curtis's office John Parre stood clutching the file
and realized that he had been made to look something of a
fool in the eyes of an employee. He was aware that if Ronnie
Walsh was alive he would not have dared to speak to Freda
in the way he had, but Ronnie was dead and matters had
to sorted out before the rot set in.

He put the file down on Freda's desk and said, "Make
sure that is put back where it belongs. And you can give
me the Board of Trade number."

To retain some dignity, Freda got through to her secretary
for the number then passed it over to John Parre who picked
up the nearest phone, asked for a line and dialled the number

himself, intent on making Freda suffer. It took time to get the person he wanted and when he did, more delay in waiting for a check to be carried out. At the end he decided it was well worth the wait.

Freda could see trouble from the expression on John's face, which turned from impatience to malice in just a second or two. He put down the phone and came close to striking Freda, holding himself in check with difficulty. "You stupid bitch," he snarled. "You've given company secrets to a perfect stranger. The only Russell they have is a junior clerk and his name is Alistaire. You've been conned, you fool."

Bulman got a cab quite quickly; the rush hour had not quite started. He was worried about the plight in which he may have left Freda Curtis. He had recognized that John Parre was out to get her one way or the other, and was vindictive enough to run a check with the BOT; he would have done the same in the circumstances. There was nothing he could do but get back to the house to meet up with Jacko and to compare notes.

He left the cab a couple of blocks from Jacko's house and arrived to find Jacko there. They compared notes to find they both had names and that they did not match. The only common denominator was that they all appeared to be Russian.

"We need to know where these London guys hang out," said Jacko.

"You don't think Benny knows?"

"No." Jacko smiled ruefully. "They're playing safe all the way down the line."

Bulman sat drinking a mug of coffee. "If we can't find them we'll have to bring them to us."

"And get back to square one with them on our tails? Nah. There has to be another way."

Bulman suddenly made up his mind. "I must find out

117

if there are any telephone messages on my answering machine."

"You can't go there."

Bulman was already dialling a number. "Knocker? This is George. George Bulman. Can you do me a favour?"

"I don't owe you one. You put me away, you bastard."

"That was years ago. I did you a favour by keeping you out of trouble. I want you to break into my flat."

"You trying to set me up?"

"Don't be daft. I want the tape on my answering machine. I can't get it myself, the place is under seige."

"So how would I get by?"

"They're looking for me, Knocker. They wouldn't know which flat you were going to if you got in. Just the tape. Help yourself to a drink while you're there." Knocker would do that anyway, reflected Bulman, and would help himself to videos.

"Where are the keys?"

"Since when have you used keys? But don't smash the bloody door down."

"I want paying for this. It might be a set up."

"I wouldn't set you or anybody up and paying is no problem. When you have the tape drop it in at the Hot Pot where I'll arrange for you to be paid off. Is that OK?"

"When do you want it?"

"Now. Keep your eyes skinned just in case."

"I'll deal with it."

Bulman hung up and turned to Jacko. "Can you ring the manager of the Hot Pot and ask him to pay Knocker, and tell him we'll square up later?"

"Sure, but I don't think the Hot Pot is a good choice; they'll probably know I go there anyway. We'll have to watch it. And so will Knocker."

Bulman shook his head. "He's getting on a bit now, but I don't envy anyone getting on the wrong side of Knocker, no matter how big they are. It's my main worry."

When Jacko had made arrangements to pay off Knocker

at the Hot Pot, Bulman rang Freda Curtis using the name she knew him by, George Russell. He thought she might well have left as it was now six o'clock, but she came through and said bitterly, "You've got a nerve. What lies have you got for me this time?"

"I thought he would probably do a check. I'm sorry. I really am."

"That's supposed to reassure me? I've lost my job. They'd have me out of the building tonight if it weren't for the fact that there are certain jobs only I can clear up."

Aware that Jacko was listening with some interest, Bulman said uneasily, "Be fair, Freda, you were on your way to losing your job before Parre saw me. The knives were out. I want a chance to explain. Can we have dinner somewhere?"

There was a cross between a cry of anguish and one of despair before she said, "Are you serious? Why on earth would I want to do that?"

"For the same reason that you answered this call. You are curious, with good cause. If I'm not BOT then who the hell am I? I am not from a rival conglomerate. I think we have a mutual interest here. We might be able to help one another."

"Mr Russell, oh I suppose that's not your real name — "

"No, but George is," he cut in.

"I'm certainly not going to call you that. Parre is trying to trace you. If I'm seen with you I'll find myself on criminal charges as well as being dismissed. It will kill off any claims I might make for wrongful dismissal."

"If we don't meet you'll be left wondering what it's all about, and I think you deserve to know. You pick the place and I'll be there. About eight-thirty?"

When Bulman put down the receiver, Jacko said, "We're opening ourselves up too much. They'll be on to us."

"They don't know we're here. As long as we're careful we should be all right."

Jacko shook his head. "You're thinking like a copper

119

instead of a villain. This woman Freda Curtis; if she was Walsh's PA I should have thought that she was one for them to watch. Unless she did it herself."

The remark had been semi-flippant but they stared at each other uneasily as the possibility caught on. "She's not the type," said Bulman.

"I never thought I'd hear an experienced copper say something like that. Does she appeal to you? She might have organized it? From where she is sitting, she might have had good cause to have him topped. She might not have been on his roster and that could have been something she wanted most."

"Shut up," snapped Bulman. "You don't know what you're talking about."

Jacko stared in surprise. He said no more, aware that he had touched a nerve and that Bulman was worried. Jacko picked up the phone again and rang the Hot Pot number. "Give me Charlie." And when Charlie came on he said, "It's Jacko here again. That package we talked about. Can you have it delivered to the video shop on the corner? Ask for Jed and tell him I'll collect it. I'll square it all up, no problem. Oh, and I'll have to keep ringing you to see if you've received it. You're better off without this number. Thanks, Charlie."

Jacko hung up and saw that Bulman was spread in an easy chair and was totally preoccupied. Jacko realized that he had upset him about Freda Curtis but it was no time to relax vigilance. He said, "I'm still uneasy about you meeting this woman."

More reasonably, Bulman replied, "If they are tailing her I'll have to be extra careful when I leave her." He glanced over at Jacko knowing him to be worried. "I can be when I want to be. Trust me."

"And if she's involved in some way?"

"Then it's vital that I do meet her. We can't run away from everything if we want a result." And then he continued, "You'd be happier if you were doing the

120

evasive tactics, wouldn't you? I can understand that, Jacko. But you couldn't handle this meeting, believe me it's my scene not yours."

Jacko roamed over to the window. "I know. We each have our part. It's just that I'm beginning to pick up nasty vibes. We're not as secure as we were and I can't put my finger on it."

Jacko rang the Hot Pot but nothing had arrived yet, which began to worry them because all Knocker had to do was to get in and take the tape and then deliver it.

They switched on the Sky News and learned that a man's body had been found on the hard shoulder of the M40 beyond Oxford. He had obviously been thrown out of a moving car, judging by the reported multiple injuries. A photograph of Bert Cooper was flashed on the screen but the police had already identified him as a missing hotel concierge. The actual cause of death was yet to be determined. Bert Cooper had not run far enough.

Jacko crossed to the trolley and poured two stiff whiskies, handing one to Bulman. The death had shaken them both, mainly because of the apparent need for it. Somewhere, someone, knew what it was that Walsh had to hide, to justify three killings so far. And where did that leave Connie Smith? She must be scared out of her wits if she had caught up with what had just happened to Bert Cooper.

Chapter Eleven

Bulman was so caught up in the need for his tape and the death of Bert Cooper that he suddenely realized that he had left little time to meet Freda Curtis. He was reluctant to go without knowing the tape was safe, but had no means of contacting Freda as by now he assumed her offices would be closed. He checked the directory but after a couple of calls realized it would be hopeless; there were too many entries and, being PA to a man as prominent as Walsh had been, guessed she would be ex-directory to keep reporters off her back.

Bulman waited at the door, ready to leave, as Jacko made one more call. Jacko put his hand over the phone. "It's there," he said in relief. He listened for a while and from his expression Bulman could see that it was not all good news. Jacko put down the phone, his face grim. "Knocker delivered the tape all right. When he arrived at your place the door was ajar, which meant someone was there or had been there. He decided to go in. He found someone going through your desk and dealt with him." Jacko held up his hands. "Don't ask. That's all Charlie has. Whether he killed him or knocked him cold I don't know. When he had dealt with the bloke, Knocker went to the answering machine and found there was no tape. He found it in the pocket of the guy he saw, so naturally he took it. We have the tape, but you'll have to ask Knocker if the other guy is still in your flat or not."

"Jesus." Bulman checked the time. "I've got to fly.

122

Knocker will have to wait until I'm back. He won't speak to you unless you know him."

"Only by reputation. Ring him when you get back. I'll nip over to the video shop and pick up the tape. That was a lucky break."

Bulman did not answer, he was already on his way, not at all sure that it was lucky.

It was a small Italian restaurant with empty bottles of Chianti and bunches of plastic grapes hanging around the place. It was clean and neat and friendly. Freda Curtis was already seated at a table for two and it was clear as Bulman went in that she was well known there.

"I hope I'm not too late," he said, as he slipped on to the chair opposite her.

"No more than I would expect from a civil servant."

"Ouch! You look splendid." She had obviously changed for him, and the pastel-coloured two piece softened her office image. He found he wanted to explain why he himself had not changed and that, at the moment, he was confined to one suit as he dare not go home because there were men with guns waiting for him. He felt shabby in her presence, which perhaps had nothing to do with how he was dressed.

"So what is your real name?" she asked, as she picked up the menu.

"George Bulman. I was once a Detective Superintendent at New Scotland Yard. I am no longer a policeman but am one of the good guys."

"You could have fooled me, and for a short time you certainly fooled John Parre."

They smiled at the recollection.

"So what's it all about, Mr Bulman? I'm here because I want to find out why you obtained a company file under false pretences and lied to me."

"Was I convincing?"

"Oh, yes. The police obviously taught you to lie well.

123

I'm not here to listen to more lies or I'll go to the police myself."

"I'm investigating aspects of Ronald Walsh's murder."

"But the police are doing that and have already been in touch with us. Be careful, Mr Bulman."

"I have an independent brief from a Government source, to look at aspects beyond the actual murder. If the police found the murderer tomorrow I would still have a role to play. There is a political slant to this. Face saving if you like. I think there are deeper issues to this than a jealous woman squeezing the trigger. I think that's what it's been made to look like, and he certainly provided enough reason for that to be believed."

"You don't think the police are able to find that out for themselves?"

"Oh, yes. I also think they'd be happy with a culprit, and that there might be a tacit agreement with the powers that be that such a result would satisfy everyone publicly. I cannot say that they have received an instruction, they would not take kindly to that, but there might well be an understanding to mutual advantage."

"So why are you needed?"

"To find the truth which actually might not be connected with the murder. There are deep, muddy waters here and it would seem the fewer who knows about them the better. I'm taking an awful risk telling you this."

"Why? Do you think I shot him?"

"You might have had good cause."

"I wasn't on his duty roster of loose women, if that's what you're suggesting."

Bulman tried to probe her guarded expression. He was taking a chance over this meeting so he took another. "From a police standpoint you might have wanted to be." He must have struck the right tone because she appeared not to be offended.

"A frustrated PA, you mean? Yes, I had an attachment to him. But it was purely professional. He paid me very well, and he always protected me against people like John Parre who really hated him because he ran rings round them. He never, at any time, tried to draw me into his sexual orbit. Our relationship simply would not have worked had he tried to. It was an understanding that worked well for us."

"And, of course, he trusted you implicitly?"

"I was probably the only one he did trust. There's always back stabbing on company boards and he knew his enemies."

"Were his enemies strong enough to kill him?"

They broke off while they ordered, and Bulman left the wine choice to Freda, really preferring a scotch.

When the waiter had gone Freda answered his question. "From what the newspapers say, the murder was committed by a woman during an assignation. Are you suggesting that might have been a cover for one of his commercial enemies?"

"It's possible. But at this stage I suppose anything is." He raised his glass in a silent toast. "As much as I would like to pin it on someone like John Parre, I don't think he, or his colleagues did it. There are reasons for saying this." He frowned as he added, "You say he trusted you, but he didn't open up on that trip to Russia did he?"

"Trusting does not necessarily mean to confide in everything."

"All right. But did he normally talk about his trips in detail?"

"Yes." Freda inclined her head. "Almost always."

"But not this particular time. So something unusual happened which he did not want to discuss, and he was morose as a result of what may have happened whilst in Russia. Is that a fair appraisal?"

"Not bad for a Board of Trade reject. Yes, that's fair."

"You didn't probe a little bit? You were not that curious at this unusual reaction?"

She smiled. "You are talking about him but you are really scrutinizing me. Of course I probed, but I knew when to stop. I learned nothing important, but his attitude suggested that there was a woman involved."

"Ronnie Walsh upset about a woman. That must have been a first."

"Don't poke fun at him. It was serious enough to keep a smile from his face for a very long time. In fact, I don't think he ever recovered, not fully anyway. Something was taken from him during that trip."

Bulman pulled the slip of paper from his pocket with the names Jacko had obtained from Benny Walker. "Penkov and Zotin. Do those names mean anything to you?"

Freda considered them for a while. "Penkov has a familiar ring to it. Zotin, I don't think I've heard of. Why?"

"They are two names a colleague of mine picked up. I think they are thugs; or if you like, hit men Russian style. When did you hear of Penkov?"

"I think it was just a call that came through some weeks ago. I remember only because the name is so unusual in this country."

"And did he speak to him?"

"I'm sure that he did. I think it was a very short call."

"I didn't notice the name amongst those he met which are mentioned in the file. But I wasn't allowed a good look. Can you help me?"

"You mean finish the job for you?"

"Well I don't think I'd be let in again."

"What would I be looking for? It is rather a large file."

"Anything out of the ordinary. What sort of business does the Russian company he visited do? Who he spent most time with. Anything at variance with normal practice."

"Every trip was different. Every country has its own way of entertaining. Variety is already there without suspicion. But I can say, without looking at the file, that the company he saw deals in arms and they have quite a large chemical division." Freda shot a warning glance across the table. "The arms side is quite legitimate. The Russians are probably the biggest European market in arms these days. They have a lot to sell."

"Did a resulting arms deal go through?"

"I don't know. If I knew all the company deals I would have been chairman."

"Chairperson," Bulman reprimanded.

"Rubbish. I don't want to be dehumanized."

"Will you do it for me?"

"You are asking me to trust a man who lied his way into our offices and lied his way out again. There is no trust to go on. Can you give me an address to go with the latest name you have given me?"

Bulman hesitated then decided to keep to the truth. "I can give you my address which you can check upon, but I am not staying there mainly because these two guys, Penkov and Zotin, and possibly others, are hanging out on my doorstep with violence in mind. I cannot tell you where I'm staying now without breaking a confidence and putting someone else at risk."

"But you don't mind me taking risks on your behalf? That's not quite fair is it?"

Bulman gave a nod to the waiter. "It certainly doesn't sound fair but there are risks and *risks*. You already know what your immediate fate with the business will be. For my part, I know of two other deaths tied in with the Walsh murder which haven't officially been connected. Three murders, Freda, not one. That doesn't sound like a *crime passionnel* does it?"

"But if I helped you wouldn't that put violent men on my doorstep too?"

Bulman could not answer. He avoided her gaze for the first time that evening and inadvertently gave her the answer.

"How would I contact you?"

"I'd have to contact you. If you'd give me your home number I could ring you there. I'm assuming you wouldn't want me to ring the office too often."

127

"I don't know how much longer I've got there. Once they know I've dealt with his affairs they'll make me clear my desk at once." Freda suddenly pushed her chair back. She ran long fingers through her hair and stared at him in despair. "I must be mad even to consider this. You could still be lying; how would I know?"

He tore a sheet from his notebook and scribbled on it. "You can ring him any time if you want a reference for me. You'll have to take pot luck on him being in but you can always leave a message." He read out the name he had written down, "Detective Chief Superintendent Walter Beatty. You might even have heard of him, he was involved in the common murders. He's an old mate of mine. He'll tell you all about me."

Freda held the slip of paper, her hand shaking. "I've already met him. But I'll still ring him. If I'm satisfied, I'll leave my ex-directory number with him and you can call him for it. That's the best I can do."

"I'm most grateful." But Bulman was far from happy; he had not wanted Wally Beatty to be contacted in this way, if only to avoid showing him the direction of enquiries Bulman himself was taking. Somehow it took something from the evening, and he could now see that Freda had an underlying fear that she had not brought with her.

Coffee arrived and they were quiet for a while, then Freda said, "Did you see any photographs in the file?"

"No. I'd hardly started to go through it when Parre arrived."

"They are probably clipped at the back. He had one group photo blown up and framed, and it's in the visitors waiting room along with others taken over the years. There were some social snaps, taken at some of the parties he attended. Would they be useful?"

"Anything would be useful, and it's always handy to be able to put faces to names. Can you get them?"

"If not the actual, I can get copies taken without too much trouble. I still need to clear you first, though."

"Of course. I'd be happier if you did. If you are still not happy after speaking to Beatty, you might try the United States Ambassador but I hope you don't have to go that far. Have you mentioned these snaps to Beatty?"

"I saw no need. Whether the other directors did is another matter. Is the American Ambassador a friend of yours?"

"I did a job for him. We became quite friendly." Realizing what she had probably let herself in for made her clearly nervous, and he hoped she would not change her mind. He was afraid to push further and he could feel that something had come between them since their meeting. It was a barrier of uncertainty which he was sure she could feel too, and he just prayed that she would go ahead and not be frightened off.

He wanted to warn her to watch her back on the way home, but that would definitely unsettle her and she might back out. He justified his silence by convincing himself that, because of the position she held, she must have been under some sort of scrutiny from day one. It was important that everything appeared near normal. The self-conviction was shaky, but he held on to it until they said goodbye outside the restaurant with a loose agreement that they would do it again. But for him, the evening was marred by his own priorities; he should have put her welfare first. As he hailed a taxi for her, he was left with a feeling of *déjà vu*.

He took all the precautions going back to Jacko's house that he should have told Freda to take. He consoled himself with the probability that she would not have known how to take evasive action anyway, and had she tried it would have been a giveaway. He was not good at it himself, but gave full concentration to doing the job until he was satisfied that he barely knew where he was going himself.

Jacko was already home by the time he returned, and was anxious and impatient. They both felt a vice tightening on them and put it down to Bert Cooper's death.

"Did you get the tape?" asked Bulman, as he took his coat off.

"Of course I got the bloody tape. I've played it back and there's a message from a bird called Anna Brenning who wants to see you, and one from a Lorna Russell who thinks she's left a message for Chief Inspector Allen. How is it that an overweight, lying, middle-aged layabout like you attracts this interest from women?"

Bulman took the proffered drink before sitting down. He checked the time on the mantlepiece clock; half eleven, too late for calling people yet he knew he must contact Lorna Russell as soon as possible. "Did Lorna leave a number?"

"I jotted it down. She important?"

"She's Connie Smith's neighbour. I'll listen to the tape after I've rung her. And I must ring Knocker to find out what happened."

"You'd better. Charlie at the Hot Pot said he'd never seen Knocker looking so rough; he looked as if he'd been done over, and from what I've heard of Knocker that's one for the Guinness Book of Records."

Lorna was still up and Bulman apologized for ringing so late. Lorna was clearly agitated and stumbled over her words until Bulman calmed her down and finally extracted from her what had happened. "Connie rang. She seemed in a dreadful state, her voice all quivering. God, she seemed scared out of her wits. She wanted to know if anyone had called on her and I brought her up to date. I told her I have your home number, but she asked me to contact you first and to give you her number only if I'm satisfied you intend to help her. She desperately needs to see someone before she does something silly."

"Give me her number."

Lorna called out a Somerset number and Bulman jotted it down and then read it back.

When the check was done Bulman said, "Destroy that number, Lorna. Burn it, flush it down the toilet, but get rid of it and don't ever admit to having had it."

130

"You're scaring me. Are you sure this is about animal activists?"

"Some of them are head cases. They can be very violent. Don't worry, Lorna, you've done the right thing by Connie. I'll look after her. Thank you very much."

"Why did you demote yourself to a Chief Inspector?" asked Jacko as Bulman put the phone down.

"Because I pulled a shabby trick." Bulman picked up the phone again and dialled the Somerset number. There was no answer. He tried again in case he had dialled the number incorrectly, but got the same result. "I'll try again in the morning. She could be out or asleep. We'll have to go down there."

He rang Knocker and held the phone away from his ear while he listened to the mass of abuse directed at him. Eventually Knocker said, "But you should have seen the other guy."

"What did you do with him?"

"I put him over my shoulder and took him downstairs and dumped him in the hall by that old fireplace right at the back."

"You left him in the hall?"

"Did you think I was going to call an ambulance? He tried to kill me. And he weighed a ton. I could have left him in your place."

"OK, OK. Was he dead?"

"I dunno. He should have been after what he tried to do to me. I need extra; you didn't mention danger."

"We'll see that you get it. I don't suppose you looked for an identity."

"Sure I did. I turned out his pockets. All he had was an automatic with a silencer attached, and some loose ammunition. I've already flogged those."

Bulman stifled a groan. "Well, thanks for getting the tape, Knocker. I appreciate it. I'll see that you get the extra in spite of what you made on the gun."

Bulman hung up and gazed at Jacko. "I'll have to leave

131

Anna Brenning till tomorrow. I suppose I'd better listen to the tape before turning in."

Jacko slipped the small tape into his own machine and played it back. It told them little more than what Jacko had already told Bulman.

"Is this Anna Brenning in the clear?" Jacko asked.

"Nobody's in the clear. I need to know more about her."

"It seems she thinks that about you too. Be careful, mate."

Bulman nodded. "Let's get some sleep and then try to reach Connie Smith in the morning."

Jacko drove. Bulman rang Anna Brenning on the car phone. She was particularly friendly and wondered if he would like to drop in for tea or even go out to dinner. He said he would on both counts but not today and could he ring her later. She seemed to be very disappointed and then she said, "I would like to maintain contact. You are different from the rest, about the only one who has not tried to make a pass. And I wondered how you are getting on with your enquiries."

"Not very well. Why? Have you thought of something that might help?"

"No. But the police have been round again, badgering me about his friends. It seems to be difficult for them to understand that he kept me away from his friends. Anyway, I'll tell you about it when I see you."

Bulman could see Jacko grinning widely, his gaze on the road. Jacko was shaking his head. "I just can't see what they see in you."

"They feel sorry for me. They want to mother me."

Jacko burst out laughing. "That's a new name for it."

"Or they just might want to kill me."

That brought it down to earth. "Is there something you're not telling me?" Jacko asked.

"No." Bulman hunched himself up in the passenger seat. He felt drowsy and found the car too hot. "It's just that

Anna Brenning sends out a different vibe every time I speak to her. She's a hot number or Walsh wouldn't have set her up; I mean she's still living in the flat he put her in. And her story is plausible and her alibi unbreakable; she simply wasn't in the country when he was killed."

"But?" Jacko turned his head for a fraction of time.

"I'd like to know more about the people she knows over here. They may not be his friends, but the chances are she had friends she didn't tell him about. I reckon it worked both ways."

"You're guessing, of course."

"Absolutely. But the more I think about it the more I believe she is too intelligent to be nothing more than a high class whore." He turned to Jacko to see how he would take his next remark. "I think it might be interesting if we broke into Anna's place."

Jacko gave no reaction. "That might be a very dodgy thing to do if she's as smart as you suggest."

"Not if I take her up on dinner."

Now Jacko reacted. "If you think I'll do the job and take all the risks while you're performing foreplay over a dinner table, forget it. But Benny Walker has some creepers on his list."

Jacko drove in silence after that, watching out for signs to Taunton. Bulman had, in the end, decided not to ring Connie. After a night thinking about it, he was now more inclined to believe that Lorna Russell herself had made the decision to pass on Connie's phone number. The more he thought about it the more convinced he became that Connie would not want to see anyone from the police. From the other end of a line Chief Inspector Allen might not sound too good to someone on the run from her enemies and the police. After discussing it with Jacko over breakfast, Bulman had decided that Lorna had panicked on behalf of Connie and had done what she considered to be the right thing, but without Connie's knowledge.

133

Nevertheless, Connie must have given her the number for whatever reason.

Bulman had obtained the address from a man he had helped who worked in Telecom. He could have obtained it by ringing Wally Beatty at Scotland Yard, but that would have put the pack at his heels.

Once Jacko was on the open road he did not want to stop, no matter how long the journey, and he just kept driving. The nearer they got to Taunton the less they talked, and their silence was driven by the same possibility. Bulman could not forget the last time he had set out to find Connie only to find a corpse, probably Connie's sister. By the time they reached Taunton both men were uneasy. They passed through the West Country town and headed towards Bishops Lydeard about five miles beyond.

Once in Bishops Lydeard, Jacko had to stop to make a couple of enquiries; the address they wanted was another mile out of town, and as it turned out, an old farm cottage with a 'for rent' board at the head of the winding track that led to the front door. Jacko pulled up beyond the open gate and turned to Bulman.

"This is history repeating itself," said Bulman morosely. "If she's there and she sees us coming down the drive the chances are she'll scarper. You circle round the back and I'll make the direct approach. I'll give you ten minutes before I start walking." They synchronized watches and Jacko climbed out, not sure how far he had to go. Bulman sat back and waited.

It was a lonely area, miserable and damp with a distant mist towards the Quantock hills. If Connie had sought isolation then she had found it, but in her profession she must have led a much more gregarious life and, if not used to it, loneliness can be a powerful enemy, a strain on the nerves and Connie would have too much time to think. She had probably given Lorna her phone number out of desperation and had probably phoned in the first place just to hear a voice she knew. Just sitting, waiting for ten minutes to pass was bad enough; silence could get to you, too much of it could eat away at stability and unnerve.

Bulman roused himself precisely on the tenth minute and climbed out, not quite closing the door so as not to break the growing silence which now bordered on the eerie. The drive was really car tracks with a rough grass centre piece. Burn marks of dirty exhausts were visible on the grass tufts at the entrance. He kept to the right hand track because the drive arched that way. Hedges lined each side making visibility poor. He trod as carefully as he could.

He suddenly came in sight of the cottage and it appeared as run down as the approaches. There was no sign of life, no smoke from the chimney yet it was cold enough for a fire. In a place so outwardly dilapidated central heating did not readily spring to mind. At the end of the drive there was open ground for about thirty yards to the cottage entrance. There was nothing Bulman could do but head straight for it and hope for the best, praying that he did not find another body.

He was half-way across when he saw the flash as a gun roared from the cottage and he fell.

Chapter Twelve

Bulman's knees hit the hard earth before he lay prone. He had nowhere to hide and the best he could do was to stay still until he knew what was happening. He peered up and could see no movement. There was no sign of Connie Smith or Jacko. He began to rise slowly, knowing he was fully exposed to anyone in the cottage. When he was shakily on his feet he lurched away at right angles to the cottage, in a self-protective effort to make further shots more difficult. With the idea of coming round on a curve so that he could approach the entrance sideways, he broke into a run. Where the hell was Jacko?

The gun roared again and Bulman dived, hearing glass shatter as he hit the ground. Then there was a piercing scream which continued until it faded to a gurgle, before the next scream rang out. Bulman clambered to his feet and ran straight for the cottage door. He crunched over broken glass and swung into the entrance to see a woman fighting furiously with a man who was trying to wrestle a pump action shotgun away from her. Jacko had his hands full.

Instead of helping Jacko subdue the squirming figure he tried to talk to her, to calm her down to convince her that she had nothing to worry about.

Jacko bawled out, "Cut that crap and hold her! She's killing me, for chrissake!"

Bulman saw the nail marks down Jacko's face, and helped to immobilize Connie who continued to scream and bite any part of them that came within reach. Jacko managed to stuff a handkerchief in her mouth as they pinned her to the chair, while Bulman bawled, "We're here to help you. We're the good guys."

It was still some time after that, that Connie Smith, exhausted and scared out of her wits, calmed down enough for Bulman's persistent words to get through to her.

"Lorna gave us your number. She's worried about you."

"Well, she shouldn't have." Fear was still strong in the voice, eyes wild and unbelieving.

"Then you shouldn't have given the number to her. Calm down and get some sense into you." Jacko, with wounds to justify his attitude, was less patient than Bulman. When she started to struggle again he added, "If I was a baddie I'd have thumped the life out of you by now. And I will if you don't calm down. Are you on drugs or something?"

The suggestion did more to settle her than anything else, for she felt affronted then – it was the one area of self-debasement she had so far avoided.

"I could murder a coffee," said Bulman and struck another right note. "It's been a long journey."

"They killed my sister," Connie blurted out. "They thought she was me."

"We know," said Bulman. "Now if we let you go, will you make that coffee for us?"

Connie was crying now but managed a nod and they gradually released her. They helped her to her feet and followed her to a kitchen which was overpowered by a Welsh dresser. Jacko found mugs while Connie wiped her tears away, although still sobbing, and filled the kettle. In old jeans and sweater and with little make-up, there was little of the call girl about her now. They said no more until they were back in the living room and Jacko had checked the shotgun.

Connie was still in a highly nervous state as she sat near the door as if ready to bolt. She could hardly meet their gaze and was clearly far from convinced that they meant her no harm.

Bulman reflected that she must have actually seen the murder of her sister whilst hiding, and was carrying both the shock of witnessing a brutal killing and the guilt of doing nothing to try to save her sister. He said as gently as he could, "There was nothing you could have done to save her. I saw her. If you were hiding you were very wise not to show yourself, or both of you would now be dead."

"I could have tried. I shall always live with what I saw."

"Don't take the blame for someone else's brutality. You couldn't have tried."

"Just who are you? What do you want?" Connie was beginning to think.

"We're not the police and we're not the people who are trying to harm you. We represent the family of Ronald Walsh, the MP who was murdered by whoever took your place." Bulman watched closely to see how she was taking this, but it was difficult to judge when she was still sitting on an emotional knife edge. He did not want to drive her back in her shell. He added, "I'm afraid I had to lie to your friend Lorna in order to get some sense from her. She thinks I'm a policeman, so if she ever mentions Chief Inspector Allen she'll be talking about me. My name is George Bulman and this is Jacko, short for Jackson."

Jacko was quite content to let Bulman do the talking; it was much more in his line. He tried to give a reassuring grin and raised his mug of coffee in a silent toast.

"Why are you running?" Bulman asked.

"I should have thought that was obvious." Connie wiped her eyes with the flat of her hand.

"I mean in the first place, before they killed your sister. What made you do a runner?"

"When the police started asking questions I got scared. I was lying to them and I could see it getting worse. And then I thought that if the other lot knew the police were questioning me, they might get twitchy. They had already done one murder so another would be nothing new to them." Connie stared Bulman straight in the eye for the first time. "I didn't know they were going to top the sod. They said they wanted to play a joke, get one back over him for something he'd done."

"How much did they pay you to go sick?"

"Three grand." Connie dropped her gaze nervously.

"Three grand? To play a joke on him? You believed that?"

"I was suspicious but I wanted to believe, and I needed the money."

"Did you know they nobbled the concierge at the hotel in the same way?"

"No. I didn't think that far."

Bulman decided not to tell her that Bert Cooper was dead. If she read about it she might not connect the two. Right now she was unstable and the wrong approach might stop her present co-operation. "Was it a woman who approached you?"

"No. From what I've read another woman took my place, but I had no idea that was going to happen. Apart from them saying they were going to play a joke I didn't know what they were up to. It seemed like easy money."

"You keep saying 'they', how many were there?"

"Two. Two men. They were big and were foreigners. One didn't speak at all and the other spoke quite well but with a terrible accent. He was quite pleasant."

"How do you think they knew where to look for you when you did a runner?"

"I don't know. They must have been watching me."

"So they knew you but killed the wrong girl?"

Jacko shot Bulman a warning glance but Bulman ignored it; he had to know.

"The men who killed my sister weren't the ones who approached me in the first place."

"Were they foreign too?"

"Two sounded like Germans; I think the other one was Russian. I don't want to talk about that any more."

139

"I understand and I'm sorry I pressed you. So how did you escape?"

"Because they thought they'd killed me. I waited until after they'd gone then hit the road and thumbed a lift. It didn't matter where. I had my purse with me so had enough money for a few days. When I reached here, after about three separate lifts, I scouted around and found this dump advertised in a local estate agency. I paid a week up front."

Bulman slowly finished his coffee. "You can't stay here. You'll get talked about in the town, a strange girl alone in a place like this. People will speculate and this is a case where it matters what they say."

"I've run out of money anyway. What can I do? I'm afraid to go to my bank; these people seem to have help everywhere."

"We can sub you for a bit. But you're best hidden in a crowd. You should really get police protection."

"No. Don't turn me over to the police. I'm guilty before the act or whatever they call it. They won't believe what I've just told you."

"Yes they will, and we can back you up. Otherwise you'll be on the run for the rest of your life and we can only help you for so long. Think, Connie. Once these blokes are collared you'll be safe."

"These blokes will never be collared because they'll get rid of anything in their way – including the police."

Jacko at last spoke, "Do you know who these geezers are? We seem to have Russians and now we have Germans. It's a funny mixture."

Connie raised her arms in a gesture of hopelessness. "I'm sorry I ever agreed to ducking the trick. I don't think I deserve to be punished by the law as well."

Feeling stuffy in the cottage, Bulman went to the front door and opened it to gaze out across the countryside. He agreed with what she said, but she couldn't continue to run away from the situation. "How did you get the gun?"

140

"It was hidden under some old sacks in a shed out the back. There was a pile of potatoes on top. The ammunition was rolled up in canvas bag. The estate agent told me the owner had died and the surviving son wanted to let it out as it was. It was obvious that nobody knew the gun was there."

Bulman turned his back on the door and gazed at Jacko. "What do you think? We can't leave her here, even if she could afford it."

"We'll have to take her back with us."

Bulman's policeman instincts warned him not to take on a material witness to a murder. He believed what she had told him, terror had forced out the truth, but the police needed to know as well. And Bulman agreed with Connie in that unless the police actually locked her up, no protection would be safe from what was beginning to look like an international organization of some strength. And yet if he suggested the police again he thought the girl might try to ditch them.

Before Bulman could reply, Jacko was on his feet staring over Bulman's shoulder to a point beyond the door and the Colt was suddenly in his hand. Connie shot up from her chair and in a no nonsense voice Jacko snapped, "Get down behind that chair, there's someone out there."

Bulman immediately stepped away from the door, closed it with his foot and grabbed the shotgun Jacko had propped up in a corner. He wasn't sure whether or not Jacko had emptied it, but it was something to hold on to.

Jacko dropped to his knees and crawled towards the back of the cottage. Bulman, meanwhile, got down and crept to the nearest window and cautiously raised his head. He could see nothing.

Connie crouched behind a dilapidated armchair, her arms round her knees and she just shivered from fright. Just when she was beginning to believe she had protection it suddenly looked very thin indeed. She was shaking with fear and near to tears again.

Bulman remained still, offering Connie the odd false

141

reassurance while he peered out hoping to see something tangible, and wondering what Jacko was up to. Jacko seemed to have disappeared altogether and there was no sound or sign of movement. A draught of air whistled in, as if the back door had been opened, but there was still no sound and the silence built up menacingly. He accepted that this was a situation which Jacko would have to control but it made him feel helpless. He called out softly, "Did you hear a car anywhere near, Connie?"

"No. Nothing. Oh God what's going to happen?"

Bulman reflected that she was probably recalling what had happened to her sister and the thought did nothing to reassure him. He opened the gun to make sure it was not loaded, and then wondered where Jacko had put the ammunition.

"Where's the ammunition for the gun, Connie?"

"I only put two cartridges in. The rest are in the shed." Her voice was still trembling and she was fast reaching a point of terror where it no longer mattered what happened.

Bulman clung to the gun because it was all he had. And then he thought he saw movement in the long grass the other side of the drive. He said nothing to Connie but kept his head down and continued to watch. The movement stopped but he was sure that he had seen something.

Time passed, and it would have been more reassuring if Jacko had put in an appearance, but the ex-soldier had gone to earth and was probably doing what he did best. Half an hour passed, during which time Bulman and Connie had hardly passed a word, and Bulman thought he could hear her quietly sobbing. If they got out of this situation he realized that there was no option but to take Connie with them.

He thought he heard a shot and Connie reacted too, for she was now moaning behind the chair, and he wished he could see her but there was little chance that she would move without help. The longer he waited the less sure he

142

was that it had been a shot and if it had, then it had been some distance away.

He wanted to do something, but there was nothing in this particular game he could do that Jacko could not do infinitely better. He must keep his nerve and wait. But the thought kept recurring: what odds were against Jacko out there? There was a limit to what he could take on, and as the time passed so slowly, he began to wonder if Jacko would come back at all.

He pulled his head back from the window, put down the empty gun, and crept across the floor to Connie. She was shivering behind the chair, afraid to, and unable to move. He put an arm round her and she clung to him as if he was a lifeline, and in a way he was. Her nails dug into his neck as one arm encircled him and he held her tight as she cried into his shoulder. He uttered useless words of comfort but the girl in his grasp had seen how her own sister had been murdered, and there was a limit to what she could take.

She did steady down after a while. She became calmer but stayed in his rough grasp and then wiped her face and her bloodshot eyes. After a while she faltered. "Now you've seen just how tough a whore is." It was self-disgust and defilement.

"Cut it out," he said. "When we get you out of here you can start again."

"Only if those bastards who are after me have been killed. That's all that will stop them. I've never been as big a fool as this and look where it's got me."

"You're not alone, Connie. Jacko is out there now trying to sort it. Give a thought or two to him."

"I'm sorry."

"I must get back to the window. Do you want to come with me? You don't have to put your head up."

"OK. I don't want to be alone."

They crept to the window Bulman had vacated, and he lifted his head again and immediately knew something was different without knowing what. Everything looked just the same. He did not understand it and decided it was a sensation rather than something he should see. He looked again. Nothing had changed that he could see, but now he really was worried about Jacko, the only consolation being that nobody had come for him and Connie, which suggested that Jacko was still out there somewhere. And then the back door opened and closed.

Jacko's voice bellowed out, "Someone was out there all right. At least two. There are marks all over the place. They must be good for I couldn't find them. I think they must be waiting for us somewhere."

Jacko saw Connie's reaction and added, "Don't worry, love. We can handle it. I've checked right round the house; they've laid nothing against the walls." He put his hand in his pocket and pulled out a handful of shotgun shells. "Found these in a shed outside." He crossed the room, picked up the shotgun and loaded it. "That might be useful." He then crossed to the telephone and lifted it to his ear. "I'm getting careless. They've cut the wire. Not by the house, I would have noticed."

"So what do we do now?"

"We get the hell out of here. Let's go for the car."

There was nothing to collect but the shotgun. Connie, like Bulman, had nothing but what she stood up in. Jacko held the Colt ready and Bulman had the shotgun as they trod warily up the rough drive with Connie between them. Jacko kept turning as if he was part of a patrol. They reached the car, crouched behind it while Jacko did a scan over the countryside until he said, "OK, get in. Connie, you flatten yourself on the rear seat."

They climbed in. Connie spread herself on the back seat and Jacko and Bulman sat as if waiting for something to happen. Jacko put the key in the ignition but still sat there, and when Bulman turned, with the shotgun held between his legs, he saw that Jacko was disturbed.

"What's the matter?" Bulman asked.

Jacko did not reply; he simply sat there with his fingers on

144

the ignition key ready to turn it, when he suddenly bawled out, "Get out now and get behind the hedge!" He rolled off his seat on to the track and stayed prone while the others, more slowly, crouched and ran to the hedge bordering the front boundary.

When they were out of sight Jacko rolled to peer under the car. He lay cursing and sweating at what he saw. He had come within a hairbreadth of blowing them all to smithereens. He knew he should have known far better, having lived with the deadly problem. He had made sure of the house and its environs because he believed that was where the danger lay. Overlooking the car was an elementary lapse which he simply could not understand. It was inexcusable and he wondered just how much more he had lost with time; he of all people.

He rolled away and considered what best to do. The bomb had been crudely fixed and without a jack it was difficult to get a better view to determine whether it was a timed device or fixed to detonate by the ignition. If training had momentarily deserted him, his last second instinct had not and for that he was grateful. He stood up and released the bonnet catch and gingerly lifted the bonnet. He could see the wiring coming up from below to the ignition.

He very carefully detached the wiring from the ignition and ran it outside the bonnet before closing it down. He took the end towards the hedge but there was insufficient to pass it through. He went round the hedge to where the others were crouching.

"They've wired the car," he said bluntly. "The detonator is under the car and without a jack I can't get at it."

"Then how was it put there?" Bulman asked scathingly, his arm round Connie to try to steady her.

"Because they must have had a bloody jack," said Jacko irritably. "I should have checked the car first. I miscalculated their intent. Anyway I don't want to move the bloody detonator. We've got to take a chance. In spite of my cock-up you've got to trust me. I think you should

145

get back to the cottage until I'm ready; there's some stuff I need to get there."

They ran back down the drive and Jacko said, "You may as well make yourselves comfortable. While they're waiting for us to blow ourselves up I don't think they'll risk coming here; they know we've got to drive off some time."

Jacko tore the wire from two side table lamps and joined them together without the precaution of insulation tape. He went back up the drive to the other side of the hedge and joined the makeshift wiring to the wire from the car. He then ran it through the hedge but it still fell far short of reaching the cottage.

With Bulman's help he searched for any spare wiring that would complete the job and eventually found it in the shed attached to an old hedge trimmer, long since rusted up, but the wiring was of good length and there was an extension coil on a crusted drum. They ran it out together and joined it, taking the loosened end back into the house where Connie lay curled up in one of the chairs in a state of numbness that really registered nothing of what they were doing.

Jacko unscrewed one of the table lamp wall plugs to connect the wires, using a small screwdriver attached to an all purpose knife he carried; Bulman watched fascinated at the calmness with which he worked. When he had finished he laid the plug on the floor near the wall socket.

Jacko stood back to appraise his handiwork as Bulman said, "You realize you're going to leave us without wheels, don't you?"

"If I've miscalculated again then it's simply not my day. We must take the chance."

Bulman, who by now knew what was in Jacko's mind said, "Well I hope it works out for you, for all our sakes. But it's a big risk."

"Not as big as me turning the ignition while we were sitting in the car. We've got to chance it."

They glanced at each other and then looked at Connie. She seemed to be unaware of what was going on around

146

her. She had lapsed into a state of shock, which at the moment, protected her.

"We stay here until I plug in, and after the dust has settled run for the hedge and stay down behind it. You'd better look after Connie. And don't forget to bring that bloody shotgun."

Bulman was not happy at that, but there was no argument he could put up except one of surrender and that was as much against his nature as Jacko's. He shook Connie gently by the shoulder. "There's going to be an explosion, love. Nothing to worry about, but when it's over and when I say run you come with me. Understand?"

Her eyes were so vacant that he wasn't sure whether she had understood or not. He saw Jacko watching him and could see that he was worried about her. There was nothing they could do but to carry on. Bulman took Connie's limp hand and held it tight, and then gave the nod to Jacko.

Jacko took a last look outside and then crossed to the wall and pushed the plug home.

At first nothing happened, for maybe two or three seconds. Bulman and Jacko had just time to exchange concerned glances when the car blew up. It cascaded out in all directions but mostly straight up in the air, a huge explosion of flame and smoke and flying chunks of metal that shook the cottage to its foundations. The walls shook and there was an earth tremor under their feet. It seemed to blow Connie from the chair for she suddenly flew forward and Bulman caught her before she collapsed to the ground. Windows rattled and there was the sound of breaking glass above their heads. Some of the metal debris hit the walls of the cottage and clattered to the ground. A series of high pitched whistles, like screaming fireworks, gave rough direction to some of the car fragments.

Jacko stood quite still, seemingly unaffected by the powerful fireball, and thinking that but for catching up on his own near carelessness, the flying pieces might well have been themselves.

147

Bulman was holding Connie tight but the explosion had brought her right back to the perils of the moment, and she was again aware of what was going on. But he was worried that the bomb might be heard in the nearby town.

Jacko had the same thought but knew it was difficult to pinpoint the direction of sound in open spaces. But the fireball itself might be spotted. He bawled out, "Let's get out of here!"

They ran up the drive towards the dark pillar of smoke pierced by deep rolls of flame shooting through, but losing height as the smoke rose. Connie, better with movement, knew that she must not drag the others behind. The debris had stopped falling by the time they reached the hedge but black dust and molten rubber still filled the air and the smell was difficult to stomach. They flung themselves behind the hedge, feeling the scorching heat as Jacko told Connie to move away from them to a better place of safety. But she would not leave them.

There was no time for argument. A car came racing along the narrow lane as if it had been waiting for this very moment, pulled up in a skid only feet from the twisted black wreckage of the car, and three armed men climbed out almost before it stopped, and approached, guns held out.

Chapter Thirteen

The view from behind the hedge was disseminated; bits of legs through the foliage, but somehow the weapons managed to stay on view as if they became the fearsome focal point. Jacko glanced nervously at Connie, scared that she might panic, but now the actual crisis was here and that among the strangers might be the ones who killed her sister, she appeared to have been injected with a new kind of courage in which revenge undoubtedly played a part. Jacko gave her a reassuring wink and carefully placed a finger to his lips to warn her not to make a sound.

The three gunmen fanned out to get as close to the wreck as the heat would allow. All three were speaking in German, but one was having difficulty with the language, and he appeared to be the leader. To Jacko, who spoke a little German, it was clear, as he had expected to happen, that they were there to make sure that they had done the job; they were looking for bits and pieces of flesh and blood, something that would tell them that three people had died in the explosion.

After a short time they were obviously concerned, and their dialogue quickened, the man who spoke bad German, getting clearly agitated and raising his voice, as he seemed to be increasingly critical of the others. Their search for human remains had so far floundered, and they started to fan out away from the epicentre and to kick amongst the smoking debris, covering themselves with fine hot dust. Their mood did not improve as they continued to find nothing but ruptured car parts.

The three behind the hedge waited anxiously and Bulman began to wonder just what Jacko had in mind. He did not rate their chances taking on three gunmen. He wondered if anyone was left in the car the men had arrived in, and when Jacko began to crawl towards the entrance where the gap was sizeable in the hedge, he realized that Jacko had the same thought. Connie came with them, unwilling to stay anywhere on her own.

Jacko reckoned that whatever small noise they made was easily covered by the gunmen who were now kicking at the burnt out car frame and everything around it as their frustration mounted. They reached the entrance and crouched behind the last section of hedge. Jacko, who was slightly in front of the others, could see the car not far away. There was a driver who had repositioned the car for a quick getaway down the lane and had kept the engine running. Even though the car now faced away from them, there was little hope of reaching it before being seen, either by the driver who remained seated in it, or the three men who appeared to have gone as far as they intended.

Jacko whispered in Bulman's ear. "They know by now we weren't in it. So they'll be wondering what we do next." As he spoke, the nearest of the three gunmen moved directly towards the entrance, presumably to search the other side of the hedge and nearer to the cottage.

The man stopped directly opposite Bulman who could see him through the hedge. Connie took a sharp intake of breath before Bulman clamped a hand over her mouth. The man called out to the others and was clearly unhappy about the situation; if the targets had not been in the car the likelihood was that they were in the cottage with guns trained up the drive. He needed the others to help him.

The man who appeared to be in control called back but reverted to his native language in time of crisis. Whatever he said, did not seem to please the man so close to the crouching three.

Bulman and Jacko were sure that they had just been

150

listening to Russian, and when Connie pulled Bulman's sleeve he guessed that she might have recognized the man. The other two gunmen came slowly towards the one by the hedge, and it was clear that their mood of triumph on arrival had completely changed and this increased the danger. Bulman noticed that Jacko had raised the Colt to a firing position and he took a firmer grip on the shotgun. The fact that there was a driver as well as the three gunmen had made a big difference. But Jacko had been right to take the chance, reflected Bulman; staying in the cottage would have made them sitting ducks.

There was a brief, angry exchange the other side of the hedge, and then one man ran past the entrance and followed the left hand border, and it was clear that he intended to cover the rear of the cottage. The remaining two stepped towards the gap of the drive, at the moment out of sight of the cottage. They were waiting for their colleague to take up position.

Jacko gave a nod to Bulman, then trained his gun on the man nearest to him while Bulman unhappily raised the shotgun. The moment they thought they were seen they would have to fire and Bulman, unused to the situation, hoped he would have the nerve.

The three remained crouched, pushed as far into the hedge as possible. The talking had stopped the other side of the hedge, and then a sharp, whispered command, and the two remaining gunmen burst through the gap running fast down the drive and separating out as they went. The moment they were out of sight round the bend Jacko burst through the gap in the other direction and ran to the car.

The driver must have seen him coming through his rear view mirror for he hung on the horn until Jacko wrenched the door open and thumped him on the side of the head. Jacko thrust the Colt against the driver's temple and snarled, "Try that again and I'll pulp your head."

Jacko bawled at the others over the top of the car, telling them to get in quickly. Bulman opened the rear door, pushed Connie in and then scrambled in after her. Jacko told Bulman to put his shotgun at the back of the driver's head while he ran round to the passenger side. He did not make it in time.

One of the Germans, shouting as he came, had heard the horn blast and came sprinting towards him, gun levelled and firing as he ran. Had he stopped to take proper aim he might have hit Jacko, and as it was the shots were too close for comfort. The more composed Jacko rolled round on the car and fired two rounds and the man fell a few feet away. Before the other two could appear Jacko jumped in the car and told the driver to move fast. It was clear that he understood what he'd been told and Jacko suspected he was one of Benny Walker's hired help.

Before they could pull away the other two men appeared from opposite directions. The Russian now fully visible, came up from behind and fired randomly into the car. Jacko hung out of the window and fired awkwardly at the approaching German who suddenly took a dive. But the Russian came on, intent on reaching the car as the driver sat immobilized by fear.

Bulman tried to turn in his seat so that he could use the shotgun, but he was totally unprepared for Connie suddenly breaking into a fury of action as she snatched it from him, and swung round on her knees to face the rear window into which she fired. The roar of the gun in the confined space and the shattering of glass caught them all by surprise, except Connie, who was raising the shotgun again, lifting it into the jagged space of the broken rear window and levelling it at the Russian who had almost reached them.

The Russian was panting hard by now, but his face was contorted with fury at being deceived by so simple a trick. He had already struck the body of the car but he wanted to get at its passengers and so put in that extra effort to come round the side. Connie fired again as he came up, and she saw his bloodied face fall away from her and then the large frame hit the ground, face down as if to hide the full horror of what she had done. She was the calmest of them all at that moment, and said, "That was for my sister, you fat bastard."

Three men lay on the ground and the driver was trembling with fear besides Jacko. Jacko turned to him and said, "I was going to make you drive, but you're now superfluous; get out."

"You can't leave me with that lot. The police will think I did it."

"Tough. Now out or you'll end up like that other bloke."

The driver made a last attempt. "Look if the Bill doesn't get me, friends of these guys will. You're passing sentence on me."

"You passed sentence on yourself when you sounded the horn. Out. *Now.*"

The driver climbed out reluctantly and stood pleading by the car as Jacko moved over to the driving seat. With the engine still running and the car an automatic Jacko put her into gear and moved off. He didn't race away, he wanted to see what the driver might do, and he was convinced that he hadn't killed the German who had come from the front. "Keep that shotgun trained on the rear. Just in case."

He did not anticipate what happened next, but had a clear view in his mirror as did Bulman, who had managed to pry the shotgun away from Connie's clutching hands. He took over her position. The second German Jacko had fired at rose as the car moved off. He saw the shotgun levelled at him and had already shown that he was not inclined to buck the odds against him, but he did retrieve his gun. As the driver stood there still in a state of shock and disbelief, the German approached, casually raised his gun and shot the driver through the head.

"Callous bastard," said Bulman in disbelief.

"He's removed the last witness in his group. He'll probably put his gun in the driver's hand and leave it to the police to try to sort out the mess. He's decided to leave the pack but they'll get him. I'm just beginning to get the hang of what we're up against. These shadows are beginning to take shape and I can't say I like what I see."

"I'm sorry, Jacko. I see the shapes too. Had I known it was going to be this bad I wouldn't have taken it on, and certainly not involved you."

"Oh, yeah! How's Connie?" Jacko asked Bulman, as if he knew that having revenged her sister, Connie would have lapsed back into her shell of fear. But he was wrong.

"I can answer for myself thank you. I feel better for having killed that scum."

It was not the language they expected. "You sure it was him?" asked Jacko.

"Completely. I suppose they'll make more effort to find me now."

"All of us, Connie." Bulman squeezed her hand. "You're not alone any more. We're all in it."

Jacko followed anything that looked like a track or minor road. He did not want to return to Bishops Lydeard, for sooner or later the police would set out from there or perhaps direct from Taunton. It was important to keep away from the main routes. None of them knew the area too well and Jacko went by instinct. While they were still not far from the cottage they saw a blue flasher moving at speed, as if being propelled along the top of the hedgerow. With three dead men back there it was time to keep their nerve.

They kept quiet until they were beyond Taunton and heading back to London and they felt safer, but the talk was desultory. Events had drained them and they were all tired, particularly Jacko who had already done what could be considered as a good day's driving getting down there.

Bulman found he was still holding the shotgun and he laid it on the floor as Connie lifted her feet. Reaction was setting in. They had killed two people and it was a situation Bulman had difficulty in coming to terms with. The killings had not been accidental, as had happened to

154

him once before, but full blooded target shooting, and Jacko in particular was not the kind of person to miss. And yet it was impossible to feel regret, and he settled back with the belief of self-defence.

When they had covered about forty miles, during which they had stopped to refuel, Jacko said, "We've got to get rid of the car. It's probably hired, but with the rear window hanging out the Bill will spot it sooner or later." He called over his shoulder in a louder voice, "And I want reimbursing for the other car Bulman. If I go to my insurance company they'll want chapter and verse of why the car got blown up. Your boss would not want me to tell them the true story and I ain't gonna lie, so whoever is paying you had better buy me a new car. It's up to them which way I play it."

It was evening by the time they reached Newbury in Berkshire, and they had travelled far more than Bulman felt was safe with the shattered rear window, which had not made life comfortable for the two in the back. They ran into the bottle neck traffic jam about which a row over a bypass still raged. On more familiar ground, Jacko knew there was a car hire and garage just out of town and hoped he could reach it before closing time. When the garage eventually came in sight, a haze of light in a descending mist, Jacko pulled in just short of the pumps. He climbed out and went into the reception, and arranged a hire for an unspecified time using a credit card to transact.

It took a little time, and Bulman and Connie became restless with lights on at the side of the road and a constant stream of traffic buzzing past them. At last Jacko appeared and came towards them. He said to Bulman, "Continue on for a hundred yards and pull in. I'll come up with the other car."

Bulman pulled out into a mass of headlights, and annoyed the other drivers by driving slowly and then making it further awkward for them as he pulled in. While he sat waiting for Jacko he wiped the steering wheel and the sides of the doors to erase fingerprints, and told Connie to clean

155

up at the back; both his and Jacko's prints were likely to be on record, if not Connie's.

Dipped headlights tucked in behind them and Jacko came round to tell them to get in the other car. There was no time to attempt to hide the car they'd arrived in. They all climbed into the Nissan Jacko had just hired, and he waited his chance to pull out and join the stream. They were more relaxed after that; the car they had just ditched held associations they did not want.

By this time, Jacko, a man used to suffering deprivation, was looking tired and strained. It was a few years since he had been a serving soldier, and although he would argue to the contrary, this day had taken it out of him. The only one to emerge with a plus was Connie, who had shed her main fears with the killing of her sister's murderer. But it was a false belief that the worst was over. Bulman and Jacko well knew that having stirred the nest the worst was to come; between Knocker and themselves they had taken out too many of the opposition. They said nothing of this to Connie.

When they finally arrived at Jacko's house he showed Connie where the blankets and sheets were, gave her a room and told her to make her own bed. In return she cooked them a late meal during which Jacko stressed that she was not to leave the house, no matter how restless she became, and that when Bulman and Jacko were out she was to answer the door to nobody nor answer the telephone. It was a low key warning, but she seemed to accept that they were not finished.

After dinner they were all exhausted, and Bulman was annoyed belatedly to find that his trousers were torn and dirty, where he had taken a couple of tumbles when approaching the cottage. Connie promised to do her best to sew them the next morning, if Jacko could supply needle and thread.

They should have slept soundly from sheer exhaustion, but not one of them had a good night, and when they met for breakfast there was a general air of hangover and depression about them. Having Connie there precluded Bulman and Jacko from discussing certain aspects, things that now must be done and which they were reluctant to voice in front of her.

It was after mid-morning before Bulman rang Anna Brenning, while Connie was mending his trousers. She seemed always to be there, and was very pleasant to him. She invited him to lunch and he accepted. It was half-past one before he arrived at her apartment.

There was a change in her which he was quick to see and late to define. She was carefully made-up and had dressed up for him in a plain but expensive dress, making him very aware of his own shabbiness which was becoming difficult to explain away; so he said nothing about it and played the eccentric just a little.

She smiled as if reading his thoughts. "What have you done to your trousers?" she asked, as she brought him a drink.

Connie had brushed the dirt off but had left a faint mark where it had been, and the sewing of the split could not be wholly disguised. "I tripped over a spanner in my garage and managed to graze my knee. Nothing serious."

"You seem to be very attached to that suit. Is it your favourite?"

He was about to think up an excuse when he saw that she was playing with him, smiling at his discomfort and gently teasing him. "It's the only one I've got," he said with reasonable truth. "I'm not a great suit man."

"There are plenty of Ronnie's suits hanging up in the bedroom. Do you think they might fit you?"

He suddenly realized it could be a trap question and yet it had been so innocently posed. "I never met the man. Dead or alive. You would know better."

"Ronnie was a big man. Why don't you try one on?

157

Seriously. They are just hanging there." She smiled impishly. "I promise not to look while you try them."

He wondered where this was leading, and whether she really believed he had only one suit. He certainly needed one, and there was no chance of getting back into his own flat without obvious dangers. It was difficult to judge what she really made of all this.

"Go on," she chided. "You won't get a better offer." She was thoughtful for a moment. "He had a weight problem and had had some suits let out. Maybe I can find them. Come on, let's try." She rose, knowing she looked good. "And I'm not having a dig at your own weight; it suits you, you would not be the same at all if you tried to lose any. You are just well made."

He decided to go along with it because he considered it important to get to know her better, and because he believed there might be a lot more to get to know. She was comfortable in the apartment and there was a certain unnaturalness about it which increasingly puzzled him.

They went into the main bedroom and the whole of one wall was covered by a fitted wardrobe. Interior lights came on as Anna slid one of the doors back. There were rows of suits all in cellophane covers.

"While you're at it, why not try some shirts, and there are plenty of socks and underwear if you are short."

Why should she think he was that short of clothes in general? Bulman reflected that if this was what Walsh had in his love nest, what was his main home like for clothes? He realized then just how wealthy Walsh had been.

"You are not superstitious, are you?" asked Anna. "I mean you have no hang-ups about wearing a dead man's clothes?"

He had not considered it but now he did, and had to confess that the idea of wearing a murdered man's clothes was bizarre; he drew a distinction between a dead man and a murdered one. He replied truthfully, "I hadn't thought about it. But you must think I'm terribly poor even to

158

consider wearing them. And if you think that, why have you let me into your home? Isn't that a risky thing to do?"

She stood with hands on hip, one leg thrust out. "That is a typical vain, male thought. You are unattached, although I find it difficult to understand why, and you are probably just neglecting yourself. Some men do in those circumstances. I never suggested you are short of money; you need a good woman to look after you." And then she said archly, "You must have recognizable qualifications to have been hired by his family to look into his death, George. Presumably they pay you good fees, given his incredible wealth." She laughed softly. "You simply don't get round to buying yourself suits."

He grinned ruefully. "You sound as if you've known me for years."

"Is that an offer for me to catch up? Look, I've got to go into the kitchen to keep an eye on things. Lunch is going to be late anyway. Just have a look through. I promise to knock on the door when I come back. Or just come out when you're ready."

When she had gone he wondered if she had ever knocked on the door for Walsh. Her charm was such that he had to keep reminding himself that she had been Walsh's number one mistress at the time he was killed, and the more he met her the easier it became for him to believe.

He did not really want to try on any suits and it had no connection with who they had belonged to. He would much prefer to go back to his flat and fill a case, but that was out of the question. And he hated trying on clothes in a shop or to be measured for them.

He sat on a bedroom chair and gazed round the room, at the pastel shades, the delicate drapes, the tasteful and expensive bedroom furniture, all very feminine and reflecting Anna Brenning. There would not be a better opportunity, so he opened the drawers and carefully searched for anything that might give an insight into this lovely German girl who spoke English so well with such a faint but delightful accent, and had finished up as a politician's mistress. It was that, over and over again, that puzzled him most, even accepting the immense charm, as well as money, that Walsh must have exuded without really trying, and which in the end might have killed him. Bulman was beginning to believe that less.

He found nothing in the bedroom that was remotely suspicious, nor in the adjoining bathroom, and nor had he expected to or he would not have been left alone in the room. When he had finished searching, not a lengthy task, he sat on a long, quilted seat at the foot of the bed and wondered just where he was getting. He wanted to maintain contact and this was one way of doing it. Humour her.

There was a discreet knock on the door and he expected her to enter, but nothing happened so he called out, "It's OK."

Anna came in wearing a little floral patterned apron over her dress. "Well? Did you find anything to interest you?"

It was the way she phrased it that made him wonder if she was playing with him. "I didn't try any on," he confessed. "I rummaged along the rails but in the end the very idea tired me out."

"Then you shouldn't keep such late nights."

Again that phrasing. Did she mean it, or was she just using an expression. I'm going paranoid, he thought. I'm seeing sinister intent in the most innocent of remarks.

She went to the wardrobe, pushed around and then unhooked a suit, took the cover off and laid the suit on the bed. "Try that on," she said. "And don't worry, they'll finish up at Oxfam if you don't have some sense. I'll give a shout when lunch is ready. If you're still undressed wear one of his dressing gowns at the other end. The cheval mirror is on the other side of the room," she added, as if he might have missed it.

He wearily undressed and threw his clothes down on the bed beside Walsh's suit. It was a mistake, for immediately he saw just how shabby his had become. He dressed in a

160

charcoal grey two piece and was surprised at the fit. It was tight but there were side buttons that could be released on the trousers, and although the jacket was tight when buttoned up, it could be worn open. He looked in the mirror and was surprised at his smartness. He slipped his hands in the side pockets and felt something in the right hand pocket, something flat which he removed. It was a head and shoulder snap of a very striking woman. He was convinced that had Anna seen it, there was no way she would have left it there, for even for her the competition was too strong. There was a haunting quality about the face.

He was still staring at it when Anna cut through his thoughts as she called out, and he realized she was just outside the door.

Chapter Fourteen

He just had time to slip the photograph into his own jacket pocket before she tapped on the door and put her head round. Seeing him dressed she came in and walked round him smiling with satisfaction. "What a change. It was made for you."

"Not quite. It's too tight but I can leave the jacket open and loosen the side buttons on the trousers."

"Here, let me help you." She came round the back of him and undid the strap and fastened it on the next button. She did the same on the other side while he lifted his arms. She was very close and he could smell her perfume. He felt an impulse to touch her but resisted, and wondered if she knew how close he had come to doing it.

"How's that?" She stood before him, appraising him and giving no indication of knowing what had passed through his mind.

"Still a little tight but bearable. Thank you, Anna." He turned to the mirror and surveyed the effect. "It does seem to make a difference."

"All the difference. There's no time to change back for lunch so you can get used to it while we eat." She gave a radiant smile, obviously pleased with herself. "Come on."

She led the way to the dining room with its three pedestal mahogany table mounted by two silver candelabras which she had not lit. Silver dishes were on a long glass hotplate mounted on a serving table. As he sat down, Bulman noticed at once that the cutlery was period silver. During his antique clock repairing days, and he still did some, he had been caught up in general antiques and *objet d'art*. It was not only an interest but a love.

"Queens pattern," he remarked.

"Is it? I wouldn't know but it is rather nice."

Anna had prepared a light, delicate flavoured soup, followed by grilled salmon in a watercress sauce with new potatoes. She had chosen the wine carefully, a German one he noted, and the meal was altogether delightful. He felt at home with her, and there was nothing stilted about them which somehow surprised him, bearing in mind they had only met twice before. He put the ease of the meeting down to Anna, who seemed to be able to adjust to his own interests. He'd had an interesting life but he was sure that Anna had too, although when he reflected on it, he knew precious little about it. They got on well together and enjoyed lunch as though they had known each other for years.

It was this feeling of instant friendship that worried Bulman. A woman like Anna had no need to waste time on the likes of him; she could aim as high as she liked. She could more than hold her own in any company, yet as far as he could see, she was almost living the life of a recluse.

"Don't you ever go out?" he asked.

"Of course I do. I need to shop."

"I meant see people. Mix. Relax. Just get away from this place and its memories for a while."

"I'm quite happy as I am. I don't want the press on my back. The moment I step out they want to know why and they just pester to a point of intrusion. It will die down and then I'll throw a party for you."

"For me? What on earth for?"

"Because you've been kind and understanding and gentle with your enquiries. You are a very nice man, George."

He felt embarrassed at that; compliments did not sit easily on Bulman. "You don't think the suit is doing that to you?

163

I mean, subconsciously you look across the table and see a blurred image of Ronnie Walsh."

"You're not a bit like Ronnie apart from size. No, I would like to get to know you better. Could we keep in touch?"

As that was the whole purpose of the exercise it was easy for him to say, "Of course. As long as you don't mind the odd question about Ronnie that I see fit to raise, relative to his murder."

"That's a horrible word." She squirmed. "I have always accepted that you have a job to do. It hasn't spoiled my pleasure."

"Nor mine."

After lunch they returned to the lounge, and as Anna put the coffee things down Bulman said, "Is there still any risk of this apartment being returned to the estate?"

"I don't think so. Ronnie knew how to cover his tracks on all sorts of matters."

And that was about the biggest indication she had yet given him. When it was time to go she insisted that he remove the suit so she could get it cleaned, but he saw it as a ruse for her to keep in touch and he knew that it wasn't for his sex appeal. She wanted to stay close and her reasons might be interesting. When he changed back into his old suit he was glad then that he had switched the snap to his own pocket.

She gave him a peck on both cheeks when he left, with a promise to ring him as soon as the suit was back; she would put it through express cleaning. It had been an interesting if confusing meeting.

When he left he found the nearest callbox and rang Scotland Yard hoping to find Beatty in. He gave his name and was put straight through. "Wally, can you spare me five minutes at your place?"

"Just about. How long will you be?"

"I am working on the probability that I'm being tailed

and I'm rather slow to shake them off. But if you sent a car for me I could be at your place in no time at all. And then you can show me a back way out."

"You crafty bugger."

"Normally you'd be right but I'm deadly serious."

"Where are you?"

The police car must have been on nearby patrol and redirected, for it arrived in little over five minutes, blue flasher going to cut through the traffic but no siren. It pulled up on double yellow lines beside the callbox. "Mr Bulman?" the driver called out.

Bulman climbed in the rear as both front seats were occupied.

"Scotland Yard, sir?"

"Thanks. And don't keep your meter running." Which produced smiles and broke the ice. The two policemen were younger generation but they seemed to know of him and they chatted on the way down. Bulman called out, "Would you know if we are being followed?"

The policeman in the passenger seat turned round. "Real cops and robbers stuff eh! It's difficult to know in heavy traffic like this, and it would usually be the other way round as you know. But we'll give it a go." And as an afterthought he added, "We've got the flasher going which makes it easier for us in traffic and not so easy for anyone following. Our instructions are to get you there fast. To hell with it, let's have the siren." The driver took off.

Beatty's office was on one of the upper floors and Bulman was shown in without waiting. The two men shook hands as Beatty observed, "You look as if you've been dragged through a hedge backwards."

Bulman laughed. "You're not too far wrong." He sat down and wasted no time by pulling out the snapshot and pushing it across the desk. "Know her?"

Beatty picked it up and gazed at it for some time before slowly shaking his head. "Nice-looking woman. Did you think I would?"

"Someone must. It belonged to Ronnie Walsh. Don't ask me how I got it. What nationality would you say she is?"

"You're better at that game than me." Beatty took another long look. "Long shot. Russian maybe. Somewhere around that way."

"She could have been born here."

"Don't piss around. You asked me for an opinion."

"It's the same as mine. Lovely, isn't she?"

"It makes a change for out there. Do you want me to put it through the computer?"

"No. Thanks just the same. That would mean a lot of people might get sight and I don't want that, not yet anyway, although I may have to come back to you. Do you know anybody in the Security Service who might help? Could you arrange a meeting for me? My old contacts seem to have all been knocked off."

"Sure." Beatty made the call himself from a number he obviously kept in his head. He then made a call on the internal network and said, "You're in luck. Robbie Andrews is in the building with SB. He can be here in ten minutes. I don't mind waiting as it's you." He looked at his watch. "You're not driving are you, so let's have a drink."

Beatty rose and opened a filing cabinet which Bulman noticed had a fair range of bottles. "For visitors," Beatty explained as he poured two large whiskies. "You're a visitor aren't you? Cheers, George."

"Cheers. Any idea who did it?"

"Oh, sure. We're pretty certain. Proving it is something again."

"Who?"

"You know better than to ask, particularly as it will probably go down as one of the great unsolved unless someone conveniently has a nervous breakdown and coughs."

"So there's a lot of protection?"

"I didn't say that."

"Did you say it was a woman?"

166

"No. And you've lost your touch. But that was the first belief and nothing has yet changed our minds. And what have you found out?"

"Well as you know, I'm not really looking for the killer. It's obvious that Home Office – or whoever – want to know what games he was playing and with whom. There's more to it than sex."

"That's for sure. I don't really know why they're using you, do you?"

"We've been over this. It's not my fault. They just don't want certain things to become public and you are public. It's political. It always bloody is. They want to sit on whatever *it* is."

"Are they stupid enough to think that we might not find it out for ourselves?"

"You've been sat on before and will be again. It's no reflection. If it's not the Government putting in an oar it's bloody Five. I'm expendable. They can blame everything on me, and they have. I need my head examined to do this."

"They know you too well, George. You're hooked old son." Beatty took another gulp of scotch. "There's no hard feelings or you wouldn't be sitting there." And then cautiously, eying Bulman with some suspicion, "Have *you* any idea who did it?"

"Not as clear cut as yours seem to be. A woman may have done it, probably did, but that doesn't tell us a thing. You'll have found out that I'm using 'Glasshouse' Willie Jackson. We've been shot at, very nearly killed and don't ask me about it; other police forces will be following that trail. It's very involved and very deep and bloody dangerous."

Beatty ventured a brief smile. "Yeah, we've heard from the Somerset police. There's a lot you're not telling me, George."

"Nothing that would lead to the arrest of Walsh's murderer. If I ever strike that lucky you'll be the first to know."

Beatty gave Bulman a hard look. "Don't be too clever,

George. I know you have a degree of protection but there is a limit. We need to see that girl again."

Bulman was spared a reply by a brief knock on the door and the entry of a stocky, round featured man with a permanent smile and steely eyes. Beatty introduced them and offered Robbie Andrews a drink which was declined.

Andrews, whose accent was ultra public school, pulled up a chair and said, "You've better bloody furniture than us, old boy."

Bulman pulled out the snapshot. "Do you recognize her?"

Andrews stared at it for some time as if photocopying it in his mind. "Where did you get this?"

"I found it lying in the street outside your HQ."

"Very funny. Don't know her at all. Is there any reason why you think I should?"

"Only a gut feeling. Pity."

Andrews was sitting slightly away from the desk, his arms resting on his legs as he leaned forward. "Look here, Bulman, I know you're doing something for Edward Marshall. I personally find it a bloody insult. He seems to think we are riddled with moles which indicates to me he's not fit for the job. And Wally here, can't be too thrilled about it. And yet you turn to us for help as soon as you're stumped."

Bulman was annoyed. He said, "In the event you have been no help at all, and Marshall's probably right not to trust you if this is your juvenile attitude. Stuff your help." Bulman rose and Beatty tried to calm things down by pointing out that he had not finished his drink. Normally it would have worked but Bulman was furious. He put the snapshot away and thanked Beatty for his time.

Half-way to the door he said to Andrews, "It will give me a lot of pleasure passing on your comments to Marshall. How the hell do they pick pricks like you?"

Beatty called out, "George, George, where can I contact you?"

168

Bulman stopped near the door. "You can't. We've gone to ground. Am I stretching it a bit if I ask for a car back? I don't want the Security Service on my tail."

"There's no need for that." Andrews stood up, his permanent smile somewhat haggard. "Look, I'm sorry, old boy. It just pisses me off when we get slaps in the face, like you being used for a job we should be doing."

Bulman said, "Wally here could have taken the same view and probably does. But he's more used to being overridden by your mob. I'm asked to do a job and if I like it I do it. We are all involved with different sections of the same job. For all I know there may be others doing things I don't know about. There are aspects about this which are at best unusual. All Marshall has done, for whatever reason, is to have made up cells, each one playing its part. I would have thought that was something you would operate yourself on occasion, without blowing your top."

"I'm sorry. You are quite right." The smile was almost back to normal. "Would you like me to take the snap with me back to HQ? Or better still, Wally can have some copies made here."

Bulman was not at all sure why he declined. He certainly did not want it widely circulated, although he was hard pushed to give himself a reason. Right now he wanted to confine the knowledge. He said, "Leave it for a bit. I just thought she was important enough to be known at your level. I'm obviously wrong. Gut feelings don't always work out." And yet it was a gut feeling that kept the snap in his pocket.

"Let me atone," Andrews suggested. He glanced at his watch. "Wally, can I use an outside line?" He rang his own office and asked to be put through to Derek North and asked him to wait for him. "Come with me back to the madhouse and it is just possible that North can help you." He looked from Bulman to Beatty. "Are we all accepting that this woman is from east of Warsaw? Good. Will you come back with me? And no, we won't follow you when you leave."

169

As they left Beatty gave Bulman a sly wink, glad that his friend had attacked the Security Service man in a way that he could not. And it had worked.

When Bulman was finally cleared to enter North's office it was late evening. Andrews made the introductions and them left them to it. Bulman liked North on sight; he was laid back and good-looking, and not prone to tantrums which was made clear as Bulman stated his own position.

"Your reputation precedes you," North said with an easy grin. "We have quite a file on you. As you'd expect. What can I do?"

Bulman handed over the snapshot and North studied it in much the same way the others had. "I've a pretty retentive memory but this one doesn't ring a bell, and it's not a face I would forget. Quite a stunner. What makes you think any of us would know?"

"I'm tired of saying the same thing but it comes down to gut feeling. This woman, in some way, was connected with Ronnie Walsh. As he travels abroad a lot she might have attracted the attention of SIS."

"We're not SIS. Shouldn't you be contacting them?"

"I'd find it more difficult to get help from them whereas, as you point out, I'm rather better known here. Also, as you very well know, there has to be an overlap of activities between the intelligence services. She may be abroad but could still become a threat here if that is her line of work. You know what I mean."

"Yes, of course. Does your gut feeling suggest this is political or criminal?"

"I've already tried the Yard and they don't know her. Well at least Wally Beatty doesn't, and if she's on file and a real threat, then I would expect him to know."

North waved the snapshot. "You don't want this run through the system?"

"Too many people would see it."

"Shouldn't that be what you want? You can't hope for individuals to know without picking the right one."

170

It was difficult to argue against the logic, but Bulman had dug his heels in and simply reiterated his doubts about the value of spreading the woman's face far and wide. But he had not come quite so empty-handed. "Are you in touch with Veida Ash?"

North raised a brow. "Is this what you've been leading up to? What do you know about her?"

"It was pretty well covered at her trial in spite of some of it being in camera. Wealthy German parents who came here during the war. She was born here. Worked for MI6 for years and gradually built up what was, and possibly still is, Europe's biggest crime ring. She used her agents around Europe and further corrupted already corrupt officialdom, particularly police abroad and more particularly the East German Stasi. She had a tremendous network, which she remote controlled from the very heart of SIS. Brilliant woman. How's she doing?"

North was smiling now, feeling easier about the position. "It took you a long time to come to the point. She was also responsible for several murders, some of them in prison. As you say, she had, no has, terrific influence but a fantastic organizing ability. She claims she never let the country down, that what she did was merely on the side. Made a massive fortune. Serving twenty-five years."

"Do you think she'll serve them?"

"With the amount of money she has around the globe and the influence she can pull even inside jail, I doubt it. She's still running what's left of her empire from prison. She's rebuilding. She'll be sprung; one way or the other. Do you think she might know the face in the snapshot?"

"As you say, she knows an awful lot of the wrong people, mostly in Europe."

"What makes you think the lady in the photograph is one of the wrong people?"

"I suppose the answer to that is I don't. It is merely the circumstances in which I found it that adds an air of mystery to her. That snap should not be hidden away but enlarged and framed."

"So you pinched it?"

"I found it. But I don't intend to tell you how. Do you think you could help me?"

North laid the snap on his desk, a finger running round its edge. "You want me to show this to Veida Ash? She's not likely to admit it, even if she recognizes it."

"That's why I would prefer you to arrange for me to see her. I know access is highly restricted."

"You think you can detect her lies?"

Bulman shrugged. "I don't know. I've never met the lady although I'm sure that would be an experience on its own. But I would like the opportunity to form my own opinion."

"She'll probably try to seduce you. She tried it on me and I'm still not sure whether or not she meant it. I had partial success in what I went for, but she's far too clever to go all the way. So you want me to get you a pass?"

"As soon as possible. I suppose she has her own phone and television?"

North nodded. "She corrupts wherever she goes. She can't help herself and she has the money to do it."

"Can't you tap her phone?"

"She's on a mobile but there would be the mother and father of all complaints if the do-gooders found out we were tapping a prisoner's phone; they would never accept that she should not be allowed one. They'd really rub that in. But she'd be careful with it, anyway. We have to find other ways and settle for an occasional victory. We'll never win the war against her. If the phone was taken away she'd find others ways of communication; it would slow her down, that's all. Better let her have it; she might one day slip up."

"So what about it?"

"If I help you I want help back. Is that reasonable?"

"Very. Depending on what sort of help you want."

"One of observation, and I'd like you to wear a bug.

You're very experienced. She's given us a list of people she's willing to sacrifice as an indication that she has seen the light and is mending her ways. But she's still protecting the big fish and always will. It would be interesting to find out her outside contacts in this country."

"Fine, but she's not likely to tell me. And I won't wear a bug. They cramp my style."

North considered it. "OK. You can form judgements." He gave Bulman a disarming smile. "And I have the feeling that you already have a few. I would respect your opinion."

"I'll do what I can. Tomorrow?"

North laughed. "That means a special pass. One of ours. They told me you are a lazy sod."

"I am. I want to get it over and get back to bed."

"I'll give you a ring — "

"No. You can't do that. I'll ring you at midday tomorrow. It can all be done by messenger and I can pick up the pass at the prison."

"If she agrees to see you."

"She'll see me." Bulman rose and held out his hand. "You've been very helpful."

"My pleasure. How's Jacko these days? Shooting as well as ever?"

Bulman returned to an agitated Jacko and Connie. "Where the bloody hell have you been?" yelled Jacko. "That was some lunch."

"After lunch I went to the Yard and then to MI5. I've got a concession to see a rather special murderess and super gang boss who's in prison. I don't suppose you know this lady?" He passed the snap across to Jacko who whistled.

"I wish I had. Before I met Georgie, of course. Where did you get it?"

"In one of Ronnie Walsh's suits which I tried on. Anna's having it cleaned and then I'll wear it instead of this load of rags."

"Then do your own mending." The call came from Connie

173

who was watching television across the room. "And your dinner is on the hotplate; we've had ours."

The two men found it difficult to discuss anything with Connie around, but short of handing her over to the police, which they had promised not to do, there was little answer except to be careful.

Bulman went into the kitchen to eat his dinner, finding himself suddenly hungry, in spite of the lunch. Jacko joined him at the kitchen table. Bulman said, "I know you're a man of action but you did more than your whack yesterday. I need to see where this snapshot takes us if anywhere at all. Don't think the heavies have finished with us. They've just been warming up."

"I know that. I was worried about you. You sure you haven't been followed?"

Bulman glanced up, touched by Jacko's unexpected concern, and the unconscious use of his first name. "I was taken to the Yard in a patrol car complete with siren and flasher. Anyone would have had a job following that."

"They'd have known you were going to a nick, wouldn't they?"

"And from there I was in the hands of Five. They brought me back part way and I did a double load of evasive action from then on. I don't want to be knocked off either, Jacko. I hope to see this woman tomorrow. We'll take it from there."

It was after four the following afternoon when Bulman went to see Veida Ash. She tried the same ploy on Bulman as she did on North. "My, they get better and better," said Veida, as Bulman looked at her across the table. "You're bigger than the last one, not as refined, but I sometimes like them rough."

"And so you should," Bulman agreed. "You can be pretty rough yourself, as surviving relatives of your victims will no doubt confirm."

"I don't have to see you," Veida retorted sharply.

174

"That's right. But you're more curious about me than I am of you. Let's conduct this without aggro and in a spirit of mutual recognition."

"I have heard about you," she said, as a peace offering. "You're obviously cleverer than you look. What do you want me to confess to?"

"Do you know this lady?" Bulman pushed the snapshot across, watching for reaction from Veida as he had never done so intensely before.

She did not pick up the snap but turned it with her finger so that she could properly study it. But even in that small movement he saw a tremor in her fingers.

Chapter Fifteen

Veida stared at the snapshot with some intensity, and as she did the fingers gradually steadied as her jaw line tightened. It had been an immense show of will. She had the sense not to speak just then, as Bulman had hoped she would, but she made sure she did not meet his gaze.

"Well?"

"Well what?" Veida's voice was normal. She had shown tremendous control.

"Do you know her?"

"Know her or recognize her?"

Bulman had given her extra time by asking a sloppy question and he was annoyed with himself. "Recognize her?"

At last she met his gaze but she had not quite won. "No, I don't recognize her." She gave a thin smile and then added, "And I don't know her either."

When he just sat there gazing alternatively at her and the snapshot it provoked her to ask, "Why would you think I would recognize her? It's a million to one chance. Have you asked the warders here if they recognize her?"

Fully recovered she was back on the victory trail, but Bulman did not forget that first tremor of the fingers when she saw the lovely face gazing up at her. "So it's not your daughter then? I mean, you'd know even if you haven't seen her for some time." North had tipped him off about various things, including the daughter, before he had finally left him.

The comment drew some blood but not the reaction it

had drawn from her during North's visit, and she made capital of it.

"So you're in touch with Derek North. I find that interesting."

"As if you didn't know." He pointed to the snap. "Lovely woman."

"Very. But my daughter looks nothing like that. That was a low shot, Bulman. Is that all you wanted from me?"

"Primarily. I'm disappointed. I thought you knew, or knew of, every top villain in Europe."

"So she's a villain? You didn't say that before."

"Where do you reckon she comes from?"

Veida tried to avoid looking at the snap again but forced herself to do so. "How the hell would I know? She could be a Chechen." She did not know why she said it and quickly wondered if Bulman was getting to her. The observation was meant to be flippant and did not really matter, but she should not have voiced it even if it did keep Bulman quiet.

Bulman, on the other hand, realized that inexplicably, he was back in the game. "That's an astute observation."

"It's shit, Bulman. Just something to say to try to keep you quiet. Putting a nationality to that face is nothing more than a guessing game and you know it." She pushed the snap across the table to him, still only using the tip of her nails. "Why don't you take a holiday? I'll come with you if you can wait a little while."

"I can't afford one, Veida."

"I can. I own a little island out in the Pacific. Just the job. Won't cost you a bean and I'll even throw in generous pocket money. Say, a hundred grand."

"Did you make the same offer to Derek North?"

Veida smiled wickedly. "He cost a little more. He's official, you see. I put him on the payroll." As Bulman smiled quietly at her, she added, "Let's face it; I could buy this bloody prison out of petty cash and then privatize it and have myself released. Money has never been my

177

problem. Why don't you join in? You need never worry again."

"With you pulling the strings I'd always be worried. As you're looking after Derek so well, I'll have a word with him and get him to give me a cut of his. I'm not demanding." While he was talking he pushed the snap back across the desk so that it was once more in front of her. "You know her, don't you?"

Caught up in the banter and convinced that she had diverted Bulman away from the snap, she was almost caught off guard. But this time her hands were under the table and he had little to go by except the instant hesitancy followed by a loquacious denial. "Just what are you trying to pull, Bulman? I don't know the woman, have never met the woman, and never want to meet the woman. Is that clear enough?"

"Oh, very. You are very impressive when you lose your rag. I must provoke you again."

But Veida was always quick to recover. "Anyway, just where the hell did you get the snap?"

He had expected the question before this. "I took it myself whilst on holiday in Chechnya. Just a face in a crowd which left a deep impression on me. I was impressed by the way you identified her nationality. Dangerous place to be these days."

"You're mad, Bulman. You must have come in with the tide, washed up on a polluted beach. You should seriously think about the island holiday. You could really lay back and rest in luxury."

"There'd be nobody to look out for me and I'd be a sitting duck for your assassins. Very easy to dispose of me in a place like that. A death cell in paradise. Great." Bulman pulled the snap towards him and slipped it in his pocket. "I really enjoyed talking to you, Veida. You are certainly no bore. When do you expect to break out?"

"I told you. When I buy the prison."

Bulman rose and smiled down at her. "Your island

will be handy then. I bet you've made sure there are no extradition laws. You will let Derek North know if you suddenly have a brain storm and remember who is in the snapshot, won't you?"

"He'll be the first to know. Think over my offer. I'd like to meet you again but you'll have to make it soon if it's to be in here."

"Dream on, Veida." Bulman tapped on the door but he knew she was planning not dreaming.

Back in her cell Veida sat on the edge of her bed staring at the dark blanket of wall opposite. Lights would go out soon and she would then use the phone. She had learned to use the buttons by touch and almost always made her calls in the dark, under the shelter of a blanket.

She sat thinking about North and Bulman, two very astute men in their very different ways. But astuteness alone could not beat her or break her, whatever conclusions they made. She was pretty certain that Bulman had scored over the snapshot, and no matter how briefly, she had convinced him she knew the woman in the snap. And that was why he had called. Where she was ahead of him was that she knew why he needed to know. He was trying to make a connection but to do that he had to know the identity of the woman.

When everyone was 'banged' up for the night and when the lights went out, she remained on the side of the bed for some time. She had a battery reading lamp which everyone knew she had, but which she used sparingly because she did not want to antagonize unnecessarily. She could buy her way through most trouble and be incredibly generous about it, but this could also make enemies and she went out of her way to avoid that as a matter of policy; villains, no matter how tough or violent, did not worry her because they knew she could always buy revenge. She virtually ran things as she always had.

But she was worried. Enquiries had taken a wrong turn.

And she respected the men who were making them. She waited until nearly midnight before making her call, keeping her voice down as she always did.

"Anna? I'm sorry to wake you. I've had Bulman here."

"Bulman? Why on earth?"

"He brought a snapshot of Yelena with him. How on earth did he get it?"

"You're asking me? Why should I know?"

"Someone must. Has he been to see you again?"

"Yes. It's important to keep in touch. I need to know what he knows."

"Then that's how he got it. You must have left it lying around."

"Don't be ridiculous. I haven't got a snap of Yelena."

"Ronnie Walsh might have had one you didn't know about and Bulman has sniffed it out. I warned you about him. This is serious because he somehow sees a connection and might finally make one."

"Then I'll have to deal with it."

"We need to know exactly what he knows before doing that. The news that's reaching me is that there are bodies lying all over the place. Bulman has called in muscle, probably some old SAS mates. It's reaching a stage where everything is going on show and that's the last thing we want. When are you seeing him again?"

"Probably tomorrow." Anna was inclined to tell Veida about the suit when it occurred to her with a shock, that the snapshot might have been in the suit pocket. She decided to say nothing about it, at the moment anyway. "I'm trying to find out where he hangs out. I can't be blatant about it without giving myself away; if he spots someone following from my place it will be obvious who put them there. I've thought of another way and I'll let you know next time. They may have the girl."

Veida was not happy about the patchy contact with Bulman. "Don't mess things up, Anna. There are aspects of your work that are weak."

180

"Then you'd better concentrate on my strengths which are lethal. None more lethal. I suggest you bear it in mind. It is us who are taking the risks; we're not sitting on our arses in jail telling others what to do."

Veida laughed. "Well, that's my strength. It's what I do best. You did a good job. Don't go stroppy on me. You'd be difficult to replace but not impossible." She hung up before Anna could reply.

Connie had gone to bed early by the time Bulman got back, and he was grateful to have time with Jacko alone. He brought Jacko up to date and told him he was convinced that Veida Ash knew the identity of the woman in the snapshot. They were sitting at the kitchen table with mugs of black coffee.

"Why is the snap so important?" asked Jacko.

"Because Walsh obviously knew her. She's tied into this somehow and Veida protected her from identification."

"You think she might have done the murder?"

"There's no way of knowing. I'm assuming she's abroad but don't ask me why. I believe the whole business stems from abroad; Germany or Russia or both."

"Get away! What a detective."

Bulman grinned, aware of how it must have sounded. "Stop taking the mickey, Jacko. I think the murderer is much nearer to home but there seems to be an awful lot of protection flying around."

"What makes you think Veida Ash is involved in this?"

"Well, the whole bloody business is clearly international, and Veida knows more about what's going on in the villainy stakes than anybody else. You must have read the trial accounts. She may not be directly involved but she would have heard on her network what was going on. She'll know about it."

"Including Walsh's murderer?"

"It wouldn't surprise me. Right through her M16 career, Veida was underestimated. I think the trial produced only

181

the tip of the iceberg. The woman has terrific vision and ability. Prison wouldn't stop her from arranging hits; she managed it the other way round and they still can't nail her for them. She's the most likely person to know what's going on in that world."

"What world are we talking about, Bulman?"

Bulman knew it was not a naïve question, that Jacko was trying to force him to get off the fence. "A politician is murdered; a philanderer. It seems that a woman did it. One woman too many is the press line. And that was how it seemed until the uglies appeared." Bulman attempted to see how Jacko was taking this but Jacko had gone into blank mode. But he was listening.

Bulman peered into his empty mug. "I don't think it's about women, except the use of them, and I don't think it's political. Veida made an unconscious remark about the woman in the snapshot; a Chechen, she said. A strange thing to say which may have had a subconscious allusion." He poured another coffee from the jug. "There's a little island off Palermo called Ustica. I don't know whether they still use it, but the Sicilian police used to 'invite' those Mafia they could pin nothing on to take a little break there to keep them out of the way for a spell. Chechnya has become a hotbed for the so-called Russian Mafia. It's a sort of no go area no matter how the Russians violated it. The Russians are reckoned to control the largest criminal organization in the world, including the American Mafia. It's the underworld's big bang. I don't see how Veida could not be involved. She has such widespread contacts, ready-made for those who need them, and at a price."

"What the hell has this got to do with a womanizing MP who got himself topped?"

Bulman pulled a face as he sipped the coffee. "This is cold." Then he looked at Jacko and gave a wide grin. "Interesting, isn't it?"

"Interesting? Are you kidding? It may be fascinating to you, mate, but to me it sounds like instant death. You can't run against a mob like that and expect to win. And losing is six feet down if you're lucky."

Bulman nodded agreement but showed no actual concern, as if he had got caught up in the mental challenge which now overshadowed the physical dangers.

Jacko thumped the table. "You'd better get real, Bulman. If what you say is true these people aren't going to let go until we're out of the way. It will be only a matter of time before they find us. However good you think I am in taking on trouble, I'm not that bloody good. Are you listening to me?"

"You don't have to shout. I understand our position just as much as you. There's no way out. We just have to carry on."

Jacko pushed his chair back. "You talk for yourself. You've conned me into this. You knew it was going to go deep. I've got Georgie to think about."

Bulman watched Jacko stand up and glare down at him. "I haven't lied to you about the dangers. We've only discovered the dangers step by step. I didn't know what we were up against. And I'm only guessing now. If you go I can't do it on my own. And what about Connie? Do you leave her to get on with it? She can't cope on her own."

Jacko picked up his empty mug and was about to throw it at the wall when he stopped, the mug still held high. His expression changed and he slowly lowered the mug and placed it gently on the table. "I'm sorry, mate. I don't know what got into me. I suppose I just realized I couldn't win and that takes some swallowing for me. I don't mind taking on anything against the odds, that's the story of my life, but to take on the impossible takes a little getting used to. You're taking it pretty well." He sat down slowly, an unusually deflated figure.

"The alternative is to let them get away with it."

"Apart from the murder, we don't know what *it* is. For myself I won't lose any sleep over the murder of a randy MP. Any politician for that matter. Maybe that is what got me down. Fighting for something I don't believe in."

"Let's get some sleep," said Bulman wearily.

They rose, pushed their chairs forward and put their mugs in the dishwasher. They left the kitchen together and went out into the hall.

Connie was sitting at the foot of the stairs, arms around drawn up knees on which she rested her chin. She was ashen. She stared up at them as if they would dispel what she had heard with a laugh or gesture and that they would say it was all a joke. But she had only to remember her sister to realize it was far from being a joke.

The two men felt wretched then, the more so because they would have to lie to comfort her and she had heard too much for that. Connie's nightmare had just got worse and the only ending she saw was one of horror.

Bulman rang Anna quite early the next morning because he wanted to keep the momentum going. She invited him to another lunch, he suggested going out, but she pointed out that she had the suit back and he could try it while she prepared something to eat. It was what he really wanted, but Jacko warned him to be careful.

Bulman did not need the warning. He was well aware that Anna was playing some sort of game. He did not believe she found him attractive enough to warrant this kind of attention. He arrived just after midday, and she had put on something flimsy and different for him. It was a seductive dress and she knew how to wear it without being too obvious.

"Do you want to try the suit on first?" she asked him before he sat down.

"Why not?"

She took him into the bedroom and the suit was on the bed, the cellophane wrapper still on, put there by the cleaners whose name was clearly printed across it. She carefully pulled the suit out and held it expertly to

184

show him before laying it on the bed. She removed the inevitable pins and labels and placed them on a bedside table, before laying the suit out on the bed again. Then she said, "They seem to have done a good job. I'll leave you to it. I'll be in the kitchen when you're ready."

When she left he gazed down at the suit as if it was an object of some interest and he supposed that in a way it was. A dead man's suit. No, a murdered man's suit. He had more qualms about wearing it than he had the previous day, but there was no denying he badly needed a change of clothes. He picked up the jacket and slowly went along the collar, running his closed fingers right round the edge, feeling carefully all the way. He did the same with the jacket hem and then finally, and this was more awkward, the body of the jacket. He realized he was taking time but it was not a job to be rushed. Satisfied that the jacket had not been tampered with he did the same with the trousers.

On this suit, as with many others in the wardrobe, turn-up trousers had returned to fashion and he finally found the bug in the turn-up of the left leg. It was hardly traceable, just the slightest swelling. A small round object had been sewn in and the difference was so slight that it could have been a slight bodge in the cloth. But suits of this quality, and the Saville Row labels were sewn inside both garments, did not have bodges in the cloth. He had half expected to find something but was still disappointed when he did it. The question now was should he wear it?

The bedroom door was ajar and Anna called out to ask if the suit had shrunk in the cleaning. He pretended not to hear and quickly removed his old suit and dressed in the charcoal. When he checked in the cheval mirror he was pleased with what he saw; he left the jacket unbuttoned for comfort. He looked as smart as at any time he could remember, but his spirits were low and it was going to be difficult to express *bonhomie* over lunch. Anna was now specifically tied in with his enquiries. It was impossible to believe that she did not know about the bug.

185

He folded his own suit, and placed it on the hanger the cleaners had provided and managed to get it in the cellophane bag to carry home. When he had finished he turned to find Anna in the open doorway watching him with a smile.

"You took your time," she said.

"I'm a slow dresser. What do you think?"

"I think I'm seeing the real George Bulman for the first time. You look terrific." She waved an arm towards the wardrobe. "Take as many as you want; they'll go for free to the charities."

"One at a time will do," he said. "It will give me an excuse to come back."

She smiled in a slightly provocative way. "That's what I hoped you would say." She pushed herself away from the door and added, "I know it's winter but I've done a salad lunch because I'm not getting too much notice from you."

He noticed she did not press for an address or telephone number as she had before. He followed her into the dining room and he could not avoid noticing that she was acting in a more feminine way than before. She did not overdo it but small movements fringed on the suggestive and were difficult to define, except for him to conclude that she could be a very sexy lady and Ronnie Walsh's attraction to her became easier to understand. She was an excellent host.

When they had finished lunch and were back in the sitting room Bulman decided to take a serious risk. He pulled out the snapshot and passed it across to Anna. "Have you ever seen this woman?"

Anna held it in a hand which rested on her crossed legs and she really scrutinized it. "Yes," she said at last. "The name escapes me for the moment but isn't this the famous Yugoslav actress?"

She had shown no sign of nerves, almost as though she had been warned and Bulman was startled into thinking that she might have been. "I don't know who she is. She

186

could be an actress with those looks. I just wondered if you might know her off the top of your head."

"Well, I'm sure I do but I can't put a name to her for the moment. I'm not a great cinema goer. I think she did a film in America." She leaned back thoughtfully. "It will come to me. Where did you get it?"

"I found it in the jacket of this suit. It's a wonder it wasn't wiped out by detergents or whatever they use." He had now stuck his neck right out. He felt it was the only way he might get anywhere.

"It was dry-cleaned, but even so I agree with you."

She gave no sign at all of being surprised or concerned. If she was acting then she had done better than Veida and that took some doing. Unless, the thought intruded again, she had been warned that he had the snap.

"Do you think she might have been one of Ronnie's earlier girlfriends; that she might be connected with his death in some way?"

"Earlier girlfriends?" Bulman asked.

"Well, that snap is not new, is it? Unless the cleaning aged it." Anna tucked her legs under her. "I can't understand why I didn't find it myself when I sent the suit off. I went through the pockets as one does when sending off cleaning." She looked questioningly at Bulman.

Bulman shrugged. "I only found it because I slipped my hands in the jacket pockets to see how I looked in front of the mirror. It would have been easy to miss." But he was thinking that if she examined the pockets before sending the suit for cleaning she would most probably have turned the pockets out, and if she had done that she would know that he was lying. He had just thrown himself in at the deep end. "Thought of the name yet?"

"No. It's on the tip of my tongue, though." She had yet to make the coffee but seemed to be in no hurry to do so. She still held the snap but was now more casual about the whole thing. "Lovely face." She leaned forward to hand it back but added with a smile, "I suppose this photo is

187

really mine. But you can have it if it helps you with your enquiries."

He slipped it back in his pocket and reflected that if she knew he was lying, equally he knew that so was she. And yet they continued like a couple of innocents.

Anna made coffee and brought his over to him. When she was seated again he decided to go all the way. The only pretence now was in outwardly dealing with the situation, in knowing that each knew the other was lying.

"Ever come across a woman called Veida Ash?" As he watched he thought he saw the barest twitch of her lips.

"Veida Ash? I certainly don't know of anyone of that name but it has a familiar ring to it as if I should know."

She is very good indeed, reflected Bulman. "There was a famous court case. You might have been in Germany at the time but East Germany was very much involved and it probably reached your press. The reason I thought you might just possibly have known her was because she was very much involved with the Stasi. Some of them worked with her. I know you suffered at the hands of the Stasi and therefore there is a link, if only tenuous."

Mention of suffering at the hands of the Stasi was the first thing that openly appeared to get to her. Anna cringed at the thought. She recovered but he could see the memory was very deep-rooted. She said with a slightly quivering voice, "If she worked with them I would hardly want to know her."

"She manipulated them. Some of them. She was far from being pro Stasi but she knew how to get to their weaknesses. She was a great corrupter and got some of them to work against their own political interests in return for a considerable financial gain."

He waited to see how Anna was taking this, but she seemed to have become withdrawn. He took a final gamble and drove in the wedge. "Of course, some of the trial was in camera, in secret, and I have to say that she did seem to be working with them politically as well. She had her bread buttered on both sides and betrayed quite a few Germans working against them."

Bulman wondered if he had gone too far. Anna was highly intelligent and might easily see his purpose. It might well depend on just how deep were her wounds from suffering at the hands of the Stasi. He stared at her, trying to seek a reaction and seeing nothing but a pale face with eyes that had glazed over to hide what was behind them.

It was some time before she responded and when she did it came in the form of a hand reaching out for her coffee. It was perfectly steady as she lifted the cup to her lips. And over the rim of the cup she shot him a cold-blooded look that chilled him.

Chapter Sixteen

The soullessness of her stare unsettled him. He had met more than his fair share of vicious criminals, murderers, rapists, some of whom were extremely frightening, but this was different. Her expression was empty yet somehow totally chilling and he could not be sure whether it was directed at him or the space in front of her. But it got to him as nothing else had.

For a short time he was rooted to his chair and yet Anna, still transmitting a terrifying warning through her ice cold gaze, was quietly sipping at her coffee as if part of her functioned normally and part was detached into some horror story. What Bulman briefly felt then was terror and his inclination was to get out fast, but he had to know what had caused her sudden switch – whatever the outcome.

As quickly as she had gone into her chilling mode she snapped out of it. She now gazed at him as if she had been in some sort of trance and had come to, not knowing what had happened. The cup shook in the saucer and she quickly put the coffee down. He thought he could detect a faint band of moisture below her hairline. Whatever had seized her now left her depleted and seemingly bewildered.

"Are you all right?" he asked.

As she looked at him her expression was quite different and warm. She offered an apologetic smile. "I'm sorry. I don't know what happened but mention of the Stasi sometimes does strange things to me."

"Was it that bad?"

"You'll never know. It is impossible for people who have

not suffered at their hands to have any idea what it was like. I'm sorry," she said again. "Let's drop the subject."

But he was convinced she knew Veida, whatever Veida's connection with the Stasi. And then it flashed through Bulman's mind that one of the men Veida had had killed in prison by proxy was believed to have been ex-Stasi; one of those who had gone on the run at the first sign of danger when the wall came down. Bulman had stirred things up and knew he would have to be extra careful. He thought that this might be a good time to leave but when he suggested it she implored him to stay a little longer.

He was convinced that he had triggered some kind of attack on her and that she needed time to readjust herself before letting him go. But conversation was never quite the same after that, and in spite of both their efforts, matters drifted until it verged on the painful. In the end he had to go and she realized that he must.

He went into the bedroom to get his old suit and swung it over his shoulder. She offered to ring for a taxi for him and he agreed to that. When the taxi arrived she wanted to come down to see him off, and he guessed she was merely hoping to hear him give the taxi driver an address so he agreed and she went down with him.

Before he got into the cab they gave each other a peck on the cheek, as if everything was back to normal but it was not. He gave his old address to the driver knowing Anna could hear him and also knowing that she knew he would change it as soon as he was on the move. He didn't know why she bothered as he was carrying what he assumed to be a directional bug on him. The association between the two had gone into a crazy dimension yet neither wanted to terminate for similar reasons, even though their positions were now clear.

He gave her a friendly wave from inside the cab and she blew him kisses in a way which made it difficult for him to recall that utterly chilling moment upstairs. Once the cab rounded the corner he sat back and tried to recover; it had all been quite a strain. After a while he tapped on the dividing window and asked to be taken to Charing Cross Station.

Anna went back to her apartment angry with herself. She poured another coffee and flung herself down on to a chair and swore in German for some minutes. It did not make her feel any better. Bulman had come more into the open but so had she, and she had known by his rigid expression that she had revealed too much of herself. At least she had learned something of him; Veida was right, he was canny and far from stupid. He had shown himself to be bold too, and in a back-handed way she had respect for him.

She wondered if it was true what he said about Veida and then realized that was exactly what he wanted her to think. Just the same, Veida was getting too bossy and one thing Anna had never liked nor would tolerate, was authority.

She finished her coffee, collected the cups and took them through to the kitchen. Returning to the lounge she went to the window and pulled the net aside to gaze down into the street. She was far less confined to the apartment than she had led Bulman to believe, but for various reasons she spent more time indoors than she wanted because she had to be careful. She lacked a real friend to talk to, but that would have to wait.

As she gazed down she saw a man standing in a doorway across the street. And suddenly he looked straight up at her windows. She stiffened as she saw him, and then as he changed position and looked up again she got a better view. She let go of the flimsy curtain and fell back, reeling against the wall, her face ashen. "No, no," she moaned. "It can't be. It can't be." She stared at the window as if she wanted to break it, and then the soulless expression that Bulman had seen returned, only now he might have interpreted it as murderous.

*   *   *

192

Bulman went into the toilets at Charing Cross Station and found himself a cubicle. He produced a penknife from his old suit which he had anticipated he might need, took off his trousers and sat on the seat so he could get at the turn-ups of the trousers. He picked away carefully at the thread with the smallest blade until he could slip the bug out.

It was little bigger than a quartz watch battery and just as flat. He held it in the palm of his hand and wondered what to do with it. He could only think that Anna herself must have sewn it in, once it was back from express cleaning; she had done a very good job. He put his trousers back on and went out into the station forecourt.

His problem was that if he destroyed the bug whoever was picking up the signals would report it to Anna. She would then know that he had found it and would realize that he had expected it all along. Would that lead to open warfare, and all the big guns were on her side, or would they both continue the pretence while still trying to extract knowledge from each other? It was a crazy situation but she could claim she knew nothing about the bug.

He did not know what the range of the bug was, but guessed it would not be all that much which meant someone was reasonably close to pick up the signals. He got on the end of the taxi queue and as it was now nudging rush hour he had a long wait. When he finally climbed in he asked for Waterloo Station, which produced a look of disgust from the driver as it would have been far quicker by underground, and once seated pulled out the bug and pushed it down the side of the seat. He got out at Waterloo and went down the escalator to the underground and caught a train back to Charing Cross. From there he took the most devious route back to Jacko's place.

At one of the underground stations he changed at he took time out to make a phone call to Freda Curtis, hoping she might still be at the office. She was and she had some photo-copies to show him, and for the third day running he arranged lunch with a lady for the following day; this time he was host.

193

He got back to the house late to find the place empty. Both Jacko and Connie had gone. He checked over the house; there was no note and the hired car was missing from the garage. There was nothing he could do but wait and hope for the best, but it was disturbing. He had great faith in Jacko and had there been trouble he would have expected to see signs of it; Jacko was not the type to go quietly.

Bulman poured himself an early drink and sat down to watch the five-forty ITN news. One of the last items was the discovery of an abandoned car near Newbury, which police thought might be connected with a triple murder at a small country town in Somerset. Put like that it sounded terrible. There had been only one murder and that was by the German who so ruthlessly killed the driver presumably supplied by Benny Walker. The others had been self-defence. There was no mention of who the men were or of what nationality or motive, except that they appeared to be gangland killings.

Listening to it like that made everything unreal, completely detached from what had actually happened and as though it was happening all over the place. Perhaps it was.

Bulman was in this mood of cynicism when he heard the sound of a car drawing up outside. He went to the window to see a strange car turning into the short drive and then it was out of sight at the side of the house as somebody opened the garage. There was no point in waiting. He went to the internal garage door to find Jacko and Connie collecting parcels from the boot.

"Give us a hand," Jacko called out. "We've changed the car and have been shopping to cheer Connie up. Haven't we, love?"

Bulman went to help. "Why didn't you leave a bloody note?" he yelled at Jacko. "I've been worried sick."

"Now you know what it feels like. We've bought you a

194

pressie to put the smile back on your face. Come on, let's get in."

They off-loaded the parcels in the lounge, most of them containing clothes for Connie. Seeing Bulman's thunderous look Jacko said, "She was bored silly. I took her out. Anyway, I thought it best to hand the car back in and buy a second-hand job from a mate of mine, which I'll trade in once this caper is over. And here's a bottle of single malt."

Connie went off to make some tea, knowing the men needed to talk. The outing had obviously done her good and Bulman begrudgingly conceded that it was the right thing to do, especially to change the car which had been hired too near to the spot where the other one had been found by the police.

Only when Connie was out of the way did Jacko remark on the suit. "Almost fits you. That one of Walsh's?"

"You know it is. Smart eh?"

"I hope you checked it for bugs." Jacko sounded worried.

"Of course I did. It was in the turn-up. I hooked it out and left it in a cab. Couldn't think of anything else to do with it."

"So it won't be long before she knows that you found it and ditched it. Well that will bring it all out into the open."

"It's already out in the open."

Jacko stared at Bulman in amazement. "So what is her reaction to that?"

"We're both pretending everything is normal. We need to keep in touch."

Jacko could not believe what he heard. "You think this is a game or something? If she planted a bug on you she has a hell of a lot to hide. I don't under-stand you."

"Not many people do. If I don't maintain contact I won't be able to take her to dinner and you won't be able to

195

break into her apartment. You'd better line up a creeper with Benny Walker."

"Don't you think she'll be expecting it, in view of what you say?"

"Maybe. But I doubt that she'll leave a reception committee for you. She wouldn't do it on her own doorstep."

"You seem pretty sure. It's me in there you're talking about. I'm the one taking the risks."

"I think she's in too deep to take that kind of stupid risk."

"You mean you think she topped Walsh?"

"How can I know? But she's in there in some way that is far from being as innocent as his mistress. There are more issues than the death of one randy MP here. And I believe Veida Ash is up to the collar of her prison uniform in it."

"Veida Ash? Oh yes, the MI6 bird inside. You've met so many people lately I'm losing touch."

"That my job. Meeting people and tucking them away if they're guilty."

"What about Germany? You said we would have to go."

"I'm not so sure that we need to now. We'll wait and see. It might depend on what you find at Anna's place."

"You've both declared open war and still believe we'll find anything? Sometimes you're just not real, Bulman."

Bulman winked at him. "You might find what she wants you to find and that might be informative. Anyway, I'm having lunch with Freda Curtis tomorrow and depending on what I find out then will depend on when I contact Anna again."

Connie brought the tea in as Jacko said, "It's bloody marvellous, isn't it? You get paid to lunch with all the birds and I get landed with the driving and hardware jobs, and supply the safe house free of charge."

"I get free Saville Row suits, too," Bulman said.

"Well I hope you found the right bug and not the one they expected you to find. You'd better get out of that suit

196

and let me look." Jacko noted Bulman's expression and knew he'd had the last word, but it was far from funny, they both knew the banter was a release.

He took Freda to Simpson's, having been lucky enough to reserve a table by telephone. He got there early so that he could escort her in and also it gave him a chance to weigh up whether or not he had company. As far as he could see he was not being followed and unless someone was chasing round London after a taxi with a directional bug in it, Anna would long since have known that her attempt to find where he was staying had failed; Jacko had found no extra bug much to Bulman's relief.

Freda arrived carrying a small document case and almost her first words were, "That suit is just like one of Ronnie's. The dark grey looked well on him." She appeared to be quite startled to see it.

It was not until they were seated that he said, "It is Ronnie's. My own suit was getting so shabby that I couldn't refuse the offer to borrow this one."

"But who on earth . . .? Not Anna Brenning?" This possibility seemed to worry her considerably.

"You know her? I somehow didn't think you would know his mistresses; I thought he might keep them tucked away from business."

"He did when he could. But many were moving in the same social and business circles, friends of friends of his, wives and daughters of friends. It's not that easy to be careful with a man like that. But you obviously know her." Her tone was almost accusing with a touch of resentment.

Bulman inclined his head in acknowledgement. "I am investigating the background to his murder. She would be one of those on the top of the list."

"You mean you suspect her but took her up on the offer of one of Ronnie's suits? You must have become very close."

Bulman gazed across at what was becoming an ever

lovelier face, and could detect the recent pressure she was suffering from the dark smudges under her eyes which themselves seemed full of pain. Freda's world had been turned upside down and he was not helping at all at the moment. He should have been more thoughtful, and then, to justify himself he said, "Freda, my suit is in tatters and I can't get back to my own place to get another. I haven't the time to shop."

"Why can't you get back?"

He may as well tell her. "There are people waiting there who would like to lay a hand or two on me. I'm in hiding, you know that or you'd be able to contact me. I had to look fair to decent with you here. How well do you know Anna Brenning?"

"You're asking me? Shouldn't I be asking you? You are obviously on extremely good terms with her."

Bulman felt wretched; the last thing he wanted to do was to hurt her, life was difficult enough for her as it was. "You know how devious I can be. I once posed as a Board of Trade Inspector."

Her expression softened a little and then she smiled. "Do you go through life being devious? How would anyone know when you are genuine?"

They ate for a while, the restaurant was full. Bulman was sorry that a degree of suspicion had crept in with Freda and he pondered on how best to deal with it. He could not fob her off with lies. She was already wary of him and it was a situation he wanted to stop. He needed her trust. When they had finished the entrée he said, "It is important to me to get to know Anna for no other reason than I think she knows far more than she has told anyone, including the police with whom I am in touch. I do realize it might be difficult for you to understand."

"I do understand." She held her head high and at the moment he could not determine whether or not she accepted what he said. Freda continued, "Anna is different from the rest. The only one of his women who was actually a high

198

class whore. In spite of his many faults it was not just sex or conquest with him; he did really like the women he slept with, but it never lasted. He sometimes used call girls but Anna did not fit into the usual mould." She dabbed her lips with a napkin. "So far as I know he never set anyone up in an apartment before. Part of his pleasure was the deception which often bordered on the downright dangerous when it came to being found out. In his affairs he remained a boy, never grew up and that led to all sorts of problems."

"Murder?"

She shook her head. "I don't know. I'm beginning to realize that I hardly knew him at all. I've never known what to make of Anna. There was something strange about the whole sordid business."

"Sordid?

"Don't you think that a married man with children setting up a woman in a private apartment is sordid? How does she come across to you?"

"I wish I could answer that. There's more to her than meets the eye, but whether it's good or bad is very difficult to say. Can't we forget her for the duration of this lunch?"

"Not while you wear that suit. It's a constant reminder." And then she appeared to relent. "Do let me know how you get on with her."

Bulman smiled at the fragile offer of peace. "I will. You'd like me to find out something really bad about her, wouldn't you?"

"Yes." The eyes had softened with the remark, as if the wish was double-edged. "She simply does not fit in with the rest. If you'll order coffee I'll produce what I have."

Bulman looked round for the waiter as Freda produced the document case and removed some papers. She cleared a little space and laid them on the table.

"You may have made notes of some of these, but here is a fairly comprehensive list of those companies and people he met during his last trip to Russia. He did some very good business deals. And there is nothing in this lot which

199

in any way looks subversive. The Russians strike a hard bargain, they have to with the country in a such a poor state, but he would not enter into anything that would not yield substantial profit to the company. And here are photocopies of snaps of some of the people he met, most of them taken after a boozy lunch by the look of them. He often brought back photographs and those that were worthy, as you have seen, grace the visitors waiting room. There's the Queen and the Duke of Edinburgh there, and Prince Charles. He only met top people."

Bulman gathered them up and slowly went through them. They were typical business groups, the Russian and the British sticking out from each other as if they wore invisible flags. Freda was right; there was a booziness about some of them, as everyone knew, some Russians could be prodigious drinkers; he himself had had sessions with Russians which should have killed them.

The photocopies had come out quite well. There was little to hold his attention because he knew none of the faces, they mainly comprised of Walsh posing with this group or that. And then he saw a face he knew.

He stared at it for so long that Freda leaned across the table and touched his hand. "Is there something wrong?"

He held it up to her. "Do you know this woman?"

She held the copy steady by placing a hand over his. "No. She's rather lovely. Why, do you?"

The snap was of two men and two women, the one Bulman referred to was standing next to Walsh but without actual physical contact as far as he could see. The other woman was older with very pleasant features but she merely served to enhance the younger woman.

"I found a snapshot of her. Just head and shoulder. Same woman."

"Where did you find it?" Freda asked.

"In this suit." Bulman tapped the pocket and then produced it from an inside pocket. "No doubt that it's the same woman, wouldn't you say?"

200

Freda took the snap from him. "Without a doubt. In his pocket? He never mentioned her, but for that matter he did not talk about the others either. Sometimes he had amusing little anecdotes which he would relate about some of the trips, but I don't recall him mentioning anything about that trip." She handed it back. "You seem to attach some importance to it. Do you know who it is?"

"No. I've been trying to find out. Have you any idea?"

"None. If you found it in his pocket Anna might know?"

"I'm convinced she does, but she played it cool and said the snap was of some Yugoslav film star." He did not tell her of Veida Ash, it would take too long and would complicate matters. "Are all the companies in here," he tapped the papers, "bone fide?"

"As far as I know. They are well known anyway."

"Tell me, how did you meet Anna?"

"Ronnie trusted me. He had to trust someone. He gave me the address in case of emergency. Strangely, he never gave me the telephone number, told me it was ex-directory even to me. I never understood that. So there were a couple of times I had to contact him there. He introduced me to her but left me to assume the connection. The only difficulty I had with that was the one I've already given you. She somehow didn't fit in. While he went over some documents I had brought along she gave me her life story, but I got the impression that she had rehearsed it until she knew it by heart and that it was important that other people knew it. She's clever and good-looking but still not his type."

"Did she strike you as cold, warm, capable of killing someone?"

"Why are you asking me? You should know the answers already."

"I'm just taking the opportunity to get someone else's opinion."

"I protected Ronnie as best I could. My view might be highly biased."

"It doesn't matter. Did she scare you in any way?"

"Yes. I caught her looking at Ronnie with an expression I would describe as scarey. It scared me anyway. Just for a second or two. Maybe she needed one in Germany but I didn't care for the fact that she had a gun in her handbag. I had only a glimpse of it but it was there. I would say she would know how to use it too. Am I being bitchy?"

"Not if you saw a gun; that would worry anybody. Did he seem scared of her?"

"Ronnie could hide his feelings." Freda locked her fingers together and twisted them as she struggled to answer. "No. I don't think he was scared. But somehow they did not act like lovers to me. You'd expect some little giveaway, some endearment, but I saw and heard nothing that convinced me they were emotionally close."

Bulman was thoughtful for some time before saying, "You seem to be the only person who has had the advantage of seeing the two together, and you obviously made good use of the time you spent there. It poses the question doesn't it?"

"What question?"

"If they were not emotionally close, then what was their relationship? What purpose was it serving?" Bulman smiled nervously. "It worries me sick to say this, but I'm beginning to see why she feels so comfortable in the apartment. And that makes me scarey too. Keep away from her, whatever temptation to see her might crop up. She might get round to wondering what you know."

Chapter Seventeen

Anna Brenning had a more anxious day than usual. She was angry that Bulman had detected the bug, which had floated in and out of range until the transponder was driving its operator mad. In the end they gave up and the bug still travelled around London.

Anna was not sure what to do about Bulman. Her gut reaction was to kill him, but that would take planning and would ultimately get more people involved. And there were enough people already stalking around, in Anna's opinion.

In a perverse way she liked playing with him. He was good company and life, at the moment and in the foreseeable future, was lonely. It was the way things had to be until the dust was well and truly settled. Yet matters could not be allowed to drift. There would come a point when she was quite sure that Bulman would have to go, and anyone who was working with him.

She was unable to contact Veida; it was a rule. It was left to Veida to contact who she felt she should but she never used the phone needlessly. There was always the fear that whatever her influence in prison, and it spread far and wide, whatever her ability to bribe and corrupt, and some were making a small fortune out of her, some things were beyond her control like staff changes and the fickleness of other prisoners who at the moment purported to be her friends.

She could not argue with Veida's strategy. It was sound and Veida had the money and the muscle. But there were aspects she could never discuss with Veida, whatever their contact, and one of those was the man she had seen in the street the previous day. That had unsettled her as nothing else could. She had not seen him since and began to wonder if she had imagined it, which is what she would prefer to believe.

The man she had seen was dead. She had killed him herself so she knew that he was dead. And yet, just for those few seconds he had stood there staring up at the windows. She did not think she had been seen and by the time she returned to the window he had gone. But it had been a tremendous jolt. She found it impossible not to go back to the window from time to time and it was becoming something of an obsession. For so usually a controlled person she found this confusing. Anna was not given to fears. She had suffered enough and had survived with an unshakable outlook from which her enemies would back away as fast as they could.

She poured herself a glass of German white wine and placed her hand round the chilled glass. The pull of the window was strong and she fought it off for a while but in the end capitulated mainly because, at the moment, there was nothing else to do.

She approached from the side, almost afraid to look, and that in itself was an unwelcome anachronism; fear was something she had discarded a long time ago and its return was disturbing. At first she tried to see through the net but the view was too blurred. Slowly she pulled a corner of the net back and just stood there, head back, and then she inched forward and scanned the spot where he had been before. And where he stood now.

She drew in her breath and could feel the thump of her heartbeat. He wore a hat and he was not looking up but it was the same man. He was standing under the canopy of the huge porch of a house almost opposite, with his hands in his pockets and legs splayed as she remembered he used to do. He had never managed to break the habit, winter or summer. He was like a wax dummy, unmoving, showing no interest in those who passed in the street just below him.

It occurred to her that she was as stationary as he. With the net held back she just stood there peering down hoping he would shift position or lift his head so that she could get a better view. The only thing that moved was a slight tremor in the hand that held the curtain. But inwardly she was in turmoil, at a loss for what to do. As she came to grips with the situation, as she gradually accepted that what she saw was not a ghost, she slowly calmed down. She could think better like this and realized what she had to do.

She let the curtain go very slowly, watching the man all the time until he was blurred again by the net. She went into the study where one wall was covered with books on open shelves and bent low to get the index volume of Encyclopedia Britannica which she removed and opened to reveal a .22 automatic pistol in a cut out section, and above it in its own nest, a silencer. She attached the one to the other, checked the magazine and that there was a round in the chamber, took the safety catch off and placed the gun in a shoulder bag she took from a collection on a wardrobe shelf in the bedroom. She put on a coat, left the flat with the long strap bag hung over her shoulder, and took the lift down.

By now she was back to normal and thinking very coolly. On arrival at the ground floor she did not step out into the street immediately but stood to one side of the porch. She was badly positioned to get a good view of the house across the street which was not precisely opposite so stepped forward.

She gazed straight at the spot where she had seen the man. He was no longer there. Still controlled she stepped into the street and walked slowly along to get a better view, should he have stepped back further under the canopy. He had gone. People were still on the street, passing by but there was nobody who resembled the man she had seen.

Dusk was falling quite quickly now, street lights flaring

out of the increasing gloom, and she told herself that that was probably the reason he had gone. But it was certainly not yet dark. She went the length of the street and back again on the other side but by now she well knew that he had gone, perhaps even into one of the houses, but it was impractical to start knocking on doors and would raise too much curiosity.

She was reluctant to return to the apartment, having the illogical feeling that if she did he would immediately reappear. The episode was unsettling. As she stood under a lamppost wondering what best to do, a man passed by and gave her a lecherous smile and she realized she must look like a tart, and that was something she had never been, although she had conjured the image that she had. The whole stupid business had left her unsettled and perhaps that was the object. She returned to her apartment anxious and frustrated.

When she put the pistol back in its hiding place she saw that she had left the cut out volume of Britannica lying open on the floor, and this lack of professionalism made her very angry. She had been thrown off balance and that hadn't happened for a very long time.

When she eventually sat down after pouring herself another glass of wine she was amazed at her own stupidity. Had she really intended to shoot someone so close to home on the London streets? The possibility unnerved her more than anything else. She had acted like a novice and she was far from being that. Sight of the man had got to her. She briefly considered calling in help, and there was plenty available, but recognized it as a personal problem, and one she would not like to get back to Veida. She must deal with it herself.

When the telephone rang she started, spilling her drink. She gazed at the ringing instrument as if it must be a wrong number. Like someone who gazes at an unopened letter trying to work out who might have sent it when all they had to do was to open it, she gazed at the ringing phone

206

as if it would supply the answer without her touching it. And then she realized that she was afraid to answer it.

This provoked her into moving. To move back into a life of fear was unacceptable, she had hardened herself too much for that. Switching off all feeling she went to the phone and picked up the receiver. She offered no name or number but simply said, "Hello." At first there was no reply but she knew someone was there. "Hello," she repeated. "Speak up or I will put the phone down."

"You mustn't do that," the caller said in German. "Is that Karen Brandt?"

"There's nobody of that name here," she replied in English. "You must have the wrong number." She had difficulty in keeping her hand still and knew she should hang up but there was something she needed to know. "Who is that?"

"You know who. You haven't forgotten your own language at least. But your English was always good, Karen."

"My name is Anna Brenning. You are obviously mixing me up with someone else." Still she did not hang up.

"I know that is your adopted name. Confused me for some time. Don't you think we should meet?"

"Whatever for? I don't even know you. Is this a joke of some kind? If it is it's in bad taste. Will you please go."

There was a dry brittle laugh. "Why don't you hang up?" Now he spoke in English, almost as good as Anna's. "But you need to know don't you? You can't get rid of me until you're sure. No, it's no joke, Karen. You owe me. To say the least. What about it?"

He was right. She did have to know, otherwise she would have finished the call after the first few words. What was bursting to come was impossible to keep in. The question was choking her yet she did not want to ask it because she already knew the answer and dreaded its confirmation.

When she did speak there was little of the usually assured Anna in the shakiness of the words. "You can't be Rudi; that's impossible."

There was a long silence then a sound she did not recognize until she realized it was a throaty chuckle coming down the line. He was laughing at her and for a time she did not know how to handle it. "You'd better believe it little sister. I'll be in touch."

But before he had finished she spat out, "Second time lucky, Rudi. I'll get you for this."

He caught the words and brought the phone back to his mouth. "You'll have to make a much better job of it this time, you murderous bitch. Go see a shrink, Karen. I'll be in touch."

She could hear the burr of the dialling tone but could not put the phone down, her hand was gripping it so tightly. She had to quell her rage and come to terms with the horrific shock before she could move. Gradually she calmed down and her features went through a myriad of changes to finish rock hard in a blanched face. In the end she put down the phone quite gently.

At last she knew for certain. She was now satisfied that there had been no bizarre impersonation. Although she had never had a really decisive view of him she was now in no doubt. The voice was a giveaway, and his English which had always been almost as good as hers. And the stance was his, as if he was imitating some American gangster, but he had often stood like that. She did not know how it had happened but it had. He had probably been looking for her ever since.

She sat down again and realized the problem had to be tackled, and she was left in no fear of how he might physically hurt her, she was too clever and ruthless for him, but he could do her irreparable harm if he decided to open his mouth. He would damage himself if he did, but it might not matter to him any more. And she had better action it before Veida got to know. It was a complication

208

from the past unconnected with what she was doing now. She needed help.

Bulman and Jacko went through the papers and photographs that Freda had provided and worked long into the night. Jacko had moved Connie into the bedroom which had a television set to stave off her boredom. She had started to talk of returning to her agency; it was the only work she knew how to do to make money and she was missing it. Meanwhile she went on the Home Office bill, which would have incensed Edward Marshall but he would never know.

When they had finished, and many cups of black coffee later, the two men, without ties and jackets by now, leaned wearily back in their chairs and decided that it might all have turned out to be a waste of time. They had names of people, companies, bare details of some of the deals, but none of it meant anything. The only pointer was the photograph of the girl and they both agreed that if they could identify her a few answers might pop out of the woodwork.

Bulman had done his best to find the answer. Those who knew, like Veida and Anna, were not going to tell him and the police in the form of Walter Beatty did not know. Maybe they all knew.

"It's the Russian Mafia," said Jacko, having difficulty in keeping awake in the too warm room.

They had been through this before. Bulman was not against the idea except that he could not conceive, on the character building he had managed regarding Ronnie Walsh, that whatever else he might have been, an out and out crook was not one of them. They had talked it over but periodically Jacko would again raise it.

Involvement did not have to be conscious. The Russian Mafia had become all powerful. As Jacko pointed out, they had recently shot Vladislav Listyev, a campaigning Russian journalist who was loved by most, and whose killing had provoked President Yeltsin to sack the police chief Vladimir

209

Pankratov for not getting the organization under control. It was running wild. But if Walsh had somehow got himself involved, in what form had it taken? He'd had boards of directors to contend with. It was difficult to see him accepting shady deals in the face of shareholders and the other directors. He would not have entered into anything that might have adversely affected his companies. So the idea lay inviting but stagnant.

"When are you taking Anna Brenning out?" Jacko yawned, surprised he was still thinking ahead.

"I'll ring her in the morning."

"You know you're sticking your head right on the block?"

"It's already on the block. We're jockeying with each other. We both know it. Judging when to stop is the name of the game."

Jacko shook his head. "Listen, matey, you are two different types entirely. You have different concepts of how to play the game. You think you can just break off when you feel there is nothing more to be gained, that you have all you need. That won't be her outlook. She'll put a bullet in your head when she thinks you are too close and too dangerous to let live."

"You sound convinced that she killed Walsh."

"It looks more like it every day. I'd like to meet this ice maiden."

Bulman tried to grin but was too tired. He said, "You'd have a lot in common. I must try to see her at least once more. If I do it on public ground it should be safe enough."

"I wouldn't bank on it. Look, I need to know when this meeting is likely to take place. I have to see Benny Walker about a creeper."

Jacko called on Benny Walker after just a few hours sleep. He did not ring because of the strong possibility of Benny refusing to see him. This time he entered by the small

210

reception office and the over-made-up receptionist got through on the intercom. He stood close to the inner door so that he could hear Benny speak.

When he went in Jacko could see that Benny had his central desk drawer open and guessed that Benny had a weapon handy. He sat in the chair he had used before and greeted Benny affably. He pointed to the wall behind Benny and observed, "I see you've got another mug-shot up to cover the bullet hole. You should have left it as part of your image."

"What do you want?" Benny spat out; he had not forgotten his humiliation.

"I told you when I was here. I want a creeper to break in a place for me. I want a refined job otherwise I'd do it myself. Once inside he can hang around while I go through the place. I just want a look round, no stealing. I just want him to get me in and to lock up again after us. Easy."

"They all sound easy. What will you be looking for?"

"That's none of your business. If it wasn't easy I wouldn't be going myself. Now do we do business or not? And you can charge a bit more for the bullet hole and the ruined photograph. No hard feelings."

When Bulman rang asking her to come out to lunch with him Anna was in two minds. It would help just to pass the time away but she really needed to know, now more than ever, just exactly what he knew and where he was aiming. She could put the pressure on him to find out whether or not he intended to opt out of the case, or did he have enough to continue; if he did then she needed to know just how far he had got. Yelena's photograph was a real complication although she would not be generally known in this country, even in security circles. But he seemed to be intent on finding out and that needed stopping.

She agreed to see him but decided that one way or another this would be the last time. For various reasons she had not had him followed since their first meeting but now she arranged for Bulman to be followed from the point they were having lunch. It no longer mattered if he made an association, it was time for things to come to a head.

He took her to The Savoy where a lunch might be prolonged and where there were plenty of other people around them. He was glad then of the use of Ronnie Walsh's suit and she chided him about it as they met in reception. As they were shown to a table he was aware of the male head turning qualities Anna could exude without really trying and in a perverse sort of way he was quite proud of her company. They appeared to be a normal, well-dressed couple and Bulman could not help but suppress a smile at what people would think if they really knew what was being enacted under their innocent noses. Their chairs were pushed in and they smiled warmly at each other across the table. Bulman could not help but reflect on the possibility that in Anna's large crocodile handbag there might be a gun.

Eddie was tall and thin with shining, hungry eyes and looked as if he needed a square meal. He wore jeans and a sweater with a loose jacket over the top. He carried no apparent tools which was a plus so far as Jacko was concerned and had come highly recommended from Benny Walker. As unscrupulous as Benny was, he ran an efficient agency and with the type of client he had, some of them murderous, he could not afford to take the slightest risk with his recommendations. Both sides of the criminal divide relied on him. So Jacko had not quibbled at the price and had paid in cash up front.

They travelled by public transport because taxi drivers had a habit of remembering faces. On arrival at the flats Jacko made sure that none of Anna's friends were evident and he went up and down the street twice with Eddie by his side and just as vigilant.

"I don't like doing jobs I haven't cased myself. Rushed jobs like this are dodgy." Eddie was turning out to be a bit of a whinger.

"It's a straightforward job. The apartment is on its own floor. And the occupant is away. It's money for old rope."

The catch on the street door was no problem to Eddie, and Jacko had warned him about the TV scanner high in the porch so they wore caps and kept their heads down. Once inside the building they removed their caps. They went up the stairs to the top floor and approached Anna's door, made sure they were alone and that the lift was stationary, and then Jacko stood aside to give Eddie space to do his job. It was at that point that Eddie really went to work and produced the tools of his trade from various specially made pockets in his jacket. So far Jacko was impressed.

Eddie started to tackle the lock when the door gave way at his touch. Startled, he swiftly drew back. "The bloody thing's open," he whispered.

Jacko came forward and as Eddie finger-tipped the door further open they could both see the rough break in marks around the frame where it had been jemmied. It was a crude job and Eddie would probably have noticed at once had he expected it and was not concentrating on the lock itself.

Eddie stood back. "I don't like this. There might be someone in there."

Jacko nodded agreement and quickly considered his options. It was not in his nature to leave without having an answer so he drew out the Colt.

At the sight of the pistol Eddie recoiled. In a scared croak he said, "What's that for? Nobody said anything about shooters."

Jacko put a finger to his lips as he pushed the door further open. "I just want to make sure. You stay there."

"You've got to be kidding. I'm not operating with shooters. You're on your own, mate." And with that he

213

headed for the stairs and skipped down them as fast as he could.

It was difficult for Jacko to blame him. He stepped into the hall and then froze as he heard someone move.

Chapter Eighteen

Jacko stood with his back to the wall, pistol raised and with his free hand silently pushed the door to. He stood for some time trying to pick up a repeat of the sound he had heard. As he looked round the hall he could not miss the fact that the four doors leading off were all open.

Bulman had given him the layout of the apartment as he knew it, but he had not entered all the rooms during his visits. But Jacko knew sufficient to know that the door facing him was the lounge and he could see something of the furnishings through the partially open door. He could also see items scattered on the floor.

He crept to the nearest door and peered through the crack by the hinges. It was a toilet and was in a state of disarray with towels and brushes scattered on the floor. A tap was running. But he could see nobody. He crept past the lounge door to the next one which was a dining room, and when he peered beyond the door he could not but help notice that the chairs had been flung haphazardly around the room and crockery and silver was everywhere. He noticed that there was another door at the end, presumably leading to the kitchen. The fourth door led to a large bedroom, a guest room as Bulman had told him, and the main bedroom led off a small inner hall off the lounge. It was a very large sumptuous apartment.

The strange thing was that he had heard nothing since that first sound which had been difficult to define. To enter by the dining room meant stepping through a minefield of broken china and glass. He decided to try the lounge. Bulman had told him there was a study leading off the lounge and that would be a logical place to search. But someone had been there before him and was probably still there. The further absence of sound might mean he himself had been heard and someone was waiting.

He rolled round the door frame of the lounge door and slid along the wall with his back to it. He leaned across and pushed the door gently against the wall to make sure no one was behind it. He faced chaos. Someone had gone berserk. The place was vandalized beyond all reason. Chairs were slashed, ornaments broken, carpets ripped and curtains torn so savagely from their pelmets that they hung in tatters. Soft down was sprouting from the jagged holes in the chairs and settees and some of it floated in the air and he felt the irritation in his nose.

There were two other doors leading off, the one opposite led to the study, part of which he could see and presumably the other led to the small inner hall, off which was the main bedroom in which Bulman had tried the suit on. A study was a good place to start a search but he held out little hope of finding anything in this mess. Had someone been searching for something or was this out and out vandalism?

He heard a sound again. More distinctly this time and then the crashing of something being flung against a wall followed by the tinkle of glass. Was there a madman in the place? As the sound had come from the study Jacko took a circuitous route to it, keeping as close to the walls as he could. The destruction continued with occasional pauses, as if whoever was there was either resting a while or seeking something else to destroy.

Jacko silently released the safety catch on the gun and edged forward towards the door. As he reached it the silence descended as if someone had heard him but he had moved too quietly and was certain he had not been heard. On reaching the door he lowered himself to one knee and tried to pick up the location of whoever was in there. Because of the state of the damage and the obvious strength used for some of the heavier breakages, he assumed it was a man in the study. He did not think there was more than one. He eased his head forward.

There were papers and books everywhere, scattered haphazardly. Shelves had been cleared. By the window, his back turned to Jacko, stood a man in a dark suit who was holding what looked like a paperweight. He was gazing out of the window, his breathing was heavy and he seemed to have run out of steam or perhaps could find nothing else to destroy.

Jacko rose slowly and stepped forward avoiding the mess covering most of the floor. He said calmly, "I have a gun pointing at your back so don't do anything stupid."

There was little reaction at first, almost as if the man had been expecting it. And then, notwithstanding the threat, he turned slowly to face Jacko who was at once warned by the wild expression in two very blue eyes. He was well built, probably in his early thirties, with a thatch of blond hair. His features were quite firm but, to Jacko, there appeared to be a weakness about the mouth.

"Who are you?" asked Jacko.

"What has that got to do with you?"

"You're German?"

"I thought my English was better than that. Yes I'm German. What are you doing here? And why do you need a gun? I'm no danger to you."

Jacko gazed round the room. "You're a bloody danger to whoever lives here. What sort of madness is this, for God's sake? You've just about ruined everything."

"That was my intention. I haven't quite finished."

"But why?"

Jacko's presence seemed to have calmed the German down. He said, "It's easy for you to ask questions with a gun pointing at me. You can see what I've been doing here. The reason is none of your business. But you, why are you here, and with a gun? Do you intend to kill someone?"

The very attitude of the German convinced Jacko that

217

it was not the first time he had faced a gun. He was not panicking, was almost indifferent to the danger and was handling matters well.

"It's for self-protection. I mean, if you consider me part of the furniture I could end up like the rest of the stuff."

"I have no fight with you. You are obviously no friend of the occupant. You still haven't answered my question."

"I came to burgle the place. Make a few bob. But you've bloodywell ruined everything."

"I hope so. If you see anything I've missed please point it out to me and I will deal with it."

"You're a cool customer, although it's difficult to accept – seeing this lot. You must have a reason for all this. What's your name?"

"Rudi Brandt. You'd be wasting your time trying to trace me, if that is what you intend. I'm officially dead. A useful condition. And I do not use that name. But that is who I am. And what is your name, sir?"

This man is taking over, Jacko reflected quickly. He's good. He formed a respect for him in spite of the inexplicable damage he had caused. "I hold the gun," he replied, trying to regain the initiative. "I don't have to answer that. Do you know who lives here?"

"Oh, yes. Do you?"

"No, I just came on spec." He gazed round again at the massive destruction. It was pointless trying to go through the mess, it had been a wasted journey. He might just as well leave Rudi Brandt to it. "So who does live here?" He wanted to be sure that Brandt was not bluffing.

Brandt was unmoved at first, then his lips trembled as he tried to speak and it was clear that he was unexpectedly emotionally disturbed. He pulled himself together and replied quietly, "An assassin."

Jacko stared. What the hell was going on? He tried what he saw as black humour to see where it would lead. "You said you're officially dead. Is she the one who killed you?"

218

He was smiling, trying to make a rapport with the hope of gaining information.

"How do you know that a woman lives here, when you said your call was speculative? You were lying."

Jacko acknowledged his blunder. "I'm not the one on trial here, mate. I'm not the one who wrecked the place."

"Just the same I think you called here for another reason. Are you the police?"

"Toting a gun like this? Don't be ridiculous. Look, why don't we both get out of here and go and have a coffee together somewhere? Then we can straighten things out and decide what to do. We might find that we are on the same side."

Brandt considered this behind a blank face and then broke into a smile which changed his grim features completely. "That's a good idea. It could be useful to both of us."

Jacko was pleased. He lowered the gun but did not put it away. Brandt picked his way through the mess and came towards the door. He seemed much more relaxed altogether and Jacko thought he was about to offer his hand as he approached. Instead he raised the paperweight he was still holding and crashed it down on Jacko's head,

Jacko fell to his knees, half unconscious and fighting for his senses. But the weight crashed down once more and he collapsed in a heap on the mess around him, blood spreading through his hair. Brandt made no effort to take the gun but stepped over the body and entered the lounge. Quite calmly he looked around at his work of destruction without showing any emotion, but obviously satisfied, for he stepped carefully towards the door and left the apartment. He pulled the door to, which was the best he could do, and ran lightly down the stairs.

The lunch was getting them nowhere. Bulman and Anna trod the verbal gangplank but each was well practised in deception in different ways. He hinted that things were

219

getting too difficult and that he may have to give up on behalf of Walsh's family and return to an easier life. She did not believe him nor that he had ever met a member of the dead politician's family, which meant that he had been employed by someone else other than the police. And that narrowed it down to an unacceptable risk. She had guessed this some time ago but was now convinced.

Killing Bulman was not without it's complications, for it might raise other difficulties she did not want. Killing a philandering politician left motives pointing mostly one way, but an investigative ex-policeman was another matter. She was also certain that the reason for the lunch was so that the apartment could be searched. She could be wrong but Bulman would not turn down such an opportunity. She smiled at that. She glanced at the time.

Seeing this Bulman called for more coffee. He was worried about Jacko because the lunch, perhaps because the conversation had dragged a little, had not taken as long as he had hoped.

Anna said, "It has been so nice seeing you again. You are so stimulating. I shall miss our meetings."

Bulman was not sure how to take that so took the easier option. "Does that mean that this is our last meeting? Are you going away?"

"Yes. I need the break."

"To Germany?"

"I have many friends there. They will be good for me."

And then Bulman thought, what the hell, we're both lying our heads off and we both know it. Go in for broke, she thinks I think it anyway. Face her with it. "The same friends who supplied the alibi for you when you killed Walsh?"

He watched her glaze over and then came that terrible look he had seen before. For a few seconds he was scared but realized that if she was going she would deal with him first anyway. Anna would not leave dangerous loose ends around.

"They gave me an alibi because it was true – I was

220

with them at the time. But you weren't joking, were you?"

"Alibis can be bought. The old style American gangster thrived on bought alibis. Probably still does. That and intimidation. But it wasn't you who paid for them was it? It was Veida with her multimillions. And that makes you the hired hand, Anna. Expendable."

She seemed about to argue the point but reached the same conclusion as he. What was the further point of pretence. "Whatever you think those alibis are solid. They are unshakable. Does your police think they can break them?"

"I doubt it. It is not something they would discuss with me. I would hazard a guess though, that they are pretty sure it was you. One mistress too many; a nice touch, Anna. A fair enough motive bearing in mind the women he had. I could be cynical and say they would have killed him one way or the other the way he was going. But you were never his mistress were you?"

The remark seemed to get to her. She froze over and said almost petulantly, "Don't be absurd. You think he set me up in such luxury for nothing?"

Bulman was pleased with her reaction. He smiled widely. "I don't think he set you up at all. I think you set him up. I was always curious as to why you had no apparent fears of being kicked out of the apartment. You seemed to be comfortable there. You were not afraid of anything going wrong." He kept her waiting for the accusation and quietly finished his coffee before saying, "The apartment is yours. You set him up. Veida's money again? Or perhaps not this time. Perhaps you have another source."

She stared at him icily. "No wonder you left the police. Or were you thrown out? You have some crazy ideas."

"It was a bit of both actually. But I didn't leave because of my crazy ideas. Come on, Anna, what's happened? Just now we were being straight with each other, well sort of, so what's suddenly gone wrong? Because I'm right about

221

the apartment? That's upset you more than my accusation of murder. What am I missing?"

"One or two screws in your head, I should think. The apartment is not mine."

"Who's then? Veida's?"

"Why don't you ask her?"

Anna said it in such a way as to convince Bulman that Veida would deny owning it, but the fact that she referred him to her made him feel that in this, Veida was not involved. And it was interesting that she no longer denied involvement with Veida. He might as well go all the way. "Does it belong to the so-called Russian Mafia, then?" As her expression closed down he knew that he had scored.

Her nostrils slightly dilated as she controlled her breathing. She had lost a little colour and she was frigid, just the faintest tremor of her fingertips and she swiftly withdrew her hands below the table. It was a little while before she answered. "I am German. What on earth would I be doing with Russian gangsters?"

"Veida's German too, well her parents were, and she deals with anybody if there's money in it. I'm almost beginning to feel sorry for you."

"Perhaps you should feel sorry for yourself." She was speaking her mind again and it sounded deadly.

"Why? Have you arranged for my execution too, before you trot off to Germany to prove you didn't do it? That was impressive shooting on Walsh, by the way. Too good really. The police knew at once that the shots were unusually accurate. A hit man's accuracy, or a hit woman." He smiled. "A hit person these days. How ridiculous that sounds. A hired killer. An assassin. You do your work well. I'm giving you the benefit of the doubt that you were not personally responsible for the cock-up when Connie Smith's sister was mutilated by mistake. And the other cock-up in Somerset. But you know all this. So why don't you tell me the name of the woman in the photograph?"

Mention of the woman helped Anna regain her senses.

222

Outwardly she had never lost her composure, in fact she had gone ice cold and would have liked to kill him then, but she had no trouble fighting that impulse and now he had revealed his own weak link. He would never find out the name of the woman in the snapshot. He was quite right to think it would explain a lot but there would be havoc if he ever found out, and that would certainly be his death warrant if one had not already be served.

She smiled now and Bulman realized he had lost in some way. "I told you," she said. "She's a Yugoslav actress. I still can't think of her name but then I'm not a cinema goer."

"No, I suppose it would interfere with your work. Assassination is a very serious business. Does it pay well these days?" He was getting flippant, losing direction. He had satisfied himself on many things, that she had killed Walsh for instance. But there was still a lot missing. There were so many factors unanswered and he felt the woman in the snapshot was the key. Maybe he should take Beatty up on his offer and circulate the snap. But his gut feeling was that it would make no difference, the answer did not lay in this country. It had all started in Russia and of that he was certain.

"Are you going to try to get the police to stop me leaving the country?" She cut across his thoughts.

"That's a matter for them. They might be glad to get rid of you. But don't worry, they're keeping a friendly eye on you even as I speak; well if it's not you then it's me. Which might make it difficult for your executioner." He gazed round the room and gave a man a few tables away a wink.

"They are watching us now?" She did not realize he had embarrassed a perfect stranger but the bluff knocked her confidence a little.

"You're the professional. You should know. You want me to have a word with them?"

"No. It's of no matter." She glanced at the time again. "I must go. Do we shake hands? For the last time? I really

223

will miss you, George. You are such an unusual man. It's a pity."

"Just one last question," he said as she was about to rise. "If you weren't Walsh's lover then what were you to him?"

She smiled sweetly, back in control. "I never said I wasn't his lover. That was you."

Bulman rose as she did. "I don't think you are any man's lover; or have ever been."

The table separated them, but she was near to coming round to strike him then, before realizing that was what he wanted in full view of other diners; witnesses to her violent nature.

She smiled again instead. "Nearly, George. You do go on trying." They walked out together as if nothing had happened and she took his arm completing the deception. Outside they both asked for taxis and without another word between them climbed in their separate cabs and went out into the Strand.

Bulman had intended to go part way, perform the usual evasive tactics and then go home. Connie had been left on her own. Instead he told the driver to take him to New Scotland Yard and took pot luck on Walter Beatty being there. And he was.

"I seem to be lucky in catching you, Wally," said Bulman as he sat down in the Chief Superintendent's office.

"No," replied Beatty. "Since my promotion I've been virtually desk bound. Not like the old days when we were roaming the seamier night spots. But I am busy so I hope you've got something for me."

"I've just had lunch with Anna Brenning. She's a paid assassin. She murdered Walsh."

"That's only news if you can prove it. We've been satisfied that it was her for some time. Her alibis, and there are a few, are tight. She stayed with people, wined and dined with people, met people. Her name is on the flight sheet both ways. Her passport carries the entry and exit stamps.

There is an awful lot to break down and meanwhile she's watertight. Unless you've got something that will break those alibis, cheerio, nice seeing you."

"What about Interpol and the Federal German Police?"

Beatty appeared insulted. "What do you take us for? They've been working on it from day one. They can't even find her background. She arrived out of thin air. Somewhere along the line she changed her whole identity and it was very well done, and I would guess, some heavy money went into it so that she could function without problems. Did she confess to you?"

"She didn't deny it when I accused her of it. I just thought you might have dug up something in Germany."

"We're still at it. I would guess that certain documentation has been destroyed at a price, never to be found again. She's made it bloody difficult for us. Is that it?"

"She wasn't Ronnie Walsh's mistress. He didn't own the apartment."

"The apartment is owned by a dummy company that was a subsidiary of another company that went bust and a list of directors have gone down the tube. It's possible that we will eventually arrive at true ownership, but at the moment we are floundering on some offshore outfits in the West Indies. Everything about her is a massive cover-up job and that means she rates high and has a lot of work in front of her, or a lot already done." Beatty twiddled with a ballpoint. "If you've accused her, you'd better watch your back day and night, George."

"She knew that I knew. I just brought it out into the open to see what might come of it. You might have told me about the apartment."

"I knew you'd get there. But we still don't know the owners ourselves. I would have told you when we do. If ever we do. Did your openness get you anywhere?"

"Not really." He rose. "OK. We're at least on the same wavelength."

Beatty nodded. "If we don't get something positive soon,

we'll send her back, although it would go against the grain. But I don't want any more executions on my patch. Look out for yourself, George."

Anna Brenning sat back in the cab and considered her position. She was satisfied about the alibis unless she ran foul of someone and they suddenly started to be rescinded and she would then be fully exposed. It was part of the hold on her but she had accepted it with open eyes. The pay was good and she enjoyed killing people, especially those she despised which was why she had regrets about George Bulman. She had got to like him and although he could lie his head off he was not a hypocrite. She like the cragginess of him and the eyes that were never hard and in which there always seemed to lurk a suspicion of humour. But he had to go and that was that. Of Ronnie Walsh she had no regrets.

The so-called tidying up jobs the Russians had overseen had been near disastrous. They had exercised no subtlety and used brute force and had managed to kill the wrong girl. And then the fracas in Somerset. It had been considered that getting rid of the riff-raff had not demanded her particular talents and professionalism, and the result was chaos, with the loss of some of their own men. Bulman had described it as a cock-up. Bulman was right.

Bulman too, was considered part of the clearing up process, so the same people would attend to it, but she would have preferred to do the job herself. At least it would have been clean and there would have been no risk of him suffering. She smiled quietly to herself as she realized the consideration that had gone into the thought. Poor, George. She would miss him.

She really did not want to return to Germany at all. It held too many sickening, often terrifying, memories. But it would be a sensible thing to do at this stage. Later she could return under yet another identity, and she had already used several. Her life was becoming lonelier. There

226

were times when she badly needed company which was why the meetings with Bulman had been double edged; she had enjoyed his company but there was absolutely no risk of her going soft on the necessity of his removal. She would send masses of flowers to his funeral out of respect. And a Get Well card which he would have appreciated if he been able to read it.

Anna was almost back to normal when the cab drew up outside her apartment block. She climbed out, paid the cabbie and gave him a generous tip and entered the building. She took the lift up and knew something was drastically wrong as soon as she left it on the top floor. There was nothing untoward immediately visible, it was the instincts instilled by her calling that made her stop outside the lift and look towards her own door.

At first she could see nothing wrong but her sense of danger was such that she opened her bag and pulled out her .22 pistol before she saw that the door had been forced. She did exactly as Jacko and Eddie had done, she pushed the door with her gloved hand and swung it back as far as it would go. It was a short while after that before she entered the hall. She saw some of the devastation as soon as she saw the open doors, all of which she had left closed.

She took one room at a time and controlled the impulse to swear and curse aloud. Everything was wrecked, wherever she looked. She took it a room at a time. She thought that whoever had done this had long since gone and she could not imagine it was done by someone Bulman had sent.

She reached the lounge and stepped into it, a shadow of the movements Jacko had made on arrival. She stepped into the lounge, gazed around, and then, through the open study door, she could just see a pair of feet and part of the legs prone inside the study. Making sure the lounge was empty and that she was not falling into a trap, she crossed carefully, gun raised until she had full view of the body lying there, the head resting

227

in a small pool of blood which also covered some of the papers and books which had been scattered around the room. She levelled the pistol at the back of the man's head.

Chapter Nineteen

As she gazed at the sprawled body Anna briefly reflected that, whatever the travesty of the scene, it had needed something like this to bring her back to basics. She saw the Colt with its laser attachment just beyond the reach of the stricken man and stepped round the body well clear of the outstretched hands. Keeping her gaze on the man she flicked the Colt away with her foot and then went further into the study to retrieve it. As she bent down she did not remove her gaze from the prone figure. Once she had the Colt she straightened and just stood there.

Jacko still had not moved but the blood had stopped flowing and had congealed on his head. Anna reached back and groped for the nearest chair, hooked it towards her, and still well clear, sat down to wait. The Colt with its attachment was too big to put in her bag so she swung round to lay it on the desk within easy reach. She was not willing to test Jacko's carotid artery in case he came to and a man with a gun like the Colt would know something of survival. She could detect no movement or sound of breathing but her guess was that he was alive. To what extent remained to be seen. She simply had to wait and that was something she could accept without qualm.

When Jacko did gradually regain consciousness he did not even twitch. Years of arduous training committed him to remaining quite still while he tried to get back his senses. He was aware of the pain at the back of his head; it was like having a hatchet in his skull, he became aware of being prone, of dust in his nostrils, of a bed of grot around him.

He could feel the cushion of the stuff but still kept his eyes closed.

Through the pain he gradually remembered what had happened, that Rudi Brandt had scored one over him and that he must have slowed down with age. The pain got worse as consciousness returned more fully. Someone was in the room, and he wondered why Rudi had stayed on. Then he picked up the faintest whiff of perfume and began to doubt his senses. He had yet to open his eyes because that might be seen by anyone there and he was far from knowing what he might do. With an ugly head wound and lying face downwards he was not in an ideal position.

As he began to think more clearly, recalled exactly what had happened, he slowly eased the lid of the eye nearest to the floor hoping it would not be seen. It was not the best of views and all he could see were papers and books and patches of carpet but with no real field of view. He was now sure someone was there. If he opened the other eye he knew it might be seen.

He must have twitched his lid for a woman with the slightest of German accents said, "I know your lying there wondering what you can do. As one professional to another, don't give it a thought. I've a gun pointing right at the hole in your head; I won't even have to make a second one. Why don't you just sit up and we'll have a chat."

Jacko thought rightly that Anna Brenning had returned. There was nothing he could do but act sensibly. He was simply too badly placed for heroics.

Jacko did not react immediately. He wanted to unscramble his mind as much as he could before facing the formidable Anna. He had to move sometime and when he felt he was ready he went through the motions of coming to and groaned a little as he made his first movements. There was no further sound from the woman as if she accepted that he would go through all the motions while wracking his brains on how to get out. She was clearly confident that there was no way he could go.

230

And then she said, "I'd help you up but I think you might take advantage so you're on your own. Don't take too long or I might lose patience and end it for you."

Jacko stirred more visibly and began to push himself up. The pain in his head became excruciating and he went dizzy and collapsed again. He was probably out for no more than a few seconds but it made him realize just how much the double blow had depleted him. He struggled up again and managed to get on all fours where he remained until his head cleared again. During this time, with both eyes open, he saw the neatest pair of women's feet he had seen for some time. The feet were small and expensively clad.

He raised his head to gaze round the room searching for something which might support him as he tried to straighten out. He used the door jamb to climb up as she said, "Don't do a runner. I don't mind shooting you in the back. You wouldn't make much more mess than this lot."

He straightened awkwardly and rolled on the jamb so that he faced her. One glance at the way she held her pistol was enough for him to know that she could use it almost without trying, and he could not miss the silencer. It would not worry her if she shot him. Bulman was right, she was a looker although just then he had great difficulty in focusing and he felt his legs go. He held on, straightened, and gave a sloppy grin. "I should take more water with it."

"How did it happen, and what are you doing here?"

"I must sit down. My legs can't carry me."

Anna stood up and threw her own chair at him. "Use that." She sat on the edge of the desk.

He straightened the chair and sank on to it with huge relief. "Thank God for that. What was the question?"

"Just answer it."

"I came here to burgle the place. There was someone already here and he clobbered me with a paperweight. I just had a glimpse of it before he struck."

"You came to burgle the place with a Colt with laser

231

beam attachment. How interesting. And did this other man have a pistol too?"

"I don't know. We didn't get that friendly. I thought I had the drop on him but he was very quick, very fired up about something. He was German too."

Anna's expression tightened. "Describe him?"

"I can do better than that, I can give you his name: Rudi Brandt. Does that mean anything to you?" He could see at once that it did. He had knocked her off balance but not enough to risk going for her. He was having difficulty in breathing.

Her own breathing had become somewhat laboured but she steadied down and asked, "How do you know?"

"Because I asked him."

"And did he ask your name?"

"He did but I wouldn't give it to him; I had the Colt pointing at his guts at the time."

"Where did you get this gun?"

"What the hell does it matter?"

"It matters because I know who you got it from. And you didn't pay for it. You did to its owner what you claim this man Brandt did to you. You didn't come here to burgle, you came to find out what you could about me. You came from Bulman."

"Bulman! I've heard of that name."

"Of course you have and don't go through a ridiculous pretence or I'll finish it now. It would be easy for me wouldn't it? The place ransacked, it screams self-defence. Did you work for Bulman?"

"Did? What's happened to him?" She was right, it was bang to rights, there was no point in pretence.

"I can't guarantee that he's still around."

"If you're not sure then you can bet that he is. If you are worried about what I found then let me tell you that I never got anywhere near to searching before I got clobbered. Anyway, where do you start looking in this mess."

232

He leaned forward and held his head in his hands. "I need to go to hospital. My head needs seeing to."

"It certainly does. You were stupid to come here. You are not going to get a doctor but you will soon end up in hospital. What did this man Brandt have to say?"

"He said that if I saw anything he had missed would I point it out to him and he would deal with it." He thought it odd that she did not question his veracity about Brandt. She knew he had not made it up as soon as he mentioned the name. So she must know him or of him. "He must be an enemy of yours to have done this, it shrieks anger and revenge – unless he's mad." Somehow she did not appear shocked at the terrible state of things, almost as if she had expected it. But she did appear to be drained.

"May I get a glass of water?"

"No you may not. You'll not need it where you're going. I'm just deciding what to do about your disposal."

"Just leave me here and push off back to Germany. I can't harm you."

"You mean George never talked to you? He kept it all to himself?"

"He is the governor. You know all about the need to know basis."

"I do. And I need to know right know before I blow your head off. What did Rudi have to say?"

Rudi? So she not only knew of him but knew him well. "Hardly anything. We were getting matey, so I thought, and were going to a pub to talk things over when he zapped me. Would you mind having a look at this for me? It's hurting like hell."

"That's the sort of thing Bulman might have said. Don't worry, I'll soon put you out of your misery. Can you see the phone anywhere?"

Jacko couldn't see it but she saw the hump of it under a pile of papers behind the desk. Jacko almost made the effort then but felt he was too weak. He would only get one chance and he had to make sure he could make it pay. As it was, he was having trouble remaining conscious.

Anna backed away behind the desk and bent down facing him, her head just above desk level as she groped for the phone on the floor. He knew what she was going to do; make sure a disposal squad was available to deal with his body once she had killed him. His adrenalin rose as he made an enormous effort to get some strength back. As weak as he was, it was now or never, life or death.

Anna was watching him the whole time, and he put on an act as if he was just about to fall off the chair from sheer exhaustion and it was not all an act. His lids drooped and he had a job opening them again. He began to fall sideways and righted himself with an effort. Anna swore as she tried to get the phone up, which was behind her, and the hand piece was well separated from the cradle. She could have glanced round to get better location but refused to take her eyes off him.

Jacko fell on to one knee just as she got a grip of the phone. He was kneeling and swaying like a mantis and she jumped to her feet and almost fired at him, but his eyes were closed and she could see that he was about to fall forward. She took the opportunity that he presented to her and glanced back to where the phone lay still partly hidden on the floor. She had to have it, she needed help. She spun round and made a grab at it as Jacko made an enormous effort, knowing it would be his last, one way or another, and hurled himself forward to the desk to push it against her, as he grabbed at the Colt which was sliding across the desk away from him.

He put his whole weight behind a desperate attempt and lunged for the gun at the same time. He felt the desk hit her body as it slid back and he saw something of her tumble as her back arched from the blow. It was not enough to hurt her but knocked her off balance. Once Jacko had his fingertips on the gun he was intent on getting full hold of it. Momentum was in his favour in that Anna was being

234

pushed away and as long as he could stop the Colt from sliding off the desk. As he grabbed it he fell to his knees again and almost passed out. He glimpsed her through the knee hole of the desk and it did not take her much longer to see him and raise her gun from an awkward position, almost on her back by now.

Jacko somehow dug up the last of his reserves and raised the Colt, hardly seeing through almost closed lids. He fired through a haze and the roar of the gun was like a massive explosion in the confines of the study. As he fired he rolled. Something zipped past his face and spattered the plaster on the wall behind him. The plop of the silencer had been drowned by noise of his own gun.

He tried to pull himself up by the side of the desk and could hear Anna moving the other side. He let himself fall again so that he was below desk level as another shot gorged a channel through the edge of the desk. He scrambled into the knee hole and could see her legs and the skirt just above her knee line. At her feet was the phone she had dropped once she realized he had got the Colt.

He could have shot her through the leg and it was not concern for her that prevented him but a sudden attack of nausea. It swelled up in his throat and he overrode it in a split second but it was sufficient time for her to move and when he looked again she had gone.

He sat in the knee hole and judged her movements by sound. There was so much grot on the floor that it was virtually impossible to miss it and the rustling of papers was quite clear. He was not in the best of positions. She must know where he was but had to be careful herself as she had no idea which way he was facing.

He edged towards the side she had been and wondered if he had the strength to lift the desk. The alternative was a good spur and he braced himself as she stopped moving and there was a deadly silence as each waited for the advantage. He shifted his position on his knees so that he now faced the way he had come. He was sure she was on the side of the desk he had been but this time she kept her legs out of view of the knee hole. There was something of a stalemate but it would end as they both knew.

The phone cradle was just by him and Jacko reached for it. He gently pulled on the wire that led to the handpiece and roped it in bit by bit so that it slid through the mess on the floor. It was essential that he had it as a unit or it would drag in flight. He lifted it up and lobbed it as he would a grenade. He barely heard the plop before the bullet hit the phone assembly and it shattered in all directions, some crashing down on to the desk. Even in the time it took him to reach up and heave under the desk top he recognized how accurate her reflex shot had been.

It helped that everything that had been on top of the desk had been removed, smashed and scattered. He lifted the desk to an angle where it overturned to form a more solid shield but at the same time he rolled away from it.

Anna was crouched in front of the desk, her gun pointing just above the top waiting for him to appear. He now faced her sideways on and he was prone. She must have seen him in her peripheral vision but before she could move he bawled, "Stay there or you've had it."

She froze but was waiting for the half chance, ready to pivot on her feet in her crouched position.

"Drop it, Anna. Just drop the gun. You'll live to fight another day. I'll kill you only if you make me."

She stayed still, an impressive pose of beauty and intent. She had never been told to drop her gun before; it was unreal and she was not sure what to do.

"We all come to it, Anna. Just drop it and come to terms with it. Try to move and you're dead. I mean it."

She let the pistol drop straight in front of her so that it was still within easy reach.

Jacko sighed. "That's wishful thinking, Anna." He aimed the gun and fired and the .22 cut a path through the papers to finish out of reach. "Couldn't resist showing off a bit," said Jacko. "Stay exactly as you are." He painfully climbed to his

236

feet, taking his time, the Colt always pointing at her which made it incredibly difficult for him but he was playing for his life; he had the advantage only so long as he could cope and every effort was both physically and mentally sapping. He got to his feet and swayed a little. During this time he was glad he had put her gun out of immediate reach; he had not been showing off but playing it safe, at the same time letting Anna know she was up against a fellow professional.

"You can stand up now," he said, "and move back to the wall by the door."

She moved back, not sure what to make of him but viewing him now in an entirely different light.

He moved sideways to where her gun had settled. He pulled it towards him with a foot and bent down from the knees to retrieve it, watching her as she had watched him. There could be no relaxation between these two. He unscrewed the silencer and slipped it in his pocket, placing the pistol in the opposite pocket. "It's a shame the Colt won't take a silencer. It would have saved all the noise."

"Your shots will have alerted my friends. They will be here any time now."

"So will the whole bloody neighbourhood, I should think." He leaned against the wall for support. "If there's anyone in the apartment underneath they would have heard, but as it's still day time, with luck they might be out. If the police come we're both in the shit so let's hope they don't. Sit on the chair, Anna. There's a couple of things to talk about." He wasn't sure that he could last out but he had to try.

She sat down primly, legs and feet together rather than the usual crossed legs pose. Her feet were slightly drawn back and he could see that she had placed herself in a position to launch herself should the opportunity arise. It was cat and mouse the whole time and she had her full faculties while he was straining to cope.

"What have you done about Bulman?" he demanded.

"He's not in my hands. It's not my problem."

"Does he know about it?"

"How would I know? We had lunch, were rather frank with one another, he accused me of murder, I regretfully told him his days were numbered. That's all."

"You told me my days were numbered, too. At least you were going to make arrangements for my funeral in the river or a rubbish tip. It wasn't too good a prediction."

"I still stand by it."

"Who's the woman in the photograph?"

The question took her completely by surprise. She stuttered over her words and for a few seconds was lost; she expected questions like that from Bulman and bullets from this man who was as good with a gun a she. She could not acknowledge that he might be better. "I don't know," she spluttered at last.

"I'm going to cut this short." With his free hand he took the silencer out, and then awkwardly, her own pistol. He screwed the silencer back on during which time the Colt wavered but not sufficiently for her to make a realistic move. He had judged the distance between them well. There was a psychological advantage in reassembling her pistol. She was forced to watch and it meant that he had changed his mind about something.

When he had finished he held the Colt in his left hand and her pistol in his right. He said, "I never did like silencers, they throw the balance too much. Now listen to me. I want the name of that woman or I'm going to change your looks, first by tearing your ears off with red hot slugs, after which I'll make it up as I go along. But you'll never look the same again. Now what is the name of the woman in the snapshot, Anna?"

"She's a Yugoslav actress. I told Bulman."

"Is that your last word?" He needed to sit down again so leaned with his back to the wall to give him support.

"That's all I know. For God's sake do you want me to make something up?"

"You've already done that." He lifted the pistol and was

238

grateful for its lightness compared with the Colt as he took aim and fired.

She jumped from the chair as the bullet whipped past her ear, scything through her hair and drawing just a trace of blood from her lobe. She had not felt so scared since years ago in East Germany. She had gone very pale and now grasped the side of the chair with knuckle white hands.

"That was one across the bows, Anna. The next one rips your ear off. You're a good-looking dame, don't turn yourself into an earless freak, you'll finish up in a side show."

"I don't know." She almost screamed the words. "I don't know."

"OK." He shrugged although he was ready to drop. He raised the pistol again and she began to shake her head from side to side to destroy his aim. He lowered the gun and said, "You'll get tired before me doing that. I have only to wait. Or I could aim at where I think the ear might be but the trouble with that is you might finish with a slug between yours eyes."

But she kept moving her head until she had to stop and at this stage her despair showed only too clearly. Her head stopped moving at last and he raised the pistol again and said, "You can stay with your head down; that's OK. Saves you seeing me take up the trigger pressure." He took aim.

"Yelena Zotov."

It was barely a mumble and Jacko could not pick up the words but realized she had given a name. "I didn't hear that."

"Yelena Zotov."

"Tell me about her."

Anna kept her head down as if she had just announced her own death sentence. "She is the girlfriend of Radomir Kochev. That is all I can tell you except to add that with that information you will not last long however good you are. We are both finished if he gets to know that I've told you. Perhaps you should have taken my ears off." She

239

raised her head then, to look him bleakly in the eye. She was sweating and for the briefest moment he felt sorry for her. He had taken her to hell and back but it was rooted in what had happened to her in the past and terrible memories had come flooding back.

He could not last much longer. His legs felt as if they would go at any moment. The pain in his head was still throbbing but he could cope with that. It had been sheer guts and will-power that had kept him going at all and an extremely rigorous training that he could never forget.

"Is there anything else you would like to tell me? For instance, what does this guy Kochev do?"

"You wouldn't want to know." And then she started talking about Bulman in a incoherent way, a jumble of meaningless words as if the strain had suddenly got to her and she had gone over the top. He tried to make sense of what she was saying but she had her head down again and the danger signals reared. He realized then that she was now trying to keep him there.

He pushed himself from the wall and almost collapsed. She was still gabbling and shaking her head from side to side. He had to get out now. He turned to the door and his legs would not move but the anxiety rising in him got him going again. Anna sat close to the door he had to pass through but she was still mumbling and he suddenly saw that the fear he was feeling was not for himself so much as for Bulman.

He turned to Anna and she smiled wildly at him, almost in triumph as she knew she was close to revenge. Jacko felt sick with apprehension and turned to her as she rose in fury.

Chapter Twenty

As exhausted as he was, he had no intention of being caught twice in the same way. As she clawed at him, raking her nails down the hand that held the Colt, he swung her own pistol across her jawline and as she fell, clipped her hard with the silencer at the base of the skull. After that he was not sure of anything.

He slowly sank beside her, fighting to stay conscious but he had been coping with it for too long and his mind rebelled. The blows that Rudi had struck had done more damage than he realized. He could resist no more and passed out in a heap.

He was not sure how long he had lain there, but as he slowly came round he was still fighting his condition. He almost panicked as he thought of Anna, and then saw her lying as he had last seen her. To climb to his knees was a far greater effort than the first time and he felt horribly sick. To his surprise he was still holding the Colt but Anna's gun had dropped uncomfortably close to her; he hooked it away. He felt behind his head and the blood had started flowing again; maybe it had never stopped.

Anna was so still she might be dead, but he was not convinced and it was this thought that motivated him most. She would always be dangerous. He pushed the Colt against her temple while he felt for her carotid artery. The pulse was weak but steady. He grabbed the other gun and struggled up using the chair she had been sitting on as a lever. He pushed his feet through the mass of paper and headed for the hall door, stumbling now and then. When he reached the door he propped himself up, looked back to see that Anna had not yet moved, and then pulled open the door and went into the hall, staggered against the opposite wall and groped for the front door. Once on the landing he rang for the lift knowing he could not manage the stairs. Only then did he stow his guns away, dismantling the silencer again to make room in his pockets.

He had an attack of vertigo and the lift started to spin. He clung on to the indicator box and closed his eyes tight. By the time he reached the ground floor the attack had lessened but he still could not walk a straight line so he had to wait and hope nobody would come. He finally reached the street and looked for a cab, leaning against the railings like a drunk.

It was some time before he could get a cab and when he did, he was thankful that the driver considered him drunk, so Jacko waved some money to convince the driver he could pay the fare. He gave the Lambeth address and knew that he should be taking a varied route but could not cope with precaution, it was difficult enough to cope at all. He had not felt as bad as this since spending four days in a foxhole in south Armagh, being discovered and savaged by a dog and beaten up by farmers. That had been a touch and go situation but he had survived that and was determined to survive this. Increasingly his scrambled thoughts turned to Bulman. Anna had actioned something against him and he wondered if Bulman realized it.

As he tried to think things through he was relieved that Anna had destroyed her phone with her own gun. He had not seen another phone in any of the rooms. He must have passed out or fallen asleep because when he woke he had lost all sense of direction and almost panicked. Memory came back and again he reflected that he should change taxis but simply had not the energy to do it. He drifted in and out of consciousness until the cabbie pulled up outside his house.

Jacko paid the driver well over the odds which bought

242

him help in getting out. The driver propped him against the outside wall and said, "You all right, mate? You want me to help you inside?"

Jacko shook his head and immediately regretted it and then unlatched the gate and stumbled up the drive. When he reached the door it was open, and he despaired; it was all happening again and he would not be able to handle it this time. He waited until he was inside the hall before he drew out Anna's gun and screwed the silencer to it. Where did he start?

He pushed himself along the wall and took it room by room as he had at Anna's apartment. There was nothing like the same amount of damage but the place had been clearly disturbed. Someone had been here. He went into every downstairs room and found nobody. The place had been left untidy, as though someone had been searching for something but otherwise nothing had been damaged.

He forced himself to go upstairs, pushing himself along the wall of the staircase. Some time later he was satisfied that the house was empty. There was no sign of Connie or Bulman. He could not even say that there were signs of a struggle, the general untidiness did not amount to that. He returned to the kitchen and made himself very strong black coffee. He had three cups and felt a little better. Apart from the disappearance of Connie and Bulman something niggled at him. He went back upstairs to Connie's room. The clothes she had bought since coming here had gone. So had a large travel case. He tried Bulman's room and found that his old suit was still there.

What had happened? He should be watching his back. If Anna's help had been here then they would be back for him, unless they had been told to deal only with Bulman at the time. On top of his pain and weariness he felt very sad and utterly depleted. As he went back to the kitchen and drank another coffee he had a fit of depression and could so easily have given up the whole affair just then.

Where were Bulman and Connie? He went into the

lounge. He had to sit down, everything was spinning again. He passed out and fell sideways on the settee. The front door was still ajar, for he had left it like that in case he had had to make a quick exit. Right now he was oblivious of everything except a sharp pain at the back of his head which penetrated unconsciousness.

The room had darkened when he came to, some time later. He had trouble opening his eyes and he did not feel any better but his head was clearer although the pain was still there. He was in an awkward position and had cramp in one leg. He pushed himself up and felt as if he had a hangover. He sat there for a while trying to make sense of everything and then he became aware that there was a light on behind him. That brought him round very quickly. He still had the guns with him and he must have partially raised one because the dark shape he suddenly saw sitting opposite him said, "It's me you silly bugger. Who's been playing football with your head?"

Bulman. Jacko could have cried in relief although afterwards he admitted that he had no idea why. "Where the hell have you been? I've been worried sick over you."

"So have I over you. I see you've been at the coffee; want some more?" Bulman rose and put more lights on as he went to the kitchen. He had obviously got things ready because he was back in a couple of minutes with the coffee.

Jacko took his cup with unsteady hands and put it on a side table. "What happened?"

"You must get that head fixed first. You need some stitches and you look as if you've lost a lot of blood. I'll take you to hospital."

"Never mind the head, the blood will build up fast enough. What happened to you and is it safe to stay here like this?"

"I've locked all windows and doors. The phone is in working order and you have a mobile and, as far as I can see, two guns in working order. There is nothing we can do until you are fit to move. Just sit back and listen and then tell me yours."

Bulman was still dressed in Walsh's suit but he had pulled the tie down which destroyed his slick image. "I had an interesting lunch with Anna during which a few truths were exchanged. I guessed she would have someone follow me from The Savoy but should have known that she would put on a full team to make sure this time. My concentration wasn't good. I was worried. I did not expect to see her again but my mind was on what she might do next or who she might kill. And I was worried about you; our lunch didn't last as long as I wanted. I went to the Yard first and should have made my move when I left, but there was a lot on my mind and I suppose I got careless.

"I arrived here by cab and as soon as I stepped out of it I noticed the front door was wide open. I don't tote a gun like you but reasoned that they couldn't have got ahead of me without knowing where we lived. So there had to be another reason for the door being open. This again took my mind off being followed.

"I dashed in the house calling out for Connie and ran upstairs to see if she was in her room watching television. A quick search and I discovered her clothes were missing with a case. I think she's done a runner. While I was upstairs I looked through her window into the street and saw two pairs of men approaching the house from different directions. They were crossing the street and had probably arrived in separate cars.

"I ran down the stairs, left the front door open to confuse them, ran to the garage side door, slipped the key out and went into the garage locking the side door behind me. I knew I couldn't stay there but I had to wait long enough to make sure they were all in the house. They wouldn't hang around outside for fear of being seen and reported. It was luck and judgement."

Bulman wiped his brow and then took a slow sip of his coffee. "There's usually a window somewhere in a garage, but you haven't got one, presumably for security reasons. I just had to judge the timing before I opened the main garage door. As it's electrically operated I used the emergency button by the door and raised it just enough to roll under it. As I reasoned that they'd be nobody blatantly stationed outside I was equally sure that they'd have someone waiting in the cars. I was in a fix because the moment I stepped onto the street I'd be seen. I rolled back in, unhooked the collapsible ladder, pushed it through and rolled back out again.

"As you know, with its recess and high wall, the garage isn't overlooked from that side of the house so I climbed onto its roof, pulled the ladder up, and lay flat pressed up against the house with the ladder close to me. I couldn't be seen from below and couldn't be seen from that side from above. I just waited until they came out and later heard the cars drive off. I wasn't taking a chance, I stayed up there and then I heard you arrive, except that I didn't know it was you although I did assume it was a taxi who had brought someone. I thought it might even be Connie returning until I heard men's voices but couldn't recognize them, and then I realized it must be you. I still waited. I had to be sure. That's it."

"You did well. But they'll be back."

"We must take that view, but they might not having realized that I must have seen or heard them and done a bunk. They wouldn't expect me to return. What they have in mind about you I've no idea."

Jacko told him. It was like reliving it but it helped him straighten his mind. "That Rudi Brandt must have dealt me a hell of a whack. It could have killed me."

"Anyone more sensitive and it might have."

Jacko smiled painfully. "Yeah. The woman in the snapshot is Yelena Zotov, girlfriend of Radomir Kochev. I'd suffered a lot getting that information and there was no way I was going to forget, whatever I felt like. But you'd better jot it down now. Do the names mean anything to you?"

246

"No. My instinct tells me not to ask Beatty or Derek North of Five. I can't tell you why but I think it's tied up with why I was used in the first place. This is the sort of information Edward Marshall wants. He's my Government contact, if I haven't mentioned it before. You did well Jacko. That titbit is worth more than a search may have revealed." He grinned in sympathy at Jacko's sorry state.

"A backhanded way to get it though." Bulman checked the time. "What are we going to do about you? You need that head examined."

"I feel a lot better than I did. The rest helped." Jacko felt the back of his head. "It seems to have stopped bleeding. It's tacky though. You know that Anna is going to look for revenge. She'll get the report of this place and we'd better get out."

"Where to?"

"I've only got my own place where Georgie is and I won't compromise her. I can't ask friends. I've got some sleeping bags in the attic, we'll have to sleep rough."

"Unless we stay at Spider Scott's place. He and Maggie won't be back from the West Indies for another week. He always leaves a set of keys with me."

"He won't thank you for that. Look, I'll take a shower. It might do the trick. And then we'll leave, wherever we go. Just keep your eyes and ears open. I'll leave one of the guns with you. You'd better have Anna's, the noise of the Colt might frighten you to death."

They were chiding each other again, a good sign. As Jacko went painfully up the stairs he called back, "We can't wait for things to happen to us. We've got them going. I have an idea about Rudi Brandt. He might be our entry."

Bulman did not ask to where, Jacko had more than earned his shower and in their separate ways they had forced the issue and got some results. The main issue was still out of reach, though. Why was Walsh assassinated, and what was Anna's role with him if not his mistress? Meanwhile Bulman tried to raise Edward Marshall on the phone but had no luck. He did not leave a message for he was not entirely sure of their future movements.

They packed canned food and bottles of water and opened up the side door to the garage with some difficulty as Bulman had left the key the other side. Jacko managed it at last and they loaded the sleeping bags in the boot of the car together with the reserve rations and anything else they might need.

Jacko had checked the magazine of Anna's gun to find that he had six rounds left. The Colt had only four, but he kept a variety of rounds hidden in a spare tyre in the garage. He filled the empty chambers and slipped some loose rounds in his pocket. He was still slow to move but he had recovered noticeably since the shower.

Watching all this, Bulman said, "You seem to be permanently ready for war. For chrissake, what arms have you got about the place?"

"They're just souvenirs from various postings I had in the SAS. Every soldier has war souvenirs. Nothing sinister."

"And I bet they all keep them in spare car tyres, too." Bulman climbed in. He noticed that Jacko closed his eyes before starting the car, as if to give his himself a last minute boost to keep him going. The door slowly raised and Jacko eased the car out.

He edged the car out on to the darkened street, and then put his foot down. In a backstreet like this there was little traffic and it was quite easy to see if someone pulled out behind them. Someone did and Jacko did some smart driving, taking corners on two wheels, remaining in the side streets, and eventually losing the tail. "I wonder how long they would have waited before busting in?"

Bulman did not answer but kept quiet while he watched Jacko and he could see that the effort was taking it out of him. Whatever Jacko said, he was not really fit to drive or do much else for that matter. But he was used to privation and

248

operating under the most arduous conditions and Bulman kept an uneasy peace.

By the time they reached Spider Scott's apartment sweat beads stood out on Jacko's forehead and he was rather pale. Still Bulman did not interfere because a row could deplete Jacko more than his effort. He *wanted* to carry on and there was no argument with that, not with Jacko. The car was parked and they had to walk round the corner to enter the building. There was no lift but there was only one flight of stairs to climb to reach Scott's place.

Bulman let them in and went to the kitchen to make them coffee. Jacko looked round the sitting room, impressed by the number of antiques and *objet d'art*. He flopped into a chair and called out, "Your mate has good taste."

"Him and Maggie," Bulman called back. "He developed his while he was on the creep. Probably the best cat burglar around at his peak. Went for the stately homes mostly. But everything you see he and Maggie bought. It's all straight." Bulman came in with the coffees and put them down.

"I was a detective sergeant when we first met. A bit of a bastard, ambitious with my one aim in life to put him back in jail. At that time, for some reason, I didn't like him at all. Then a couple of things happened during some of the grey jobs I did for the Security Service who also used his special talents, and I realized they were fixing to get him back inside once he had helped them out. By then I was a detective inspector and it riled me to see what they were doing to him. I began to see him in a different light and, of course, most of us mellow over the years. And Maggie, who's a super woman, did more than her bit to keep him on the straight and narrow. It wasn't easy for him simply because he loved his work. We became very close friends over the years which was quite remarkable because he hated coppers as much as I hated villains."

249

Jacko listened to this and detected something of the soft spot in Bulman he suspected to be there. Entering Scott's place had obviously affected Bulman emotionally.

"We won't need to use their beds; I'll bring the sleeping bags up later. Have you thought what we're going to do about Connie?" Jacko asked.

"Nothing. Where do we start looking? The police are searching for her anyway, so all we can hope is that they find her first. She's been lucky so far. The probabilty is that she's gone back to work. She threatened to before, said she needed the money. There's nothing we can do. What was it you said about Rudi Brandt?"

"I reckon he's keeping an eye on Anna most of the time. He must have seen her go out for lunch and chose his moment. And Anna knows about him. It was amazing; her place was like a tip with anything breakable broken. The study was a mass of papers, not just letters or documents, but all the unused stationery was scattered everywhere including newspapers, books and magazines. A lot of hatred had gone into that wreckage. And yet the state of the place did not seems to distress her. Mention of his name got a reaction but it was as though she had expected something like that to happen. It was weird. I mean, the bloody place was wrecked and yet she took it so calmly. I think we should go back there tonight."

"You're crazy. She'll have called in help to clean up the place so she won't be alone."

"No, not that. I reckon this Rudi is camping out for whatever reason. He might be dealing with her a stage at a time. If I'm right then he's watching her as much as he can and probably wants her to know."

"She'd make a move against him. She has enough help."

"There's something here we're not latching on to. She knew the name as soon as I mentioned it. My guess is that it's something personal. The destruction was an act of revenge and it won't end there. Maybe he wants to destroy

250

her bit by bit, make her suffer. I can't think of any other reason for doing what he did. It could be that she doesn't want to call in help. She may have a reason for keeping it to herself. I would also guess the advantage is with him. I bet he knows just when to fade away. He's just one more shadow in this lark. We don't go looking for her, George, but for him. He's got information we need. Cheaper than going to Germany and, I bet, more effective."

"If he's there."

"Sure, if he's there. But I don't think he's finished with her yet, not by a long chalk."

"You're not fit enough, Jacko. Look what he did to you."

"I was suckered. That won't happen again."

"No gun play, Jacko. God knows what trouble we're already in when it catches up with us."

"It's all been self-defence."

"Sure. But with so many dead bodies around no jury will believe it. We just pray it doesn't come back to us because I'm an accessory."

"You'll have to dig out your connections. Look, let's stop pissing around. Do we or don't we?"

"OK. But I think we should have a night's sleep and then go for it."

"You'd better keep Anna's pistol. Just for show," Jacko added hastily as he saw Bulman's expression. "Let's go in for broke. If he's not there let's go for her. Why don't we have a bite to eat now and then we'll feel better."

They moved into the kitchen but Bulman was worried; he knew just how reckless Jacko could be. The scrap meal was going to taste like the Last Supper. The gun felt very uncomfortable in his pocket yet for all his misgivings he knew he might need it. And that worried him the more. It was, after all, a particularly deadly assassin they were after and she had all the help she needed, probably each one a killer.

When they climbed into their sleeping bags Jacko was

barely awake. He slept through to lunch time next day and when he did wake he cursed Bulman for not rousing him sooner. They set off three hours later, an uneasy silence between them.

Chapter Twenty-One

They travelled for about ten minutes and Bulman's broodiness was showing enough for Jacko to remark, "What's on your mind apart from this caper?"

Bulman did not reply directly. "Do you mind if I use the mobile?"

"You don't have to ask." Jacko kept his gaze on the road. Traffic was thick now and they were back in the main stream.

Bulman tapped out the number, relieved when he got a call signal. It rang out for so long he almost hung up. He heard the voice just in time.

"Bulman here. I've been trying to get you. Do you know of someone called Radomir Kochev? You do." Bulman sat and listened, giving nothing away to Jacko. "That's interesting if not downright scary. And Yelena Zotov? No? Then I've got one for you; she's Kochev's girlfriend." He sat back and listened impassively aware that Jacko was straining to hear. Bulman said, "I've made no mention of Kochev to Wally Beatty at the Yard nor have I mentioned him to Derek North of Five. It seems that I did the right thing. They will both surely have heard of Kochev if what you say is true. So why shouldn't they be told? I see. I've mentioned Yelena Zotov to them both because I have been trying to trace her. They both claim they don't know her and in view of the fact that you don't, they were probably speaking the truth which must have been hard for Five."

Bulman sat back and listened for a while before saying, "Veida Ash is wrapped up in this somewhere. Whether she's

253

actually running it, is another matter. I would guess she's co-operating with another crowd, one possibly even bigger than her own and probably much more ruthless and that's saying a lot. OK, I've a better idea of what to do and what it's about." He rested the phone on the shelf.

"Well?" demanded Jacko.

"Radomir Kochev is a Russian gangster who's so evil he gives all the others a good name. He's top dog over there and wields the power that matters."

Jacko whistled. "Are you saying that Walsh was tied in with him?"

"In some way. He must have been. It begins to make sense."

"It doesn't to me, mate. I thought that, as business men go, Walsh was straight. You'd better explain."

"I can't explain. Anyway I don't know yet."

Bulman mused for a while and Jacko did not waste his time trying to push him. Bulman said, "It accounts for the mixture of Russians and Germans we've come across. Kochev and Veida. My God, what a combination. Anna is only part of a team; a deadly, important part, but expendable. And I think she knows it." Bulman turned in his seat to face Jacko. "You were right. This business with Rudi Brandt is something she wants to keep apart from the rest, maybe for her own safety."

Jacko jockeyed through the thickening traffic. "Keep quiet for a bit. There are a lot of idiots on the road. It makes you wonder just what we're up against though, doesn't it?

In spite of Jacko's driving skills it took much longer than they had expected to thread through to Anna's part of town. For most of the way the traffic was solid. Jacko did not approach Anna's place directly but drove round a couple of blocks away looking for somewhere to park. He did not hurry and went round in different directions while Bulman joined him in checking on being followed, they were certain they were not, but it was possible they might pick up a different type of threat nearer to Anna's.

Finally Jacko found a place to park not too far a walk from Anna's. They climbed out and locked the car and walked slowly back the way they had come, until they found an intersection that ran at right angles to the top of the street Anna lived in.

"Are you all right, Jacko?"

"Sure. Do I look dodgy?"

"I just want to make sure you're up to what you want to do. You want to wring his bloody neck, don't you? Just be sure you can do it. If he's there."

"He'll be there. If not now then at some other time. We'll have to persevere. I don't think this guy will give up."

They reached Anna's street and stuck together as they walked along, seemingly chatting and in no particular hurry. They kept to the opposite side of the street to where Anna lived and where Rudi Brandt was more likely to be, if he was watching her movements.

Jacko was on the inside as he was more versed in spotting danger in tight situations. Bulman glanced up at Anna's place as they went past and could see that her lights were on. He told Jacko who was pleased because there would be more likelihood of Rudi making his vigil if she was at home. They reached the end of the street and turned the corner. They did not stop until they reached the next corner.

"I didn't see a thing," said Jacko.

They weren't alone on the streets but there were not many people about. "We'll have to go round again," said Bulman. "This time from this end."

They changed positions so that Jacko remained on the inside and started out again. Jacko suddenly grabbed Bulman and pulled him to the nearest railings and quickly turned his back to the street. "That's him," he whispered urgently. "The guy coming from across the street who hived off towards Anna's."

"You could hardly have got a glimpse and it's pretty murky. Are you sure?"

"A glimpse is all I needed. I shall never forget that bastard." Jacko still kept his back turned although the man who Jacko claimed to be Rudi had gone. "Have you got a piece of paper?"

Bulman took out his notebook and tore off a sheet and handed it over.

"My guess is," said Jacko, "that he'll take up position in one of the doorways." He grabbed Bulman's arm. "I wonder if he's rented a room in one of them. There are plenty of flats and at the shabbier end probably bed-sits. I carry the paper. The moment I spot him I look at the paper as if searching for the address, we talk about it, and you mount the steps to check the door number. You can even ask him. Leave the rest to me."

It was reasonable; Bulman accepted that Jacko could not approach the front door for fear of being recognized. But he did not like the idea. It had not been thought through. They changed positions again with Jacko now on the outside and set off.

The piece of paper made all the difference, for held before them, they could peer at it under street lamps, and gaze openly into doorways trying to find the number, and it enabled them to argue a little to delay them further.

They located a man lurking in a doorway quite quickly. He was well back, hardly detectable to anyone except someone like Jacko, and too indistinct to be recognized. Anna's block was at an angle to where he stood but he would have had a clear view of the entrance. They went past, then backtracked a little, both looking at the paper and complaining of the bad light. They peered up into the porch as if trying to locate the number, Jacko keeping just behind Bulman. Numbers on these buildings were notoriously badly marked and some not at all. Jacko gave Bulman a nudge.

"I'd better go and see," said Bulman grudgingly. He

started up the steps and near the top he said, "I'm so sorry, I didn't see you standing there." He grinned in the darkness. "Hasn't she shown up?" And when he got no response to that he added, "Maybe you can help me. We're looking for number twenty-seven." He peered at the paper he had taken with him and held it out. "A Mrs Anderton? Says she has rooms to let. Have we got the right street?" He held the paper out further.

Rudi, who simply wanted to get rid of him, stepped from the shadows to glance at the proffered paper as if to be helpful, took one glance at a sheet that was clearly blank even in the poor light, sprung back, hand reaching inside his pocket and bumped into Jacko who had raced up the steps to ram the Colt into Rudi's neck.

"You're not doing it a second time, Rudi. Take your hand out, without the gun." Bulman stood in front of Rudi to make sure he did.

Rudi raised his hands while Jacko told Bulman to withdraw his gun, which Bulman did, together with a long bladed knife in a sheath.

"What, no paperweight?" said Jacko. "We're going for a walk, Rudi. We need to talk. And depending on that we'll decide what to do with you next. You nearly killed me you bastard so don't try anything."

"Where are you taking me?"

Jacko could not help but notice Rudi's seeming lack of concern at his position and it made him ponder on what other tricks he might produce. "Watch him all the time," said Jacko to Bulman. "He's a crafty sod. We're taking you somewhere quiet where we won't be interrupted."

"Then why don't you take me to my apartment where we can be comfortable."

"Because I don't trust you."

"Look, I'm sorry I hit you. I didn't know where I stood with you. I couldn't take a chance. Afterwards I realized I had done the wrong thing. It will be easier for you to keep an eye on me in my apartment."

"Where is it?" This came from Bulman.

"We are standing in the porch. I have rooms on the top floor at the back, which is why I have to stand here to watch Anna."

"Give my friend the keys. He'll go first, then you, and then me. You know the form, try anything and I'll do you. I mean that. Which will mean that Anna survives."

"We talk. There is nobody in the apartment. I live there alone." Rudi handed over the keys. "The big one is for the front door here, and the smaller two for the apartment."

Bulman unlocked the door, groped for a light switch where Rudi told him it would be and preceded the others up the stairs, not at all happy. It was true that they had to talk somewhere but they could have driven back to Scott's place, although he would not have been happy about that either should something go wrong.

They climbed the stairs with Jacko slightly behind Rudi, the Colt not actually touching him so that the German could not roll off the barrel. They reached the top, the quality of the interior of the house nowhere near the luxury of the block across the way. Bulman unlocked the mortice and the Yale and, without really thinking about it, drew out Anna's pistol and pushed the door back. He examined the rooms, there were only three, a bedroom, sitting room, and a large kitchen with a bathroom just off it. The furnishings were utilitarian and he suspected they belonged to the landlord.

He called out to Jacko who propelled Rudi forward into the sitting room and then Bulman closed the door behind them. But Rudi was fascinated by the gun Bulman was holding. As Jacko made him sit down with his back to the door Rudi said to Bulman almost breathlessly, "Where did you get that gun?"

Jacko sat down facing the door and opposite Rudi. He answered for Bulman who was moving round to take up a position behind and out of sight of Rudi. "I took it from Anna."

258

Rudi was suspicious. "I know it's Anna's. It is her favourite pistol. She's had it for many years. You took it from her? But that is incredulous. Was she asleep?"

"After you left me for dead she came back and we had a fight and she lost."

"Good God. That is difficult to believe."

"I'm not asking you to believe. My friend behind you is just as deadly with that gun as Anna was. Let's get some straight answers and see where it leads."

"It will be easier to answer you knowing that you took her gun. So you are enemies?"

"It looks like it. She'll certainly try to kill me next time we meet; in fact she tried it then. Let's get on with it. Just who are you, Rudi?"

"I am Anna's brother."

Whatever they had been expecting it was not that. The two bore no obvious resemblance. And yet when they looked again, now with different intent, there was a detectable likeness.

"I saw the brotherly love you showed in her apartment. Did she burn your teddy bear when you were kids?" Jacko was doing the questioning because threats might become a necessity and he was better at physical intimidation than Bulman.

"No," replied Rudi quite calmly. "She tried to kill me."

Jacko looked over Rudi's shoulder to catch Bulman's eye and could see that he was just as shocked. The readiness of the answers was at first a drawback, suggesting that Rudi was saying anything that entered his head until he added, "I am telling you this now because I want to avoid physical pain or maiming, and because I begin to see that we are on the same side in that we want Anna's destruction. Maybe we have our different ideas of doing this but the aim is the same."

"How did she try?"

Rudi glanced over his shoulder. "With the gun your friend is holding. She fired three shots into me and left me

259

for dead. It is a miracle, and a tribute to excellent surgeons that I lived." Rudi stood up. "No tricks," he assured them. He removed his jacket and pulled his shirt up to show three entry marks, still red around the rims like active craters and one perilously close to the heart. He turned so that Bulman could see too. "I was in hospital for four months. In intensive care a good deal of that time. It was touch and go." He tucked his shirt back in and put on his jacket and sat down.

"She wasn't such a good shot then," observed Jacko. "You should have seen what she did to the last guy." There had been press photographs of the body. "Why did she do it?"

"You are right about her shooting. It was before she became a paid assassin. Before she shot me she shot our mother but was more successful with her. She used more rounds and got a couple of shots off to her head. Mother died at once."

"I begin to see why you wrecked her flat. You still haven't said why she did it."

Bulman was content to leave the questioning to Jacko and it was going well; he had no wish to stop the flow of information.

Rudi began to flounder and it was clear that he would rather not answer. "It does not matter why. Anna was always wild."

"But was she insane as well? We're talking matricide here."

"There were problems within the family. It's over."

"No it's not, Rudi, or you wouldn't be here on a mission of revenge. It's not over for you. We want a little light on this, it might provide some insight into why she does these murders."

Rudi gazed at the floor. He wanted to withhold information but could see the futility of it. In the end he decided it did not matter to these two men; what mattered was getting at Anna and maybe they could help him.

"They were terrible days in East Germany. The easiest way to live was to go along with the regime. It was all powerful. It did not make for an ideal life, there was no such thing for ordinary mortals in East Germany. Anna couldn't do that. She did one spell in prison. She was a radical, always in trouble and always being saved from further prison or worse by me or my mother."

Sitting behind Rudi, Bulman heard the slight catch in his voice as he started to relive something he wanted to forget. In a way he got a better feel for the German than Jacko who faced him.

"To get her out of trouble meant concessions on mother's and my part. We found a way of nullifying her efforts which would have put anyone else in jail, or they would simply have disappeared." Rudi glanced up and Jacko was surprised to see tears in his eyes; his fingers intertwined and gripped tightly.

"When the Eastern Bloc collapsed and the wall came down problems of a different kind emerged. When the Stasi records were released to the public Anna spent days going through them. We tried to talk her out of it but she was intent on proving that her attitude had been right. She eventually found out that both mother and I had been reporting her activities to the Stasi all along. As we saw it we had saved her. As she saw it she had been betrayed by her own mother and brother. It was a tremendous shock to her. She never forgave either of us and from that day we ceased to exist as a family. She brooded until revenge became an obsession. She shot us both on the same day in the same room and disappeared. As she saw it I suppose we deserved it. It's ironic that what we did kept her alive to do what she did."

Rudi spread his hands in a pleading gesture. "I don't know if we did the right thing. In her eyes certainly not. And now the coin is reversed and I want my own revenge, not for what she did to me but for what she did to Mother. I can never forgive her for that."

There was a long silence before Jacko said, "How did you trace her?"

"Well, I guessed she had gone abroad. The whole family were always good linguists and I knew she excelled in English, as I did at the time. I guessed she had gone to America or Britain and would certainly have changed her identity. It seems that she teemed up with an organization who could easily change her background.

"She set herself off into crime and became a murderer. I have a German friend who is a foreign correspondent on one of our newspapers and he has friends on some of the English papers. I gave him names she might use. Brenning was one because it was the name of a particular friend of hers who was killed by the Stasi. I had given photographs and eventually got one back. None of this was connected with the MP who was murdered. Not then, anyway. There were changes in her appearance, of course. Her hair was a different colour and perhaps she'd had minor facial surgery. But there was no way I couldn't recognize my murderous sister when I saw her. I came over straight away."

Bulman and Jacko looked for the flaws and there were openings for some, and an uneasy silence developed. But some aspects were still not clear.

From behind Rudi, Bulman said, "If you wanted revenge why didn't you just kill her? Presumably, you had the chance."

"I wanted her to suffer first, as I've suffered since that day. She was never caught and while she was free there was always a chance that she might try again. I decided to take the fight to her. The first shock was when she saw me through her window while I stood on view. I knew she would see me sooner or later and it would unnerve her. Later I telephoned her and that really got to her. Then I wrecked her apartment and the next logical step is to dispose of her."

"You think it will be that easy?" asked Bulman. "My friend here had a devil of a job just escaping."

"I could have killed her then," Jacko retorted. "But we have to operate within the law." Jacko caught Bulman's look of total disbelief.

"So why hasn't she been arrested?" Rudi was becoming confused.

"Because there is no evidence against her. She has cast iron alibis in Germany."

Bulman said, "Can we change the subject for a moment? Do you know a man called Radomir Kochev?"

Rudi tried to turn round but Jacko stopped him with a flick of the Colt. "Do you mean the Russian gangster? Everybody knows of him."

"Evidently not this side of the Channel," said Bulman. "Does Yelena Zotov mean anything to you?"

Rudi gave it consideration. "No. Should it?"

Bulman ignored the counter-question. "We think Anna is tied up with this Radomir Kochev and with a woman who is in prison here but still runs a massive crime syndicate. Veida Ash."

"I know of her. There was a scandal in Germany about her too. She had a bad influence on some of the Stasi. Stasi records concerning her were destroyed and nobody found out who did it. You say she's tied in with Kochev? That would be a formidable combination. And Anna is working with them? I would have thought she would have had more sense."

"Why do you say that?" Bulman left his post and came round to the side of Rudi; he found it impossible to conduct an interview with someone's back.

"She's always been her own person. She is strong as you know. She would operate independently."

"Perhaps she thought she could. The probability is that she's paying the price for a new identity and guaranteed alibis. She would have difficulty in arranging those things efficiently on her own. She has protection and for that she loses her freedom. Do you think she is planning on trying to opt out?"

Rudi spread his arms. "How can I know? You've only just told me of her involvement with these people."

"OK, do you think she will try to return to Germany?"

"If she feels up against a wall she might. She wouldn't run away from me. She will expect to finish me. I'm probably her only failure."

"You're taking it calmly, Rudi."

"That's because I have other ideas." Rudi smiled sadly. "Is that all?"

"Almost. Do you know anything about Ronald Walsh's murder?"

Rudi appeared genuinely surprised. "How would I know about that? I would find it easy to accept if you think my sister did it."

Bulman and Jacko exchanged glances. "We'd better go across there," said Jacko.

Rudi suddenly looked alarmed. He was agitated as he said, "To Anna's? Why would you go there? This is no longer your problem."

"It's always been our problem, matey. Why do you think we should let her go, after what she did to me?"

"She is my sister and I will deal with her."

Bulman tried to calm Rudi down. "All we want to do is to find a link between Kochev, Yelena and Ronnie Walsh. We think Anna has the answers. And we also want to know Anna's link with Walsh. I think that's reasonable, don't you?"

"And you think she will tell you? Just like that?"

Jacko took a tighter grip on the Colt. He saw trouble ahead. "Not just like that. We'll do whatever it takes."

"Beat her? Torture her? Just now you were claiming that you had to operate within the law."

"Well, now, it depends whose law we're talking about. If we operate within *her* laws we might get what we want." Jacko considered he was being reasonable.

"Then take me with you."

"You'll probably kill her. If we go that far we won't get

a thing. We have to know, Rudi. Once we know you can do what you like with her. We'll give you a ring from her place. What's your number?" Bulman pulled out his notepad.

But Rudi was restless and it was clear that he had no intention of leaving it to them. He had co-operated, he wanted a little back. He wasn't interested in Yelena and Kochev or Walsh. He was so restless that both Jacko and Bulman thought he might be reckless enough to make a run for the door – even knowing he was unlikely to reach it. Bulman moved back to his original position between the door and Rudi.

"Take me with you," Rudi pleaded again. "I can be of help. It will be three to one. I will help you find out what you want then you leave her to me. Anyway, she may have help over there. There have been men coming all day, I suppose to clean up the mess I left and to change the lock. I made it difficult for her."

Bulman and Jacko exchanged worried glances again and Bulman put his own interpretation on Jacko's thoughts. If they left Rudi here they would have to tie him up to make sure he did not follow. He was about to make a suggestion when Rudi made one for him.

"How do you think you can get in? I have a gadget I brought over with me, a kind of master key that will get us past the street door. Have you? And if you tried to break her door down she would pick you off as you came in. Take me with you. I will ring the bell while you two stay out of view of the spy hole. She will let me in. I go in and you rush in behind me. What do you think?"

"What makes you think she'll let you in?" Jacko was suspicious.

"When she shot Mother and me it was in a fit of ice cold rage; she had to do it. Now she is a professional killer she thinks things out first, weighs the odds. And she is still curious about me, how I survived, what has happened meanwhile, how I got on to her. She knows I want to kill her and she now knows I intend to do it slowly. She does not know what plans I've laid, what help I may have. She will want to know all these things before squeezing the trigger. Believe me, I'm your only way in. You help me and I'll help you."

Bulman nodded to Jacko. It was certainly the easiest way in. "You agree to let us question her first? No funny business? And then we leave her to you. It could save all our problems."

"I won't break my word. You do your business and then I'll do mine."

It all sounded too easy, as if Anna was a helpless sitting duck. It was difficult to imagine. And Rudi remained an unknown quantity, whatever his assertions.

Jacko rose, still holding the gun. "It's the best offer we've had yet. Let's go."

Chapter Twenty-Two

They kept the same formation as before, Bulman first, then Rudi, and Jacko bringing up the rear as they went down the stairs. The atmosphere between them was different from on the way up but was difficult to define. On the one hand they were easier with each other but on the other, somehow, the suspicion was heightened. They had all agreed on the action but nobody was sure about it.

Half-way down, Rudi said, "Do I get to know your names, gentlemen?"

Bulman called back over his shoulder, "I'm George Bulman. Anna already knows that. My friend behind you has no name. When he was a baby he was found abandoned in a cardboard box on a doorstep and was called X." Bulman had spoken quite seriously. It was better that Jacko retained his anonymity as long as possible.

They reached the hall and gathered behind the door without losing shape. Rudi said, "I'd better get on to the porch first and when I'm sure she's there and it's safe to cross I'll call you."

"I'll do that," said Jacko dryly. "George, you keep your gun handy." It was suspicion all the way.

It was sensible to put the hall light out while they opened the front door, but if they did Bulman would lose sight of Rudi. In the end Jacko opened the door with the light on and slipped out quickly. He immediately went to the darkest spot where Rudi had stood. It was a good observation point. Across at an angle he could easily see that Anna's lights were still on. He stood there for a few seconds to see if he could detect anyone at the window and then tapped on the door.

The door opened fractionally after the light was switched off and Rudi complained of Bulman pushing him. They had yet to reach the apartment but trust was already wearing thin. They stood in the porch, all three hunched together. Rudi wanted to cross the street one at a time but Jacko, who automatically took over these sort of operations, said they could all go together and this they did with two guns concealed beneath coats, very much ready for anything Rudi might try to pull.

Once across Rudi said, "When you have finished with Anna I will need her gun. The one you have, Mr Bulman. It would be poetic justice to use that on her. Have I your word that you will not call the police once you have left?"

It seemed to Bulman an odd time to be thrashing out these sort of problems but they assured Rudi he would be left to do whatever he wanted to do. The whole business was bizarre. They were talking as if the matter was already settled and it would all be a pushover, instead of thinking they were facing a professional assassin who had killed efficiently and would have no problem doing so again. Anna would always be dangerous, and would always have something up her sleeve. This was no sacrificial lamb they were on their way to see but a trained, cold blooded killer.

As they mounted the steps, Bulman reflected that there were times when Rudi still saw his sister as just that, and not as she had become. There were flashes when he seemed to see the whole thing as some sort of game. Revenge, yes, but he seemed to think it would be so easy. He was not worried about the outcome when he should certainly be. And Bulman could not help but wonder where that would lead.

They kept their heads down to nullify the effect of the TV scanner but, in any case, the porch light was not on. Rudi opened the street door and they passed across the wide hall to the lift, and entered in the same order with Bulman

268

leading. But in the lift the atmosphere tightened and even Rudi seemed to recognize that the next few minutes would be crucial. They stepped out of the lift and stood there in a group, as if reluctant to perform the next step. It was the only indecisive moment they showed. As if a button had been pressed they came to their senses and moved in a group towards the door. When they reached it Rudi stood in front of it while Bulman and Jacko took up positions either side with pistols raised and ready. It was time.

Rudi rang the bell and stood plumb in front of the spy hole. When he was satisfied Anna was viewing him he raised his arms and called out, "I'm unarmed. I want to talk."

Nothing happened in response to that and he began to think she would not let him in. He gazed at the spot where he had crudely smashed the lock and, as he expected, saw that the woodwork had been repaired and the lock must have been replaced. He rang again and this time the door opened immediately and Anna stood before him, a gun in her hand which was similar to the one Jacko had taken.

"You won't need that," he said, and stepped towards her. It was the best warning he could give them so that they knew she was armed.

"Of course I'll need it," she replied. "I have to finish a bodged job."

"In your own apartment? Come, Anna, you could not have forgotten so much." He stepped forward again to make room for the others to get in and the next thing he knew was being knocked flat from behind. The blow had pushed Rudi into Anna before he went down and she was close to shooting him then. But as Rudi sprawled, Jacko, who had dropped to his knees, smashed the Colt down hard on Anna's gun hand and she screamed out with pain. As he tried to take her gun she fought desperately in spite of the pain and it was not until Rudi climbed to his knees to help, that Jacko finally managed to get hold of it. Behind them Bulman simply found it impossible to get past.

Anna finally lost balance and fell back, and they all

269

managed to rush in. Bulman closed the door behind them and Jacko and Rudi pulled a struggling Anna to a chair while Jacko was bawling out, "Calm down. We just want to ask some questions and then we'll leave you alone. Sit there."

She sat holding her wrist which was already swollen and strangely misshapen and Jacko guessed that he must have broken it.

Bulman, who had also seen the state of the wrist, went to the kitchen and soaked a towel in cold water and returned to bind it round Anna's wrist. She was clearly in a lot of pain.

Jacko gazed round in wonderment. The place had been tidied, and there were three new chairs. Two of the old ones remained and had been pushed against one wall, presumably to await removal, seats still torn, but they, and the ripped carpet, remained the only visible reminder of the dreadful damage that had been done by Rudi. Shelves were bare of ornaments and gave an empty feel to the place but it was obvious that a massive clearing up operation had taken place. Rudi seemed to be totally unaffected by the change.

They sat in separate chairs, the settee forming the blank end of a triangle. Bulman took over from there. He noticed Anna shoot a glance at the gun he was holding and smiled at her. "It's not the impression you had of me, was it? Gun toting? As you can see your friends failed again and I'm alive and well. Anna, if you will give us some straight answers to a few questions we'll be on our way. We are not asking for a confession. All we want is information, not retribution. What was the connection between Kochev, Walsh and Yelena?"

"I'd be putting a contract on myself if I told you that."

Bulman glanced at Rudi who was showing some of his old impatience. "You mean you'd rather keep it in the family? That's a bit short-sighted isn't it? Right now your life isn't worth a nickel. We're offering you a sporting chance."

270

Anna sat back sullenly. The side of her face was swollen and blue where Jacko had caught her when he was last here. And she was cradling her wrist. Bulman supposed that nobody had reported to her the failure of the attempt on him. Otherwise she might not have opened the door at all. She was going through a bad patch, but as he watched her Bulman was convinced that she was far from finished; someone like Anna would be a proficient shot with either hand, and he gazed around the room for likely accessibility points for hidden weapons. She would be prepared.

"What about it then?" he said in quite a friendly way, which seemed to irritate both Jacko and Rudi.

"I can see no reason why I should help you."

"You owe it to me, Anna. You tried to top me, and my friend here. We've disarmed your brother to keep him in line. If we get no answers we might just as well give Rudi the guns and walk out. Dammit, I'm not asking much."

"I'm afraid you are, George. I'd never get work again."

"As a killer? Is that what you want? You'll slow down with time. And they'll find a successor whose first job will be to dispose of you. Nothing changes. Get out of it while you can. You're bright, you'll think of something."

"With Rudi around? He wants to kill me by instalments. Which means I still have one more job to do, whether I like it or not."

"So you won't co-operate?"

"There are too many reasons why I can't."

"Which means I'll have to let my friend loose on you, and you already know about him. Or let Rudi take his revenge."

"I have to take that chance. You don't know what I'm up against."

"Actually, I do. OK, I'm going to tell you what I think has happened. If I'm right it might persuade you to fill in any gaps."

Bulman leaned forward, arms on knees, and gazed at Anna, seeing nothing but hostility. Whether it was aimed at him or the others he could not be sure. He hoped she might have just a spark for him and not try to make a smoke screen.

"Radomir Kochev is the biggest influence in the Russian Mafia. It was his organization, probably linking with Veida Ash, who got you out of Germany after shooting your mother and Rudi, and he supplied a new identity for you in return for the odd hit and probably used you in other ways. You were probably sent to Russia to be trained.

"Ronnie Walsh walked straight into the honey trap set for him when he went to Russia on his last business trip. A renowned womanizer, how could he resist the charms of someone like Yelena Zotov? The KGB no longer existed in their old form. He was safe. He had overlooked the new shape of things to come in Russia. He probably saw or knew of it, but Yelena was a great temptation to get just a little careless and, really, what was the harm? He was not forcing her against her will. She was a very eager partner, someone he might bring back to England for a while. What he did not know was that she was Kochev's mistress and acting on his orders. OK so far?"

Anna made no reply; she stared at the floor in a moody silence that was hardly a denial.

"You've hit the button," said Rudi. "I know my sister."

"The age-old rig, Walsh and Yelena were caught at it by Kochev himself, who threatened to blow our Ronnie's brains out there and then. At this stage Kochev gets over his message of power. There was public outrage when a popular TV journalist was shot dead on the streets of Moscow, but nobody has yet paid the price and if someone eventually does, he will probably be a sacrificial goat. Such is the power of Kochev. At the moment they are running wild, just as gangsters did in America in the Twenties and Thirties."

Bulman noticed that Anna had changed her position slightly and was now sideways to him. He hoped Jacko had noticed it too. He continued, watching Anna closely, and

272

keeping a tight hold on her favourite gun. "Kochev points out that a British businessman has already been killed in Moscow but will let Walsh off the hook at a price. He wants his money laundered through Walsh's chain of companies. Walsh wouldn't be the first, but by far the biggest.

"It is here I flounder a bit. Walsh was a strange mixture of honesty and immorality. He would be frightened, terrified even, anyone would in those circumstances because life meant nothing to someone like Kochev. But I can't somehow see him doing it for those reasons. Can you enlighten me? You know I've got most of it."

"Can someone make me a sling for this?" She held up her broken wrist. "It's agonizing."

Nobody wanted to move. They were all watching her. Jacko said to Rudi, "Go find something to make a sling. A tea towel, anything."

Rudi was appalled. "I'm not helping that bitch even if her head was coming off. I'm glad it's hurting."

Bulman said, "I'll go. I'll make a proper job of it but only when you've filled in the gaps. The quicker you answer, the better for you. What's missing in what I said?"

Anna continued to hold her wrist up against her body. She looked across surlily, her gaze dropping as it reached his, and from then on she seemed to be talking to the carpet.

She had trouble at first, during which time Rudi jibed her and almost sent her back into her shell, but eventually she said, "You are right about Ronnie. He could be quite strong. But he was taken to a special place, his lids were forced apart and his head held still in a clamp, and he was forced to watch the slow agonizing torture of someone who had offended Kochev and to listen to the terrible screams for mercy until the poor wretch was finally put out of his misery. At least I kill clean. What Ronnie witnessed was threatened against his wife and children if he did not help with the laundering. It was a no contest."

Nobody said a word for quite a while until Anna added,

"Now you know what I'm up against. It's not just dying but the terrifying manner of it."

There was no argument, not even from Rudi.

Bulman said, "You were really Walsh's captor, weren't you? You were there to make him toe the line; a constant threat, a reminder of the torture in Moscow. Would I be right in saying that even so, he reached a point where he couldn't go on and threatened to pull out whatever happened? Perhaps he realized how difficult it would be for him to pull it off with so many other directors around him. He had managed so far with the smaller subsidiaries but could do no more." Bulman paused and tried to catch Anna's eye but she was still in that strange half turned position.

Bulman continued, "And then you received instructions, probably from Veida, to kill him. He was now a threat, a waverer. With him out of the way they would try to hold on to the venues they had. That's why Kochev, with Veida's help, sent over such a large labour force. And what a mess they made. The planting of the wig, gun and contact lenses down in Hampshire to incriminate Connie Smith was pathetic and they killed the wrong girl anyway. The trouble was they never had time to acclimatize, were mixed races and Britain was not Russia and Germany, and they could not operate in quite the same way. Even the traffic system was against them. But as time goes on they'll feel more at home and there will be a lot of trouble. Am I right?"

Anna looked sideways at him. "There were instructions to kill him. I've never admitted doing it although you've accused me of it and seem to think I confessed. But it was obviously done on Kochev's instructions. Haven't I earned the sling, now? This wrist needs medical attention."

"Of course." Bulman rose and left for the kitchen. He rummaged around and found a first aid box in one of the cupboards. As he unfastened the box to search for a sling he could hear the murmur of voices coming through the open door of the lounge. He found the sling, unfolded it and then

274

made a triangle so that he could tie it round Anna's neck. And then he heard two shots that froze him to the spot. All he could think of was that they had not come from Jacko's Colt, which was like canon exploding, and that Rudi was unarmed. He rammed the sling in his pocket and pulled out Anna's pistol which he had stuffed into his waistband and hurried to the door.

He crouched down at the side of the door, and could see nobody but Rudi, who lay sprawled sideways in his chair with blood seeping over the arm. There was no sign of Jacko or Anna.

On his hands and knees Bulman crept into the room and caught sight of Jacko crouched behind his upturned chair which he had presumably rolled back upon and was now using as a shield. He followed the direction of Jacko's gaze and crept round the back of the chair where Rudi lay slumped. And then he heard Anna speak from the other side of the chair and her voice seemed to come from where he had last seen her.

"George, if you're there, please bring that sling. I won't shoot you or your friend. I don't want any more complications than I've got and shooting you would bring plenty. Bring me the sling and go."

It was Jacko who answered. "If you want the sling throw your gun over here. Anyway, with Rudi out of the way why don't you get it yourself?"

"And be gunned down by you? You're as much a professional as me."

"Do as he says, Anna," Bulman called out. "Throw your gun out and you'll be in no danger from either of us. I've got your sling with me."

"I'll accept your word, George, but not your friend's."

"He'll only fire in self-defence. He'll honour my word. Just throw the bloody thing out."

The pistol came arching through the air and almost hit Jacko on the head. He grabbed it before it spun away, pulled out the magazine, and pulled back the breech to unload the round in it. He then called out, "I'm standing up. Cover me, George."

Both men rose and were well enough separated to split the target effectively. Anna was sitting as they had last seen her and was still holding her wrist. She must have had a gun tucked down the side of the chair and fired left-handed.

"I don't like failures," she said, almost as if nothing much had happened. "Rudi was my main danger. He wouldn't have given up." She turned her head to give Bulman a semblance of a smile. "I was banking on you going for the sling, George. I knew you had a soft centre. You are really a nice man and I'm sorry to have done this to you. You narrowed the odds for me, but I really do need it."

Bulman tossed this sling to her; he had no intention now of going near her, she was capable of too many surprises.

Anna managed the sling awkwardly. While she struggled with it she said, "Are you walking away from me as you promised?"

Jacko looked at Bulman who replied, "Yes. We got what we came for. Unless the police can break your alibi there's not a lot they can do. They'll probably be glad to see the back of you, if you're going to Germany." He stepped round Rudi's chair again and viewed the damage. Rudi's head was on the arm of the chair and facing him, and he suddenly saw the suspicion of movement in the lids. And then the eyes opened wide for a second or two and were pleading with him, and with deep shock he realized why.

He stepped away again. "He was unarmed," he accused Anna.

"He would have done the same to me. Goodbye, George. Take your friend with you. I don't like him."

Bulman headed for the door and stopped when he reached it. "That's because he's too good for you."

Jacko, who had gone round the other way to join him, gave a wave of farewell. "You're not bad, Anna," he said grudgingly.

Bulman turned towards Rudi for the last time. He tossed Anna's gun on to the lap of the inert Rudi. "He asked if I would make sure I gave it to him, once we had settled things with you. He wanted to kill you with the gun you tried to kill him with. It won't be of much use to him now. You didn't give him the chance. Cheers, Anna. We won't be meeting again."

Bulman and Jacko left the lounge and headed for the front door. Bulman opened the door, they both stepped through but Bulman held the door open and grabbed Jacko's arm as he went towards the lift. After a few seconds the two men heard the plop of a silenced gun followed by a muted scream from Anna, and then another shot and then silence.

"Let's get the hell out of here." Bulman raced for the stairs.

"He was still alive, you bastard," Jacko panted, as they ran down the stairs.

Bulman did not reply until they were in the street, walking briskly towards the direction of the car. "I kept my word, that's all. It was between the two of them. Anyway, it was justice, the 'settled out of court' variety."

"But Rudi is still alive, for God's sake. We should ring for an ambulance."

"No. Where did you park that bloody car?" They hurried on. "He was barely alive. He just willed himself to hold on long enough to finish the job. He'll have died a happy man and Anna would have got her just desserts."

When they were out of sight of the building they slowed down to get their breath. Bulman was panting heavily by now. "I must contact Marshall." He paused to get his breath. "I'm too bloody old for these capers," he complained.

Jacko was astounded. "What the hell are you talking about? You've just acted as judge, jury, and executioner."

He slapped Bulman on the back. "Never mind Marshall. Let him wait. You ring Freda Curtis and take her out again, and remember that rust never settles on a moving target."

ANNA Preinning (first
Conni Smith sick ✓

Marshall PFS (gov)

Derek Nelson